On Liberty's Watch

Tifani Clark

Also in the Soul Saver Series:

Shadow of a Life

Haven Waiting

On Liberty's Watch

Tifani Clark

On Liberty's Watch by Tifani Clark

© Tifani Clark 2015

Cover Design: Sherry Gammon of Wordpainting Covers
Cover images © via DepositPhotos
Fer Gregory
Вера Загородная
Lisa Combs

ISBN-13: 978-0692468661
ISBN-10: 0692468668

An ABCD Publishing Book

http://www.tifaniclark.blogspot.com

Dedicated to the four children who keep me on my toes.

TABLE OF CONTENTS

Prologue 1
Chapter 1 4
Chapter 2 11
Chapter 3 21
Chapter 4 29
Chapter 5 37
Chapter 6 48
Chapter 7 58
Chapter 8 68
Chapter 9 81
Chapter 10 91
Chapter 11 99
Chapter 12 106
Chapter 13 113
Chapter 14 121
Chapter 15 131
Chapter 16 140
Chapter 17 149
Chapter 18 158
Chapter 19 170
Chapter 20 181
Chapter 21 190
Chapter 22 199
Chapter 23 210
Chapter 24 221
Chapter 25 229
Chapter 26 239
Chapter 27 247
Chapter 28 255
Chapter 29 264
Chapter 30 272
Chapter 31 282
Chapter 32 291
Chapter 33 296
Author's Note 299

On Liberty's Watch

Tifani Clark

Prologue

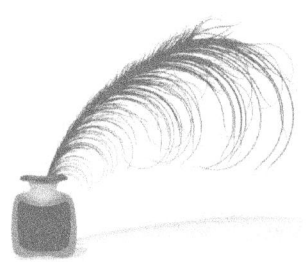

When everything in your life changes—everything you believe, everything you know, everything you are—you have to find yourself again. But finding yourself isn't as easy as it sounds.

I know. I've been lost more than once.

Whenever I thought I was getting close to feeling normal that summer, life would throw another curveball at me and I'd find myself right back at the beginning of my search.

My name is Jamie Peters. I was almost sixteen, I lived in Marion, Massachusetts, and I'd recently found out I was a soul saver.

Yes, it's as serious as it sounds.

I hadn't always known about my gift—or problem, depending on how you want to look at it. I found out about it at the end of my sophomore year when I caught a girl following me around. The girl was a ghost named Sophia.

Yes, a real ghost.

I didn't believe in ghosts before that point and when she told me I laughed in her face. I mean, really? Who would believe that some people become ghosts when they die? Who would believe ghosts

1

could make themselves visible whenever they wanted to? Who would believe ghosts could be physically touched? Who would believe ghosts could live among humans—not that ghosts aren't humans—without anyone ever having a clue? It took some time, but Sophia wore me down. She convinced me that I was her soul saver and it would be my job to help her finish her business so she could move to the afterlife, wherever that is.

I did help her. I reunited her with a long lost boyfriend (Nick) and successfully fought off her evil stepparents—aka my distant ancestors. They all were extricated. That means they left this world. The crazy business with Sophia and Nick left me in possession of an antique map. My friends—Peter and Camille—were in on the ghost secret and were convinced that the map would lead to gold and jewelry and riches galore. I never felt that way. Chalk it up to my soul saver instincts. A soul saver is drawn to things that will help the ghost they're trying to save. They're connected to their ghost in ways I can't really describe. It's like finding a long lost sibling or having a child to take care of. Weird, I know.

Anyway, the map didn't lead us to treasure, but it did lead us to another ghost named Haven—a friend of my distant ancestors. And... Haven was a witch. Her secret was discovered and she was hung during the Salem witch trials back in the 1600s. Totally crazy, but true. The map marked the place where her spell book had remained buried for centuries. Before she died, Haven accidentally let an evil spirit thing out from the underworld and I had to help send him back before she could be extricated.

All of this craziness occurred in less than two month's time. I was emotionally drained and physically tired. Putting every thought into one thing for days on end can do that to you, I guess. Before all the ghosts started showing up, I'd been completely normal—boring even. I got good grades, I hung out with Camille, and I read a lot of books.

My parents separated when I was six and my dad raised me alone. Mom never really gave an explanation for her absence. I always assumed she wasn't cut out for motherhood. She *did* try to act like a teenager still. Mom would come around once in a while, but never for more than a few days at a time. Sometimes I'd go months without seeing her.

Mom showed up for one of those random visits when Haven happened to be around. Much to my horror, she found out I was a soul saver. Even more horrifying, Mom revealed she too was a soul saver. That's why she left Dad and me in Marion in the first place. She wanted the thrill of adventure with ghosts and couldn't get that being a housewife. It took my mind a long time to wrap itself around that information.

Anyway, Mom invited me to stay with her for the rest of the summer. I knew I needed to go. Truthfully, I missed the feelings I had when I was connected to a ghost. I missed having a purpose in my life. I needed to know if I should break ties with everyone I knew and throw myself into the soul saving business full-time ... just like Mom.

I only had until the end of the summer to decide something that would affect the rest of my life.

Chapter 1

I stared at the ground as I walked so I wouldn't have to squint in the lowering sun. I glanced at my watch again and shook my head. I wouldn't get there on time and I didn't like to be late. No, scratch that. I *hated* to be late. I could thank Dad for that character trait. He didn't know the meaning of the word. Mom, on the other hand, lived by her own schedule—one that didn't include actual time. Her days consisted of morning, afternoon, and evening. If she said she'd do something in the morning, it could happen anytime between the hours of eight and twelve. I blamed her for my current tardiness. Peter and I agreed to meet at our favorite spot by the Sippican Harbor at 7:30 that night, but Mom called at seven and wouldn't stop talking. I'd been waiting for that phone call since three in the afternoon.

I quickened my pace as I neared the harbor and tried to put myself in a better mood. A scraping sound caught my attention and I turned to look over my shoulder. Nothing. I turned around again, but kept my head up, shielding my eyes from the sun with my hand. Another scrape sounded behind me and I whirled around, coming to a complete stop.

"Hello?" I called.

A bird rose up from a nearby tree and flew off in the opposite direction, but nothing else seemed to be around. "Hello?" I called again, quieter that time.

A prickly sensation started at the base of my spine and traveled up my back. The little hairs on my neck stood up and I shivered. My heart beat faster as I recognized the sensation. I'd been around enough ghosts that summer to know when another presence was around. I wasn't alone. Thoughts of demons and evil spirits crossed my mind as my eyes darted from tree to tree, trying to catch a glimpse of something or someone that didn't want to be seen.

"Who's following me?" My voice shook and I took a deep breath to steady it.

A hand touched my shoulder. I screamed and whirled around at the same time I jumped back.

"Whoa. No need for fists."

Peter.

"You jerk!" I looked down at my clenched hands and then slugged him in the shoulder.

"What was that for?"

"You scared me!" I complained. "I thought you were a ghost."

Peter turned on his puppy dog eyes and grinned. I fought against doing the same thing, but lost the battle when my lips curled up.

"With how often you're followed by ghosts, I wouldn't think you'd be scared of them anymore," Peter said as we turned and walked the rest of the way to the harbor.

"After dealing with the demonic Samson I'm a little wary. You should be, too."

"True. I wouldn't want you to stab me again."

"Let's not talk about that tonight. In fact, let's not talk about ghosts at all."

Peter slipped his hand into mine and pulled me down to the grass with him. "You know, you're going to miss the sunsets here when

5

you leave."

I looked up at the ever-darkening sky lit with all shades of pink and orange and hints of purple. "It's not like I'm going to be gone forever. It'll be six or seven weeks ... max."

"A lot can happen in six or seven weeks. Just think about the last month and a half."

I closed my eyes and thought about Sophia and Nick and Haven. I missed them. I knew I'd always have a little pain in my heart, but I wouldn't trade knowing them to get rid of that pain.

I opened my eyes just as a burst of light shot across the sky. "Did you see that?"

"See what?"

"The shooting star."

"I missed it. Did you make a wish?"

"I thought you were only supposed to wish on the first star you see."

"Nope. Shooting stars are even better. Just close your eyes and wish. Maybe it's not too late."

I laughed as I closed my eyes and made a wish, feeling absolutely ridiculous. "There. Are you happy now?"

"Only if the wish had anything to do with me and you and more adventures with crazy people."

I lay down and rolled to my side, propping my head up on my elbow. "I thought we agreed that we weren't going to talk about ghosts tonight," I said with a half-smile.

"Who said anything about ghosts? That word never came out of my mouth." Peter fought a smile.

"Maybe not specifically, but referencing our adventures is the same thing as talking about them."

"Okay. Sorry. What do you want to talk about then?"

I rolled onto my back and folded my arms under my head. I didn't know what I wanted to talk about and it worried me. I'd had a crush on Peter for almost as long as I could remember. He'd always been a friend, but not a close one. That is, until Sophia came along. She found out about my crush and pushed us together. I'm glad she helped, but part of me worried that Peter didn't like the real me. Before I became a soul saver, he'd occasionally chat with me, but that was about the extent of our relationship. Jamie the soul saver kept him entertained with wild adventures. Without a ghost around, would I still be exciting enough to keep him interested?

"Umm . . ." My mind came up blank on subject matters. "How are your Red Sox doing this year?" There. *Sports are a safe topic, right?*

"They're looking great so far. Dad got us tickets to two of the home games. The first one's in a couple of weeks."

"How's that pitcher doing, you know, the one who hurt his arm at the end of last season? What's his name?"

Peter sighed and sat up, facing me. "Jamie, I know you. You don't really want to talk about sports. You might as well just talk about the weather."

"I know a little bit about sports. I used to be somewhat of a tomboy, remember?"

"Sure, back in elementary school."

"Well . . . we *have* been having great weather. I mean, it's dark now and I'm not even cold at all."

Peter laughed and stood. He reached down and pulled me up to stand next to him. My heart beat harder when he slowly slid his hands around my waist. "Why do you want to avoid talking about ghosts so much?"

"Because." I closed my eyes and took a deep breath. "I need to know if we can hang out when there's not a ghost involved."

"Isn't that what we're doing right now? And didn't we go to a movie a week or two ago? It was just the two of us."

"Yeah, but we talked about Haven's map most of the time."

"What are you trying to say?"

"Would you like me if I wasn't a soul saver?"

"Of course. I liked you before I ever knew anything about ghosts."

"Before Sophia came along you never asked me out, held my hand, or," I felt my face turn red, "kissed me."

Peter dropped his hands and shoved them in his pockets. "Sorry. I guess I just never had the guts to ask you out. I've never had a girlfriend before. I guess I just figured I'd get around to it eventually."

That's what I'd been trying to get at. "Do you think of me as your . . . girlfriend?" I asked hesitantly. I really hated awkward conversations and avoided them at all costs. After the words left my mouth I thought about bolting, but knew I'd eventually have to face him.

Peter ran his fingers through his hair and shifted from one foot to another. "I haven't really—"

"Wait! Don't answer that." I put a finger on his lips to silence him.

Peter lifted his eyebrows and stared at me.

"When I leave with my mom, you and I won't see each other for a while. Maybe we can both decide how serious we want to be after that. I mean, there's no rush, right?" For some reason, I felt like I needed to give Peter every opportunity to run. My parents had been separated for almost a decade. My dad still cared about my mom and it wasn't fair the way she ditched him to chase ghosts. I worried that I was on a fast track to becoming an exact replica of my mother. Ghosts were my life. I couldn't bring myself to do to Peter what my mom had done to my dad.

He smiled. "Sure. And it's not like you're going to be very far. Boston's barely an hour away. I'll come visit you. We can hang out in the city."

"I'd like that."

"You can go to a Sox game with me and my dad when we come

up."

"It's a deal. Just don't expect me to be able to name any of the players."

"Not only will I expect you to name them all, I'll expect you to know all of their positions, numbers, batting averages, and any minor league clubs they played with." He paused and the twinkle I loved so much sparked in his eye. "There'll be a test. You better study."

"Is that a challenge?"

"Maybe."

I made a mental note to memorize stats during some of the downtime with my mom. I had a feeling there'd be a lot of it. Years before, she and a couple of friends started a soul saving business. They'd help a ghost figure out what to do to extricate in exchange for "inheriting" all of the ghosts assets when they left. I had the impression the three of them barely scraped by, moving from city to city, and ghost to ghost, trying to keep the high they had when they were helping someone. I got it, really I did. I knew the feeling all too well. But, constantly searching for the next high was something an addict would do. I didn't want to be like that. Even more, I worried that I'd *already* arrived at that point.

"Okay. No more sports talk and no more ghost talk. Let's go to Grandma's Café. I need a milkshake," Peter said.

We walked home from Grandma's Café while sipping the remainder of our milkshakes through red and white striped straws. Peter offered to call for a ride, but I didn't mind the walk. I'd be leaving in the morning and it was my last night with him.

"You'll call me if anything exciting comes up, right?" Peter asked as he kept pace beside me.

"Of course. But not until I call Camille and my dad. And your

9

friends Scott and Jason. And maybe Jason's girlfriend, Lana. I mean, I've never talked to her, but I really should get to know everyone better," I teased.

"Ouch."

"And I'd probably call my neighbor, Mrs. White. Remember how you ruined her rosebushes when you tried to teach Haven how to ride a bike?" I teased.

"I think your memory is a little mixed up. The rosebushes were fine until you got jealous of me helping Haven."

I couldn't argue with that. It had pretty much been my fault . . . and I *had* been jealous. "Jealous? Me? Never," I said anyway.

We'd arrived at my house and stood on the walk leading to my front porch. "Thanks for hanging out tonight," Peter said.

"I had fun."

He took a step closer to me. "Don't forget to call."

I felt my heart speed up. "I will."

He slipped his hands around my waist and I held my breath. His kiss only lasted a second, but it made my head spin.

As if I wasn't already confused enough.

Chapter 2

D ad!" I stood at the top of the stairs and called down. "Have you seen my blue sneakers with the pink stripes? I need to pack them!"

He appeared at the bottom of the stairs. Dad took a half-day off work—a rare thing for him—so he'd be there when I left with my mom. As Dean of Academic Affairs at nearby Newton University, he stayed more than busy. My parents were polar opposites. Mom laughed a lot, went on crazy adventures, and tried to dress like an eighteen-year-old. Dad rarely took off his suits and thought having fun meant loosening your tie a little and playing a game of Scrabble. Don't get me wrong, I loved him and appreciated everything he did for me, but serious was his middle name. I guess that's why neither Mom nor I had the guts to confide in him about ghosts.

"Have you looked in your closet?" Dad answered.

"Yes. And in the bathroom. And under my bed." A thought came to me. "Wait! I think I know where they are." I ran back into my room and opened my closet door again. The breeze it created moved the hangers full of clothing. I stared at the clothes hanging down. Some of the items had belonged to Sophia. I really missed her . . .

11

"Don't think about ghosts right now," I said aloud and forced myself to look away.

My backpack lay in the corner of my closet, right where I'd tossed it after the last day of school. The pockets bulged with the remnants of my locker and final assignments handed back by teachers. I grabbed the bag and unzipped it. Yep. My shoes. Right on top of the rest of my nasty gym clothes.

Wrinkling my nose, I stared at the crumpled clothing. "Maybe I should just burn these," I muttered to myself.

My phone vibrated in my pocket as I emerged from the closet with the sweaty shorts and shirt hanging between my thumb and index finger. I dropped them in my laundry basket before pulling the phone from my pocket.

Camille.

"What's up?" I answered.

"Have you left yet?"

"No. Mom's supposed to be here in an hour. So probably three hours."

"Good. I want to come say goodbye. I still can't believe you're going to leave me for the rest of the summer. What am I supposed to do by myself?"

"I'm sure you'll think of something. Even if I were around, would you hang out with me or would you spend all your time with Travis?" Camille had been dating Travis Andrews for a couple of months.

Silence filled the other end of the call.

"Cam?"

"I'm not really sure if Travis and I are still going out."

"Seriously? What happened? I thought you'd be the new 'it' couple next year?"

"I don't know. I'm starting to get kind of bored with him, you know what I mean?"

I didn't know what she meant. Peter was the only guy I'd ever gone out with more than once and I couldn't imagine being bored with him. "Uh huh," I lied.

"All he ever wants to do is go to a movie or rent a movie or . . . stuff. It gets old." I heard her take a deep breath on the other end of the line. "I told him I was bored and we kind of got in a fight. I'm not really sure where we stand now."

"Oh. I'm sorry." I picked at a loose string on my comforter. "Just don't be like Allison."

"Hey! That's just mean. And totally uncalled for."

I grinned to myself. "You're right. Totally uncalled for." Allison, Camille's older sister, would be a senior the next year. She looked like a beauty queen and changed boyfriends faster than I changed my socks. Every time a new guy came along she insisted he was 'the one.' Cam and I had been making fun of her behind her back for years.

"I'm on my way to your house right now," Camille said. "See ya in a minute."

I hung up the phone and tossed the blue sneakers into my giant duffle bag. I had to squish the contents around to get the zipper closed all the way. Packing for the move to Boston proved to be harder than I thought it would be since I didn't know how much room I'd have in my mom's apartment. I didn't want to bring too much, but it would be better than regretting leaving things behind. I sat on the edge of my bed, tapping my foot on the ground as I continued to fidget with the hem of my comforter. I hadn't lived with my mom for ten years. *What did I agree to?*

The doorbell rang. I stepped to my open window and looked down at the front porch. "I'm up here, Cam. Just come up," I called through the open window.

She burst through my bedroom door a minute later and walked straight to my bed. At least she had the decency to kick off her flip flops before shoving my duffle bag aside and throwing herself across my pillows. For some reason, everyone who entered my room—ghosts or living—bypassed the rocking chair and headed straight for my antique four-poster bed.

"Are you sure I can't come with you?" Camille whined.

"I'm sure. Mom's going to Boston to help a ghost and we all know how you handle that kind of thing," I said. "Besides, she's renting a two bedroom apartment with her friends. I'll be sleeping on the couch as it is."

"Promise you'll call or text at least once a day."

"Promise."

The doorbell rang again a while later and I looked out the window. Mom stood on the porch. She wore a yellow sundress with a wide hat. My heart sped up and my palms began to sweat. I took a deep breath and willed my body to stop reacting as if I'd never met her before.

"She's here," I said as I turned around slowly. "I guess it's time to go."

Camille frowned. "I miss you already."

"It's nice to know my absence will be noticed."

"Peter's going to miss you, too."

"Maybe."

I heaved the strap of the duffle bag onto my shoulder and shoved my purse and a backpack full of books into Camille's arms. "Carry this for me."

Mom watched from the bottom of the stairs as I stumbled down them with my load. "Are you ready?" she asked

"I think so."

"Oh. Hi, Cam!"

"Hi, Lillian." Camille gave Mom a hug. They were more alike than my mom and me. If I suddenly disappeared when they were together neither would even notice.

"If you forget anything, we can buy it in Boston. It's not like we're going to a foreign country," she giggled.

"I'll see you later, Dad." I wrapped my arms around his neck. We weren't much for hugging, but my impending absence had to be bothering him. We'd been apart before, mostly when he went on business trips, but we'd never been apart because of Mom. As soon as I agreed to live with her for the rest of the summer he started making elaborate plans for all the things we'd do in the fall. I think he worried that I'd choose to stay with her permanently.

"Stay in touch and call me if you need anything. Or if you need me to come get you," Dad whispered into my hair.

"I will." When the familiar sting of tears came to my eyes I pulled my arms away and turned around. Through the open front door I could see two passengers waiting in a van."Let's go before we make your friends wait."

In the last twenty-four hours I'd said goodbye to Peter, Camille and Dad. That didn't even include all the ghosts I'd had to say goodbye to that summer. There could be only one conclusion from all of that. I really hated goodbyes.

Mom and I tossed my luggage in the back of the van and climbed in. Dad and Camille waved from the porch as we pulled away from the curb. Changing my mind was out of the question at that point. *Boston, here I come!*

"This is Steven and Portia. They're the other two-thirds of my soul saving trio." Mom nodded to the driver and the woman sitting in the seat next to him.

"It's nice to meet you," I said. "Mom said you all agreed I could stay with you for a while. Thanks."

"Jamesie, when are you going to stop calling me Mom? It makes me feel old. I tell you that all the time."

I forced a smile as I turned to her. "I'll stop calling you Mom when you stop calling me Jamesie."

Mom's eyes widened. "But I love my nickname for you."

15

"And I like calling you Mom."

Portia cleared her throat in the front seat. "I'm glad Lillian's finally letting us meet her daughter. We've been living together for years, but she's never introduced us."

"I didn't want you to accidentally say something about ghosts," Mom said.

"Little did you know, you'd been visiting a fellow soul saver every time you went home," Steven added.

"Tell us about your soul saving experiences, Jamie. We can share some of ours," Portia said. "We've got an hour until we're in Boston. We might as well make good use of the time." She swiveled around in her seat, giving me her full attention. I liked her immediately. She looked to be in her late twenties and wore her dark brown hair—the same color as mine—in a casual ponytail. Steven looked to be about her same age. *Just how casual is their relationship?*

We spent the next hour telling stories and swapping tales. Talking with people who'd gone through the exact feelings and emotions I'd gone through lifted my spirits. Portia's initial experience with a ghost was almost identical to my mom's. Both had been leading normal lives when they were sought out by ghosts looking to be extricated. Neither could give it up so they actively searched for other souls to save.

Steven's first experience differed from the other two. After his grandfather passed away during his second year of college, Steven believed he caught a glimpse of him sitting in his favorite chair. The moment only lasted a few seconds, but Steven couldn't shake the impression. He spent his free time looking for proof of the existence of ghosts and that led him to Mom and Portia. The three of them formed their business and had been working together for years.

"How do you advertise?" I asked as we sat at yet another red light. "No offense, but I can imagine placing ads in the newspaper might draw out a lot of crazies."

"You're right," Mom said. "We tried that in the beginning and got all kinds of weird calls. Now that we've established ourselves in the ghost world, we advertise by word of mouth only. We have a long waiting list."

"Does packing up and moving to a new place every few months ever get old?"

Portia grinned from the front seat. "More than you can possibly imagine. But, that being said, I'd rather move five times a year than get a normal job."

I turned to my mom as Steven inched the van forward through the traffic. "No offense, Mom, but I grew up thinking you couldn't hold a job and that's why you moved so much."

All three of them laughed. "You're not the only one who thinks that about us," Steven said, making eye contact with me in the rearview mirror. "My parents have pretty much disowned me because they're too embarrassed by my lifestyle."

Portia nodded in agreement. "I'd be rich if I had a dollar for every time someone asked me when I'm going to finally settle down."

A moment later, the GPS on the dashboard came to life. "*Arriving at destination.*"

My jittery nerves came back and I bounced my leg up and down as I glanced out my window. The apartment building where we'd be staying didn't look too bad. The neighborhood had lots of trees and its own park out front. A couple of little kids played on the jungle gym while two young mothers sat on a bench and talked.

Steven pushed his door open. "I'll run get the keys from the manager's office. Since we're paid up, he said he'd just walk us through real quick. You know, do an initial inspection."

A few minutes later, Steven emerged from the office door with a short man who could stand to lose a few pounds—or a hundred. However, it wasn't his girth that drew my attention. An enormous handle bar mustache jutted out from the sides of his face.

17

Steven motioned for us to follow and we piled out of the van. "This is Mr. Nelson," he said. "He manages this complex and the one next to it."

The man stuck his hand out and shook Portia and Mom's hands. When he got to me, he frowned and stepped back, shooting a glare at Steven. "I thought you said you were only going to have three people living up there. It's only got two bedrooms," he said gruffly, his Boston accent unmistakable.

"This is my daughter," Mom jumped in. "She's just here to visit while we move in. She's not permanent."

I'm not a permanent part of Mom's life. No surprise there.

Mr. Nelson grunted something in response and turned around. His mustache followed him. "Come on. I'll show you the apartment."

We followed Mr. Nelson to an elevator bank and took the lift up to the fifth floor. The building had eight floors in all. I'd never lived in multi-family housing and I cringed at the thought of strangers lurking behind every door. Back in Marion, I could go into any room in the house and look out a window. The widow's walk coming off the attic had the best views of Sippican Harbor. That's where Peter kissed me for the first time.

"As you'll see, your views are pretty good for the city," Mr. Nelson said as he unlocked the door and handed the key to Steven.

I followed the others into the room and looked through the living room window. The concrete structure next door blocked everything—even the sun. "Where?" I said without thinking. Mom giggled, but shushed me anyway.

I stepped closer to the window and peered out. If I stood on tiptoes at just the right angle, I could see Boston Harbor in the not-so-far distance. The mast of a tall ship bobbed in and out of my view. I closed my eyes and breathed deeply. Until that moment, I didn't understand how much the water meant to me. The apartments on the other side of the complex looked out over the little park. But, despite all the concrete, I preferred our view solely because of that tiny sliver of harbor.

"Take a few minutes and walk through the apartment. If you find anything wrong, now is the time to point it out. Otherwise, I'll charge you for it," Mr. Nelson said while staring at his watch and twirling one side of his mustache between his fingers.

I followed Mom into the kitchen and began opening cupboards and drawers. The refrigerator and freezer were both cold, the burners on the stove heated up, and the microwave turned on. Three barstools were pushed next to the counter, a small table with four chairs rested in the dining area, and the living room had a simple beige couch with two matching chairs. A coffee table separated them. Steven and Portia emerged from the hallway and reported that everything worked as it should in the bathroom and bedrooms. The furnished apartment might have been small, but it was in good condition.

"Great. I'll be on my way then," Mr. Nelson said. "There are laundry rooms on the fourth floor and the first floor. Try to respect your neighbors with your noise and, last but not least, don't think you're the exception to the rule when it comes to pets. I don't care if it spends all its time in a cage or knows how to do its business in the toilet. No pets means no pets. If you need me, you know where the office is." He turned on his heel and disappeared into the hall before anyone could respond.

Portia shut the door behind him. "He's a joy, isn't he?"

I cringed. "Does it always feel like you're being judged when you move to a new place?"

Mom exchanged looks with her partners. "Actually, yeah. I'm sure our living situation raises a few eyebrows all by itself."

"And the fact that we always want to sign short leases," Steven added.

Portia shrugged. "Let people judge. I don't care."

The trio had dropped off a load of boxes at a friend's house earlier in the week. Since none of them owned very much, unpacking their few belongings barely took any time.

I decided it might be nice not to have a permanent residence. Letting go of things would be a lot easier. *Of course, it might make letting go of family easy, too.*

At ten o'clock, Mom stretched and yawned. "I'm going to bed. Do you have everything you need, Jamie?"

I glanced at the couch. "I'll be fine. One blanket should be plenty this time of year."

Portia stood and disappeared into the room she'd share with mom. Steven had already retreated to the other room earlier.

"Thanks for agreeing to come," Mom said when we were alone in the room. "I think this is going to be good for both of us."

"Thanks for inviting me."

"Get some sleep. Tomorrow you'll see how we operate. Our new ghost is coming over."

"A new ghost. I can't wait."

Chapter 3

Rise and shine, Jamesie . . . I mean Jamie."

I heard the distant voice, but couldn't quite pull myself from my sleep-induced coma. The too-soft couch and I battled all night and I'd barely gotten any sleep. Not that I'd slept well at all over the last couple of months. I forced my eyes open and blinked against the light a couple of times. Mom stood over me with a giant grin on her face.

I rubbed my eyes. "What time is it?"

"Nine. I thought you were an early riser."

"I thought I was too." My voice sounded gravelly.

"Do you want some breakfast? There's some cereal and milk in the kitchen."

"Thanks." I closed my eyes again.

"Uhh . . . you can't go back to sleep. The new ghost is going to be here at nine-thirty. We need the couch. You know, to pow-wow."

I opened my eyes again. "Right. Sorry. I'll jump in the shower and get out of your way. Can I store my duffle bag in your room?"

"Uh huh. You can just toss your blanket on my bed, too. It's the one under the window."

I took a record-setting shower and dressed just as fast. I wanted to observe the new ghost right from the beginning, but I didn't want to look like a clueless teenager. I pulled my hair up with a gold clip and replaced the tiny silver stud earrings in my ears with gold hoops. I applied a little makeup, a skill I finally understood, and emerged from the bathroom just as a knock sounded on the apartment door.

I waited in the shadows of the hall as the soul saving trio opened the door and greeted the newcomer. Steven's deep voice made introductions and then another male voice responded.

When the foursome came into my view, I took a long look at the new guy. He towered over Mom and Portia in his gray suit with a red and yellow tie. I guessed his age to be somewhere in his mid to late twenties. His shock of red hair stood out the most.

In the past, I'd felt a connection to the ghosts I helped almost immediately. I didn't always understand the feelings, but something inside told me I wanted to be around them. The ghost in front of me gave me the opposite feeling. His presence made me want to take a step back. He saw me standing in the hall and our eyes met. I couldn't bring myself to look away and judging by the way he narrowed his eyes at me, I don't think he could either.

Mom interrupted our staring contest. "Jamie, this is Myles Westing. Myles, this is my daughter, Jamie."

Myles finally broke eye contact and turned his eyes to my mom. I let out a long breath, not aware I'd been holding it.

"Your daughter?" Myles said. "You don't look old enough to have a daughter that age."

Mom giggled and patted him on the forearm. "What can I say? You do crazy things when you're young."

I started to roll my eyes, but stopped mid-roll, not wanting everyone else to see. True, Mom had been young when she had me, but not *that* young. And she'd already been married to Dad when I came along. It wasn't like I was the product of a teen pregnancy the way she made it sound.

"And she knows about my kind already?" Myles continued.

Mom nodded proudly. "She's already been the soul saver for several people. Not bad, huh?"

Myles looked my way again before Steven ushered him to one of the beige chairs. Mom and Portia sat on the couch and Steven dropped into the other chair. I took up residence on one of the barstools. I kept my back to the group, but tried to crunch my cereal flakes quietly so I could hear everything they said. They weren't trying to keep any of it a secret, but they hadn't exactly invited me to join them either.

"Tell us exactly when and where you lived," Portia said to Myles.

"I was born on March 2, 1896, and died on September 7, 1923. I spent my entire life here in Boston. My family has been here since the 1600s. Some of them were instrumental during the Revolutionary War," he said proudly.

"So you're 27?" Mom asked.

"Sure, I guess. If you don't count all the years since I died."

"Sometimes age matters," Steven said while scribbling something in a notebook. "Are any of your family members still alive? Particularly ones that knew you before you died?"

Myles raised his eyebrows. "Still alive? Nope. That would be a really long life."

"Long, but not unheard of. What about your own children? Or a young niece or nephew you were fond of?" Portia asked.

"Never married. No children. No siblings. No nieces or nephews. I was an only child." Myles chuckled and I glanced over my shoulder to take another peek at him. "Actually, I can't answer that last one for sure. My dad took off when I was sixteen or seventeen. Who knows? I could have a dozen siblings out there somewhere."

Everyone's head popped up. They definitely found his joke to be

23

more serious than he himself thought.

"You never saw your dad again? At all?" Mom asked.

"Never."

The ghost in the living room had my full attention. I stopped chewing my cereal and turned on the barstool until I could just see Myles out of the corner of my eye.

"Have you tried to find him since you died?" Steven asked.

Myles stretched his legs and crossed his arms over his chest. "Not really. He was a jerk in life. Why would I want to see him when I'm dead?"

Portia's mouth dropped open. "He could be the key to your extrication. Haven't you been curious?"

Myles shook his head. "Not really. He didn't have much to do with my life."

"Sometimes unfinished business is the last thing you'd expect it to be," Mom said. "That's why it's harder for some ghosts to figure it out than others."

"You can look into it, but I don't think you'll find that dear old dad is the problem."

"What do *you* think is the problem?" Steven asked.

"If I had a clue, do you think I would have come to you guys?"

I stuffed the last bite of my cereal in my mouth and stepped around the counter to put the bowl in the dishwasher. I leaned my elbows on the countertop and watched the scene in the living room—observing without interfering.

Mom cleared her throat. "Next question. How did you die? Death has something to do with extrication more often than not."

Myles blew out his breath. "My death. Now that's a great question. Well . . . I was shot. I went out for a late night stroll one evening and out of nowhere a stray bullet hit me in the chest."

No one seemed fazed be Myles' revelation. I could only imagine the things the soul saving trio had heard during their years in the business.

"What do you mean by a stray bullet?" Portia asked.

Myles stared at Portia for a few seconds before answering. "I mean someone fired and I was in the way."

"How many gunshots were there?" Mom asked.

"I have no idea. I only remember the one. It all happened so fast."

"How do you know it was a stray bullet? Are you sure you weren't the target?" Portia asked. I liked her way of thinking.

"I didn't live in the best neighborhood. That's how poor kids raised with deadbeat dads end up. Not very fitting for someone whose family came from such strong colonial roots. My ancestors practically built this town before and after the war." Myles sat up straighter. "Someone had to take care of my mother after my dad walked out. I did the best I could to support her, but we lived in an area where cops looked the other way. I guess I could have been the target. Maybe someone wanted to rob me."

"After you died, didn't you become a ghost immediately?" Mom asked.

"Yeah. So what?"

"You should have seen the shooter as a ghost."

Myles paused before shaking his head. "I didn't get a good look at him."

"He's lying," I said from my place behind the kitchen counter. I surprised myself. The reaction came from my gut and I didn't expect it to come out verbally. My face burned and my hands became clammy as all eyes in the apartment turned to stare at me.

Myles narrowed his eyes at me. "Excuse me?"

"You're lying," I said again. "Or you're at least leaving part of the story out." I straightened, trying to look more confident in calling his bluff than I felt. My soul saver intuition must have kicked in because I knew without a doubt that he wasn't being truthful.

"*Are* you lying?" Mom asked Myles.

A small smile tugged at the corners of his lips. "I don't know about lying, but I might have left out a few details."

"Maybe you better start over and not leave anything out this time," Steven said. "If you don't tell us everything, you're just wasting our time and yours and you might as well leave."

Myles sat up and rested his elbows on his knees. "I wasn't just out for a stroll. I was visiting one of the underground clubs."

"You mean one of the illegal ones," Portia said. "This was during prohibition, right?"

"Right."

"And?" Portia prompted.

"I had a few ties to the mob. I honestly didn't get a good look at my killer, but I've always guessed that he belonged to a rival gang or maybe someone the mob bosses angered. Who knows?"

"You're talking about the Irish mob?" Steven said.

Myles gave a small nod.

Steven's indifference changed as he took new interest in the man in front of him. "Just how close were your ties?"

"I wasn't an official member, but they watched out for me in exchange for the occasional favor. And before you ask, the answer is no. I never killed anyone for them."

Steven narrowed his eyes. "What exactly did you do for them then?"

Myles sighed deeply. "I'm not proud of it. I did some stupid things in my life. When you're broke and hungry you learn a few tricks for getting what you want."

"So you were a con man," I said, still unable to keep my mouth shut. The first ghost I helped had been raised by habitual con artists and she died because of it. My dislike for the man on the couch grew.

"I guess you could call it that," Myles said.

"Are you even a ghost? Maybe this is a con, too." *Why can't I keep my stupid mouth shut?*

"Jamie—" Mom started to speak, but Myles cut her off.

"It's fine. I *should* prove to you who I am."

Myles stood and snapped his fingers, vanishing into the air as he did so. The room fell silent. A stunt like that would have gotten a few gasps or screams in a normal crowd, but no one in the apartment—including myself—seemed the least bit disturbed by it. I expected Myles to reappear a moment later in the spot where he'd been standing. Instead, he popped up on the other side of the counter, his back to the living room. He leaned toward me, his face so close to mine I could feel his warm breath. I gasped.

"Listen, girl," he whispered so only I could hear. "I don't know what your problem is, but I suggest you mind your own business and let me mind mine. Got it? I don't want some moody teenager ruining my chances at extrication."

"If anyone ruins anything, it will be you," I whispered back, silently begging my heart to stop pounding so hard.

Myles turned around and returned to the chair next to Steven's. I clasped my hands behind my back so no one would see them shaking. *Why does this guy bother me so much?*

"Obviously, you're what you say you are," Portia said with a quick glance in my direction. "I think we need to get more information on your ties to the mob and what exactly you did for them. Maybe your extrication would come if you righted a wrong."

"No one's alive still, remember?" Myles said.

"Maybe not, but their descendants are," Steven said. "You never know what will tip the cards. Just let us do our jobs and we'll try to make the process as quick and painless as possible."

"I'm going to look for information about your missing father." Mom turned to a clean sheet of paper in her notebook and handed it to Myles. "Write down his full name and any information you know

27

about him so I can get an idea where to start. You'd be surprised what you can find online these days."

Myles scribbled on the notepad and handed it back to my mom. "Anything else?"

"Yep. Mob names." Steven handed his notepad to Myles and the ghost wrote again.

"We'll keep in touch. I'm sure we'll have more questions soon. Do you have any questions for us before you leave?" Portia asked.

Myles looked at me before responding. I swallowed hard. "I'm good for now," he said.

Myles might not have been the most scrupulous of characters, but I didn't have any reason not to trust him. He'd come to my mom and her friends because he wanted to leave his ghost life behind. Nothing wrong with that. Besides, some would argue that the last ghost I'd helped—Haven—was pretty sketchy herself. After all, a Salem witch who invites an evil spirit from the underworld to reside on earth isn't exactly the kind of person you bring home to meet your family. Despite the fact that he might be sincere, I planned on giving Myles Westing a wide berth.

As the front door shut behind him, I couldn't help but wonder if he'd really gone. For all I knew, he turned into his invisible self and came right back in. I might never truly be alone.

Chapter 4

Mom convinced herself that Myles' dad would be the key to his extrication, Steven insisted it had something to do with the mob, and Portia wavered between the two. Me? I had no clue. With the ghosts I'd helped in the past, I'd been their "official" soul saver which gave me some extra sense on what direction to take. Doing it without a connection to the ghost couldn't be easy, but that's how Mom, Portia, and Steven always had to do it.

"Find out anything interesting about Myles yet?" I asked Mom. She sat on a barstool in the kitchen with her laptop open on the counter in front of her. Her tanned legs stuck out from her short shorts and I frowned when I realized her legs looked better than mine. Her bare feet revealed toes painted bright purple with yellow smiley faces.

"Actually, I did," Mom answered. "I found a marriage license for Myles' parents. Job and Esther Westing. They're both bible names I think. Isn't that funny?" She laughed.

I raised my eyebrows at her. "That's not uncommon, is it? Why is that funny?"

29

"I don't know. It just made me laugh." She giggled again for affect. I waited patiently for her to get to her point. She stopped laughing, cleared her throat, and continued. "Anyway, his parents weren't married until September of 1895."

"Should that mean something to me?"

"Myles was born in March of the next year. Esther must have already been pregnant when she got married. Seems a little scandalous for that time period. If people knew about it, I'm sure it caused problems. Anyway, it makes me wonder if his parents ever loved each other or if they only got married because Myles was on his way."

I sat down on one of the stools next to her and wrapped my own bare feet around the legs. "Most people wouldn't think twice about a pregnancy these days."

"No kidding, but back then . . ." She stared at the screen again.

"They divorced later, so they must not have cared too much," I said.

"True, but they didn't get divorced for almost twenty years. And I'm not even sure if they actually got a divorce. Myles said his dad took off. He never said they got divorced."

"That story sounds familiar." The words were out of my mouth before I could stop them and for the millionth time that day I wished I could learn to keep my mouth shut.

Mom's smile disappeared. She reached over and put her hand on mine. "I honestly loved your father when I married him. We weren't pretending. And I *still* care about him."

"Just not enough to live with him. And not enough to let him go."

"Let him go?"

My eyes darted around the room as I looked for Stephen and Portia, hoping they'd save me from the awkward conversation. Neither of them were around. I took a deep breath. "You've left Dad hanging for a decade. Isn't that long enough to know if you're going to get back together? What if he wanted to date someone? He couldn't because the two of you are technically still married and he's too much of a gentleman."

Mom raised her eyebrows in surprise. "Dad wants to date someone?"

"No. I mean, I don't know. Maybe. He doesn't talk about stuff like that."

"Your dad doesn't want a divorce."

"How do you know?"

"I've asked."

That little tidbit was news to me. "You have?"

She nodded. "On more than one occasion. I'm fine either way. Ghosts are my life now. But, I figure it's only fair to him to give him a choice. He insists on letting it play out the way everything is right now. If things change in the future . . . well, we can revisit the subject again."

The room seemed to spin and I dropped my head into my hands. I'd always assumed Mom didn't divorce Dad out of some sort of selfish agenda. Dad still cared about her, but I didn't know he cared so deeply he wouldn't take her up on the offer of a divorce. "You mean you can revisit the subject if this ghost business doesn't work out?"

Mom shrugged. "Or, if I ever think he's ready to hear the truth of why I left, maybe that will change things."

"Maybe I should tell him. It might be nice not to sneak around."

"Do you really think he'd believe you?"

"I honestly don't know. If I took a ghost with me and they showed him what they could do, maybe he'd believe. I mean, why wouldn't he? I'm more concerned about him banning me from helping other ghosts. And he'd be crushed that I've lied to him so much lately. I feel awful about it."

"Do you see why I left?"

31

It made a little more sense. "I see why you left, but it wasn't the only choice you had. You could've stayed and just not said anything."

"I wouldn't have been a good mother if all my thoughts were consumed with trying to find another ghost to help and not letting your dad find out about it. Maybe I did make the wrong choice and maybe I didn't. We can't change anything now. And you know what? I think you turned out pretty good. Your dad's done a good job."

Maybe mom and I weren't going to be best friends and sing campfire songs together, but I finally felt like I understood her. When she left home, she *was* thinking about me and Dad and trying to do what she thought would be best for all of us. I'd never considered that. The picture I'd formed of her in my mind was one of a selfish woman pretending to still be a teenager. Since I'd been staying with her, the immaturity I hated had disappeared. *Maybe her behavior was her own nervous way of dealing with things.*

I climbed off the stool and retrieved my shoes from the coat closet near the front door. "I'm going for a walk. I'll stay close and I've got my phone if you need me."

Mom's eyes returned to her screen. "Have fun. I'll just keep plugging away in here."

The humidity hit me as soon as I stepped through the door of our building. I stopped twice to lift my hair from my neck after it started to stick. Pulling it into a ponytail before I left the apartment would have made sense. I walked toward the little park on the opposite side of the complex. A few other tenants were outside enjoying the warm day. Three children chased each other around the playground area, laughing and calling to one another, and a young couple sat on a blanket with a pizza box open in front of them. I could smell the cheese from where I walked and my stomach growled. Maybe I'd suggest we order pizza for dinner.

"You're new here, right?"

Not watching where I walked, I jumped back at the sound of a voice in front of me. I almost stepped off the sidewalk. A boy close to my age stood in front of me with a wide grin.

"Sorry. I didn't mean to scare you," he said. "I'm Daniel."

"Hi," I said as I shook the hand he offered. My heart fluttered when our hands touched and color rose to my cheeks. Daniel was cute. *Really* cute. Not boy-next-door kind of cute like Peter, but make-your-heart-skip-a-beat-if-he-smiles-at-you kind of cute.

Daniel continued to stare at me expectantly. I didn't know what he wanted. "Do you have a name or do you prefer to be called Hey You?" he finally said.

"Oh, sorry," I said, blushing even more. "I'm Jamie."

"I saw you carrying boxes in yesterday. I guess I should've offered to help, but I was on my way out."

"We didn't have much to move in. We're in one of the furnished apartments."

"We? How many are in your family?"

"Actually, my mom is living here with a couple of roommates. I'm just visiting her for the summer. You?"

"Just me and my uncle. We're on the fifth floor."

"Same here."

His eyes narrowed. "Wait . . . there's only one empty apartment on my floor. Did you move into 512?"

I nodded.

"You're right across the hall from me. Now I feel even worse that I didn't stop."

"Really, don't feel bad. There were four of us working and it only took an hour to carry everything up in the elevator. We're already completely unpacked. No big deal."

"Good. Well, it was nice meeting you . . . Jamie, right?"

I nodded again.

He glanced at his watch and then at the building. "I'm supposed to be somewhere. I'll see ya around."

I smiled as he walked off. For the first time since I developed a crush on Peter, I'd met a guy who made me temporarily forget Peter even existed.

"How was your walk?" Mom asked when I stepped back through the door an hour later, desperately in need of a second shower. She sat next to Steven on the couch.

"Good," I said. "It's hot out there."

"I guess it's a good thing I've been inside all day."

I motioned toward the papers spread out on the coffee table. "Did you find anything else?"

"Tons! Come see."

"So apparently Job Westing, Myles' dad, *did* have another family."

I sat down in one of the chairs and leaned forward. "After he left Myles' mom?"

"Nope. His dad must have been quite the jerk. He had another family at the same time he was living with Myles and Esther," Steven added.

"No way."

"It looks that way. The father's name on the birth certificates of these two children," Steven held up two sheets of paper, "is Job Westing. His birth date matches the Job Westing on Myles' birth certificate." He held up a third sheet of paper.

"Okay . . ."

"These two kids were born in Boston in 1901 and 1903. They weren't that much younger than Myles," Mom said.

"Are you sure it's the same Job Westing?"

Mom nodded. "Pretty sure. It's not that common of a name and on the census records, the two younger kids are listed as living with their mother only. It says she never married."

"Do you think Myles' mom knew about the second family?" I asked.

"We don't know. Myles is coming over first thing in the morning to take us to some spots where he used to live and work. We'll tell him what we've learned then."

The door opened and Portia stepped through, her arms loaded with grocery bags.

"It's *so* hot out there," Portia said.

I helped her set the bags on the kitchen counter. "That's exactly what I said when I walked in."

"I drove to the store in the air conditioned van and still couldn't cool down. I'm making lasagna for dinner. Is that okay?"

"Sounds great." I stared at the array of ingredients Portia pulled from her bags. "Are you making it from scratch?"

"Of course. Is there any other way?"

"Dad and I cook lasagna all the time. We open the box and stick it in the oven for an hour."

Portia laughed. "That's not cooking. That's reheating. Want to help me? It's not as hard as it looks."

I glanced at Mom. She and Steven still sat on the couch, deep in discussion about the pile of papers in front of them. "Sure. I can try."

Portia and I went to work. I cooked the noodles and browned Italian sausage while she seasoned tomatoes.

"What do you like to do? I mean, when you're not saving lost souls," Portia asked.

Why do adults always ask this question? "Umm . . . I read. A lot. Or I hang out with my friends."

"Yeah? What do you do with your friends?"

I could barely think of anything. We went to movies and wandered around town. Sometimes I watched Camille paint her nails or she painted mine. I couldn't seem to hold the little brushes steady enough to paint my own. "Not a lot. I love Marion, but there's not

35

much to do there." My life sounded boring.

"What about guys? Surely someone as cute as you has a boyfriend."

I thought of Peter and looked away so she wouldn't see my reaction. And then for some strange reason my thoughts turned to Daniel. "No official boyfriend," I answered.

"Don't let her kid you," Mom called from across the room. "She's totally got a boyfriend."

Portia raised her eyebrows. "I think there's a story here."

"We're good friends and we date sometimes, but there's nothing official."

Mom rolled her eyes. "Maybe you should make it official. I like Peter. You need to flirt more. If you do, I'll bet he makes it official by fall."

My face burned. "We'll see."

"Sorry I brought up the subject," Portia whispered to me after Steven pulled Mom's attention back to the papers in front of them.

"It's fine," I said. "And thanks for teaching me to cook."

"Any time. Your mom, Steven, and I have an unspoken arrangement. Steven manages the financial side of our business, Lillian manages the ghosts, and I'm usually the one who cooks and maintains the day to day household stuff wherever we are. I'll gladly let you help whenever you want."

When it came time to layer the lasagna, I struggled to hold the slippery noodles and they kept jumping out of the casserole dish and onto the counter. Portia assured me that no matter how it looked, it would taste perfect. She was right. The thick layers of meat and garlicky sauce held together by drippy cheese tasted better than anything I'd had all summer. Good thing I didn't ask to order pizza.

Chapter 5

We're leaving in half an hour, Jamie," Mom called from the kitchen. I stretched my legs until they reached the end of the couch, but I didn't stand. No sense in getting up before the one shower was available. After only two days, I really missed having a bathroom all to myself.

"Leaving?" I asked as I rubbed my eyes. "Where are we going?"

"I told you yesterday. We're going with Myles to see where he used to live and work. Remember? Aren't you coming?"

"I didn't know I was invited."

Mom walked into the living room and sat down on one of the chairs. "Of course you're invited. I thought that's why you came here this summer, to see how we operate."

It had nothing to do with wanting to hang out with my absentee mother. "Yeah, well, that was before I met Myles."

"What's wrong with Myles?" Mom asked in surprise.

"He's kind of a jerk."

"What makes you say that?"

"He hung out with the Irish mob at illegal bars and conned

37

people."

"That was a long time ago. One thing you'll quickly learn about ghosts is that they're usually good people who made a few errors in judgment when they were alive. When they come to us, it's because they want to fix those mistakes. We shouldn't judge them for wanting to patch up whatever went wrong."

"Sorry. Maybe I judged him too quickly. There was just something about him that rubbed me the wrong way."

"I won't tell him."

"I'm guessing he figured out I don't like him all on his own." I sat up and stretched my legs out in front of me. "Would it be a big deal if I just stayed here today?"

"Not at all. I don't want to force you into helping us this summer, but know that you're always invited, okay?"

"Thanks. Maybe I'll keep looking things up online while you're gone."

"That's a good idea. We were going to look up information about Myles' death yesterday, but none of us had any time. Let me know if you can find anything out about that, will you?"

"Sure. Have fun with the mobster."

Mom laughed and gave me a little hug before she walked back to her bedroom. She and the others were gone when I emerged from the shower twenty minutes later. I poured myself a bowl of the same cereal I'd eaten for breakfast the day before and took it to the table. Picking up the closest chair, I scooted it to an angle where I could see the sliver of Boston Harbor through the living room window.

As an only child with a father who worked a lot, much of my life was spent alone. Since I started hanging out with ghosts, I usually had someone around all the time—whether I wanted them there or not. I'd kind of gotten used to having someone else to talk to. That morning, solitude didn't seem as appealing as it usually did.

I texted Camille, but she didn't respond. I poured myself a second bowl of cereal and returned to my solitude. "Maybe Peter will want to talk to me," I mumbled as I texted him.

"*What's up?*" He texted back almost immediately.

"*Not a lot. Just sitting in the apartment while Mom and her friends are off trying to save a lost soul.*"

"*You're not helping?*"

"*The ghost is a jerk.*"

"*I'm calling you.*"

I waited thirty seconds before my phone rang. "Hey," I answered.

"It's easier to have a full conversation when I'm not typing on a little screen," Peter said.

"True."

"So the new ghost is a jerk?"

I spent a few minutes telling Peter about Myles Westing and the weird feeling he gave me.

"The guy sounds like a real winner."

"Exactly. I'm the only one that thinks so, though. Mom thinks I'm judging him too soon. She's probably right."

"Not necessarily. You're good about trusting your gut."

"Yeah, but I'm not his soul saver. My gut feelings come when I'm actually connected to someone." I sighed. "Mom wants me to look into his death while they're gone today. Is it bad that I intend to dig up dirt on him?"

Peter laughed. "I wouldn't expect anything less from you. You always look for the negative first."

"I do not."

Silence.

I smiled to myself. "Okay, I do. It's not always a bad thing, though."

I stood from the chair and carried the carton of milk back to the refrigerator. Balancing the milk and my phone in one hand while trying to open the refrigerator with the other proved to be harder

39

than it looked. I finally got a good grip on the door handle and yanked. The door popped open and the pan of leftover lasagna flew out as if it had a mind of its own. It hit the ground with a loud thud, splattering red sauce all over the kitchen and my white t-shirt.

"Crap!" I yelled into the phone.

"What happened?"

"*I* happened. I swear I'm so clumsy. I need to hang up so I can do a load of laundry."

"Sounds . . . thrilling. Have fun with your mom and the new ghost."

"Thanks."

We ended the call and I hurried into mom's bedroom to dig out another shirt to wear. My wardrobe pretty much consisted of t-shirts and jeans—except in the summer when I daringly exchanged the jeans for shorts. After pulling a clean yellow t-shirt over my head, I pawed through Mom's laundry hamper for enough clothes to make a load. I scrounged up all the quarters I could find in my purse and grabbed a container of detergent out of the hall closet. Having a washer and dryer at our home in Marion, I had no idea how much it would cost to do a load of laundry. "One more thing I miss about having an actual home," I muttered as I opened the front door.

Much to my surprise, and a little to my horror, the door across the hall opened at the exact same time. Daniel stepped out, holding a laundry basket of his own. *Please let him not have heard me talking to myself.* I couldn't quite break the habit—another consequence of being an only child.

"Morning," he said. "It's Jamie, right?"

"Uh huh. Daniel?" There was no way I would have forgotten the name of someone who looked the way he did.

"Yep."

I locked the apartment door behind myself while Daniel did the same thing to his door. Desperate for some sort of conversation starter, I searched my brain for anything remotely interesting. Talking to hot guys wasn't my strongest ability. I took a deep breath and turned around. "Could you explain to me where the laundry room is? The building manager told us where it was when we moved in, but I didn't pay attention." *There. A completely innocent question.*

Daniel grinned, showing off a dimple in one cheek. "Sure. There're two of them and they aren't that hard to find. There's one on the fourth floor and one on the first floor, but I'll let you in on a secret. Even though it's technically closer, skip the one on the fourth floor. The washers don't spin the clothes out as much so it takes forever for them to dry. Plus, Mrs. Hayley hangs out in there *all* the time. She's nice enough for an elderly lady, but she'll talk your ear off."

"Thanks for the warning. First floor it is."

I followed Daniel to the elevator and he stood to the side so I could step on first. We didn't talk while the elevator descended, and I found myself wishing I'd just gone to the fourth floor laundry room. Daniel didn't seem bothered by the silence, but it made me anxious.

The laundry room was right off the elevator. I carried my basket to the nearest available machine and set it down. Daniel took the machine next to me. I piled the dirty clothes in and then stared at the machine, trying to figure out how to turn it on. I stuffed every quarter I brought into the metal change holder, but it wasn't enough. *This is so completely embarrassing. Where's a good hole to crawl into when you need one?* I started to pull the clothes back out of the washer, but stopped when I felt a hand on my shoulder.

"Uhh . . . need help?" Daniel asked.

"I'm fine. I didn't bring enough money down. I'm not used to doing laundry this way, I guess. I'll just have to come back down later." I didn't turn around. My face was so warm, even my ears burned.

"It's crazy what they charge for these things. It's not any better at

41

one of the Laundromats in town, though. Here." Daniel reached over me and began feeding quarters into my machine.

"Hey! You don't have to do that. Really. I just need to go upstairs and get some more money."

He shrugged. "It's not a big deal."

"Thanks." I smiled. "I'll pay you back. I promise."

"I'm not worried about it."

When both machines were running, I followed Daniel to a row of plastic chairs pushed against one wall.

"Have you always lived in Boston?" Daniel asked.

"I've lived here for exactly two days."

"Wow. That's a long time."

"What about you?" I asked.

"I've always lived here."

"You don't have an accent," I said without thinking.

Daniel laughed. "Is that a requirement of residents?"

"No. Sorry." I twisted my hands together in my lap.

"Don't be. It's not the first time someone's said that to me. I guess I sound like my parents and they didn't have accents. They weren't native to the city."

"Where are your parents?" I asked, but then realized it might be a sensitive subject. "I mean, you don't have to tell me if you don't want to."

Daniel slid down in his chair and crossed his arms over his chest. "I don't mind. They both passed away. That's why I live with my uncle. Charlie is his name."

"Sorry about your parents."

"They've been gone for a long time so I'm used to it." He smiled and I struggled to take my eyes off him. He completely fascinated me. *How can one guy be so cute?*

"You said you're living with your mom, right?" he said.

I continued to twist my hands in my lap. "Yeah. My dad and I live down in Marion. I've been there my whole life. My parents are separated."

"Sorry. That's got to be hard."

"It's pretty much the only life I know. I haven't lived with Mom since I was six. This is a new experience for me."

"Do you get along with her?"

"Yes. That's kind of the strange part, though. It seems like all my friends fight with their parents now and then, but I never do. I think it's because we're *not* close. There's nothing to fight about. I mean, you wouldn't fight with a complete stranger, would you?"

Daniel nodded slowly. "I get your point, but I wouldn't worry about it too much. I didn't fight with my parents and I think we had a pretty good relationship."

"You probably think I'm an idiot. I can't run a washing machine and I babble on to someone I barely met about my messed up life. Sorry."

Daniel threw his head back and laughed out loud. I liked the sound of it. "I've seen some really messed up families, J. You seem okay to me. And for the record, I *don't* think you're an idiot."

J? He's giving me a nickname already?

We continued to talk and by the time the washers beeped, I felt like we were old friends. I let my hands drop to my sides, no longer feeling the need to fidget.

"Thanks for entertaining me." I examined the white t-shirt I pulled from the washer. All the red spots had come out and I smiled to myself. "Maybe I'll see you around."

"You're not going to dry your clothes?" Daniel asked with a raise of the eyebrows. "I can give you quarters for the dryer."

"Not these. I'm hanging them to dry. Thanks for the offer. I promise I'll pay you back later."

"I'll tell you what. Go out with me tomorrow night and we'll call it even."

My heart stopped beating. Literally. *Did the cutest guy in history seriously just ask me out?* "Umm . . . I . . ." The offer came out of nowhere and I didn't know how to respond.

"If you don't want to, that's fine. And you don't have to repay me."

"No! I mean, no. I'll go. It sounds fun."

"How about I come get you around seven tomorrow?"

My mouth still hung open and I made a conscious effort to close it. "Sure. That sounds great."

We exchanged cell numbers and I took my basket of wet clothes back to the apartment. I walked up all the flights of stairs instead of using the elevator. After all, I had a lot of excited energy to burn.

"Myles Westing," I muttered as I typed the name into the internet search engine. "September 7, 1923." I hoped my search would magically produce an obituary, but it didn't. None of the search results had anything to do with Myles Westing the ghost.

Not giving up, I tried a site where burials all over the country were listed. I sat up straighter in my chair when I saw one hit pop up under Myles' name. "Names of deceased believe to be buried in Potter's Field," I read aloud. Myles Westing's name appeared at the bottom of the alphabetical list. "I found you. Now, to figure out where Potter's Field is." If other ghosts resided in the cemetery, they might know Myles and be willing to talk."

I returned to the original search engine and typed: Potter's Field Boston. My search turned up definitions more than anything else and I learned that Potter's Field referred to any grave where unknown or poor are buried. I wouldn't find out where Myles had been buried unless I asked him. He'd want to know why I was snooping into his business and I didn't want to have that conversation. I'd just have to look for something else.

Next, I searched through scanned copies of old Boston Herald editions. The images were fuzzy, but readable. I started with the date Myles died and worked forward, finding something on the day after his birth.

> *The body of Boston resident Myles Westing was found by a man who wishes to remain anonymous near the city park on Layton Street, at 7:14 a.m., the morning of September 7. Police believe Westing was illegally intoxicated at the time of the shooting.*
>
> *Captain Willard of the Boston Police Department stated that no witnesses have come forward and ask that anyone who may have been in the area of Layton and Third Streets on the evening of the sixth or early morning of the seventh please notify them immediately.*

"Come on. Say something I don't already know." I stopped reading the article long enough to gulp some water from the water bottle next to me. Up to that point, the details proved Myles' story. Maybe I judged him too soon.

> *According to copies of court records owned by this paper, Westing has had numerous run-ins with the police and has been incarcerated for theft on more than one occasion. Westing also had known ties to one of the local gangs and police have not ruled out the possibility that the shooting could be related to those connections.*
>
> *This reporter made attempts to contact Esther Westing, the deceased's mother, but those attempts were not successful. Ms. Westing's last known address was the same as her son's, but neighbors claim they have not seen her for years and that Myles Westing*

lived alone. More on this case will be printed as it becomes available.

"He did lie," I whispered. "He said he lived with his mother, but she'd already moved somewhere when he died. Why would he lie about that?"

The front door opened and I jumped in surprise. Mom and her partners stepped through the doorway. I frowned when Myles followed behind them. Not wanting him to see what I'd been reading, I quickly closed my laptop and leaned my elbows on it.

"How was your day?" I asked to the room in general.

"Not bad," Portia responded first. "I got to see more of the city than I ever have before."

"I don't know if I saw more than I've seen in the past, but I definitely saw areas I've never been," Mom added.

"Or ever thought I'd go," Steven mumbled.

Myles plopped into a chair at the table. "I warned you that I was raised in a seedy area."

"Did you find anything that might help?" I asked.

"That remains to be seen," Steven answered. "It'll take us a while to retrace all his steps and see where we need to focus our efforts."

"So, Myles." I tried to sound nonchalant. "What happened to your mother after you died? If you were her sole provider, there must not have been anyone left to take care of her. That's sad."

Myles slowly turned his head toward me and stared as if he could see right through me. He knew I had ulterior motives. "After my death, she moved to a boarding house where she could share a room with other unfortunate ladies in similar situations. She baked bread for the neighbors and barely scraped by. She died of heart failure."

His response would sound genuine enough to the casual listener, but to me it sounded rehearsed and overly dramatized. I absolutely couldn't figure the ghost out. If he really wanted to be extricated, why wouldn't he be honest about the details of his past? Maybe he didn't want to be extricated. Maybe the whole thing was a game. Once a con man always a con man? Maybe *we* were his latest targets.

Chapter 6

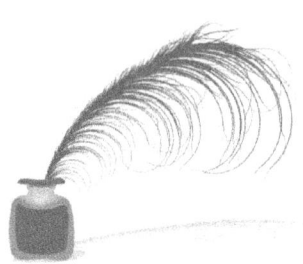

Camille didn't return my text from first thing in the morning until everyone else had gone to bed. I almost didn't answer it.

"*Sorry. Allison hid my phone. I hate her,*" she texted.

"*It's ok.*"

"*How's Boston?*"

"*Good, I guess. I haven't actually gone anywhere yet,*" I texted.

"*Sounds super fun.*"

"*Thrilling. The new ghost is a jerk so I don't really want to help him. You'd hate him, too.*"

"*Sorry.*"

I started to type something about Daniel, but then hesitated. *Camille has no problem getting dates and finding guys that like her. What if she comes to visit sometime and he sees her and forgets all about me?* I shook my head. I was being ridiculous. "*I met a guy.*"

"*???*"

"*He's really nice. And cute.*"

"*You forgot about Peter that fast?*"

"*I didn't forget about him. This guy lives by us and he asked me out. He seems nice.*"

"*Whatever.*"

I shook my head at the phone. "*What's that supposed to mean?*"

"*Doesn't seem like you.*"

"*Maybe if I go out with Daniel, I'll know how I really feel about Peter.*"

"*Ok. But don't tell Peter. It'll crush him,*" she texted.

"*I won't if you don't.*"

I put my phone down and crawled under the blankets on the couch. *Would* it crush Peter if he knew I had a date with someone else? We'd agreed to wait until the end of summer to make any relationship decisions, but we never said anything about dating other people.

"What if Peter dates while I'm gone?" I whispered to myself in the dark. Yep. No question it would devastate me. I chewed on my lip and tried to push the image of him with another girl from my mind.

"Do you want to come with us today?" Mom asked at eight the next morning. Too many sleep-deprived nights made the thought of getting up send a wave of depression washing over me.

"I'm not sure," I answered.

"Does it make a difference if you know that Myles and Steven will be off doing stuff while Portia and I go together?"

I sat up. "That makes a huge difference. I'll come."

I really wanted to tell them about Myles' lies after they came home the night before, but he stayed until ten and then I didn't know if he'd actually left or if he lurked behind in his invisible form to see what we'd say when he wasn't present. I'd probably been overreacting, but I didn't want to tip him off and not know it.

"When do you think we'll be back?" I asked Mom as she pulled

49

the van out of the parking lot at the apartment complex.

"I have no idea. Why? Do you have a date?" she laughed and kept driving.

My mouth dropped open and it took me a while to respond. "Uhh . . . actually, I *do* have a date."

Mom giggled again, but Portia turned and stared at me. "I think she's being serious, Lillian."

Mom glanced at me in the rearview mirror. "Seriously?" she asked.

"Uh huh."

"We've only been here a couple of days. Who do you have a date with?"

"I met—"

"Is Peter coming to visit already? I like him," Mom said, cutting me off. "You'll like him too, Portia. Maybe you should invite all your friends up for a day sometime."

I sighed in exasperation. "It's not with Peter. I met a guy when I went for a walk the other day. He lives in our complex. He's sixteen. We talked again when I did laundry yesterday and he asked me out. Oh, and he lives across the hall from us." I spoke so fast I had to take a deep breath when I finished my explanation.

Mom's eyes met mine in the rearview mirror. A grin spread across her face. "This is totally not like you."

I shrugged. "Maybe I'm changing."

Portia leaned closer to Mom. "Are you going to let her go?"

"Why wouldn't I?" Mom said in surprise.

Portia frowned. "You haven't met him. You don't know his family. What if he's a serial killer?" She glanced at me in the backseat. "Not that I don't trust your judgment, Jamie."

I smiled at the idea of Daniel being a serial killer. He'd been a complete gentleman when we talked the day before. Of course, that didn't necessarily mean anything. In Marion, everyone had known everyone else forever and if you said yes to a date you knew exactly what you were getting into.

"Maybe she's right. If I'm going to be your guardian for the summer, I should probably screen your dates," Mom said. "Does your dad meet your dates and their parents before you leave with them?"

Of all the times for Mom to take a parenting stand...thanks, Portia. "Other than Peter, I've been on two dates. One of them Dad arranged himself," I said.

"Can you have his mom call me before you go?" She wasn't going to let it drop.

"His mom is dead. So is his dad. He lives with his uncle named Charlie. And no, I haven't met Charlie."

"What time is your date? Maybe I'll just run across the hall and talk to his uncle before you leave."

I pictured how that meeting would end. Mom would try to flirt with Charlie and she'd end up embarrassing me. Worse, she might try to flirt with Daniel.

Portia turned around from the front seat again and scrunched up her face. "Sorry!" she mouthed.

"It's fine," I mouthed back. "By the way, Myles lied to you again," I said aloud.

"What are you talking about?" Mom asked.

"I looked into his death like you said. Most of it was true, but he lied about his mom."

"Really," Portia exchanged glances with Mom before turning back to me. "We suspected he still hasn't been completely truthful. That's why we split up today. We figured we could talk more openly and look into things he might not want us to see if Steven kept him occupied."

Relief washed over me. I'd been afraid that I'd have to convince them that something wasn't right about their new ghost.

51

"It's so strange. Why wouldn't he just be honest about everything? I mean, does he really want to be extricated or not?" Portia continued.

"It's like he's playing some kind of game," I said.

Mom sighed. "We've never had a ghost not be honest with us before."

"Sorry. I must be the jinx. Maybe you better send me back to Marion."

"I suspect that he does want to be extricated, but lying and deceiving has been something he's done for so long, he can't figure out how to stop."

"You're probably right," Portia agreed. "We'll just be extra cautious. And don't hesitate to tell us if something doesn't seem right to you, Jamie."

After explaining what I learned about Myles' mom to them, we made the office of the Boston Herald our first stop of the day. An overly talkative but helpful lady with a huge wad of gum in her mouth helped us print off a copy of the article I'd found. She also found editions of the paper where Myles' name was listed on court records. We returned to the van with a file folder full of documents and growling stomachs.

"Let's find somewhere to eat. I'm starving," Mom said.

We chose a little café around the corner and sat at one of the tables on the front sidewalk. Mom spread the new documents in front of us.

Portia picked up one sheet and narrowed her eyes. "Apparently his minor crimes weren't so minor after all."

I looked over her shoulder at the paper she held. "Sure, but only if you consider armed robbery and assault on an officer major."

"He only served six months for the assault. How long did he serve for the bank robbery?" Mom asked.

I picked up a different sheet of paper. "Three years. He died after

52

only being out of prison for two months. That might be important. Maybe someone he ticked off in prison got released and did him in."

"Lillian, why haven't you brought your daughter along before now? I like the way she thinks," Portia said between bites of her salad.

"I would have if she'd confided in me sooner." Mom elbowed me playfully.

I tucked my hair behind my ears. "You could have confided in me, too, you know. And to be truthful, I didn't confide in you. You just caught me in a moment of weakness with an out-of-control ghost."

"Yeah, how *did* you find out about her?" Portia asked Mom.

"You tell her, Jamie. It's your story." Mom took a giant bite of her sandwich and looked at me expectantly.

"Fine. The last ghost I saved was a witch from Salem. A real witch. When she died, she accidentally released an evil spirit and I had to send him back by learning to cast spells."

Portia coughed and had to sip water before talking. "You're kidding."

"I wish."

"That's insane!" Her mouth hung open.

"Anyway, I was practicing spells one afternoon and I made some of the furniture float. I couldn't figure out how to get it back down and Haven—that was the name of the ghost—wasn't around. Mom walked in and saw the furniture before I had a chance to fix it."

Portia shook her head. "That's one of the best—and most unbelievable—stories I've heard in a long time."

At the time of the incident, I'd been horrified. Now that a little time had passed, I could laugh at the situation. If only Dad knew what had happened in his living room that day.

"Can you still cast spells?" Portia asked. "I'm still trying to comprehend the whole witch thing."

I shook my head. "Nope. The magic was tied to Haven's spell

book. It's been destroyed. I'm completely normal now."

"Except that you're a soul saver." Mom tossed her napkin onto her plate and pushed away from the table. "We should probably get back to this case. What's next on our agenda?"

"Do we know where Myles was buried?" Portia asked Mom. "You know ghosts like to hang around their bodies. Maybe another one is around and could help us."

"I thought of the exact same thing, but I don't think you're going to have much luck there," I said. "Myles didn't get a normal burial. No one, including his missing mother, came to claim his body. I found a reference online that said he was buried in Potter's Field. It didn't indicate where. And I didn't dare ask."

Mom pulled out her phone and started typing. "I don't mind asking. I'll text Steven and tell him to ask Myles."

"Let's keep looking into the death of Esther Westing. If we know when she died, it might make a difference." Portia started to say something else, but then stopped. She tilted her head back and forth and narrowed her eyes. She looked from me to Mom before clearing her throat and asking, "What if Esther died before Myles? The article said she hadn't been seen for a while. Maybe it's because she was already dead."

"You think Myles killed her," I whispered.

Portia raised her arms and then dropped them again. "The only thing I know for sure is that this case is way more twisted than we originally thought."

I jumped into the shower as soon as we got home at five. Myles and Steven hadn't returned and I hoped to be on my date before they got back. I climbed out of the shower, dried off, and wrapped a towel around my head. Steam clouded the bathroom mirror and I wiped it away with another towel, feeling the need to see the entire room. Ever since I started helping ghosts, I'd had a paranoia that someone might be lurking around when I showered.

I used Mom and Portia's bedroom to dress. I'd only packed two skirts—the only two skirts I actually owned, unless you counted the clothes I "inherited" from Sophia. If I had it my way, I'd wear shorts or jeans all the time. Or better yet, sweat pants. I chose the pale blue skirt and paired it with a yellow shirt. Dropping my hands to my side, I turned around three times in front of the long mirror mounted on the closet door. "Casual yet dressy," I said. "And I can still get away with wearing flip flops."

I combed through my hair, but when it came time to actually do something with it, I didn't know where to begin. Mom was far girlier than me. "Mom!" I called while continuing to stare at my image in the mirror. She didn't respond so I called even louder. "Mom!"

Nothing.

"Lillian!" I finally yelled.

The door opened and I whirled around, expecting to see Mom standing there, but Portia stuck her head through the crack instead. "Did you need something, hon?"

"Oh. Sorry. I was just going to see if Mom wanted to help me with my hair."

Portia came all the way into the room and stood next to me in front of the mirror. "I can help you if you want."

"It's not a big deal. Where's Mom?"

Portia glanced at the open bedroom door. "She . . . umm . . . stepped out while you were in the shower."

I turned away from the mirror and faced her. "Stepped out where?"

"I'm sorry. Don't hate me. I guess since I said something this morning, she decided to go across the hall and meet your date's uncle."

I closed my eyes and took a deep breath. "You're kidding, right?"

55

"Sorry."

I opened my eyes and crossed the room to the door in two giant steps. "This is *so* embarrassing. I can't even go on this date now. Daniel's going to think I live with a crazy person."

I stormed down the hall with Portia on my heels. Gritting my teeth, I yanked the front door open, but Portia reached around me and pushed it shut before I could leave the apartment. She stepped in front of me and leaned her back against the closed door, her arms spread out as if she'd use her body to keep me from leaving the apartment if necessary.

"You'll make it worse if you go over there. I promise," she said.

"I think it's already at its worst."

"Why are you so convinced that Lillian is going to embarrass you?"

"Because, that's what she always does."

"How?"

"I don't know. She just does."

Portia dropped her arms from the door and crossed them over her chest. "I don't think she does anything different than anyone else's parents. You're just reacting this way because you need something to be mad at her for. I know she hasn't been there for you in a long time. And honestly, I'm on your side on that issue. But she's trying now. She really wants to make the whole being a mom thing work, but she's struggling. She's just as scared about this as you."

Portia turned on a smile and put her hands on my shoulders. "Teenagers are supposed to be embarrassed by their parents. It's a rule. My parents were horrifyingly embarrassing when I was a teenager. My dad would sit on the front porch and wait for all of my dates to come so he could talk to them first. When we got home at night, he would still be sitting there, making sure there were no goodnight kisses. I used to hate him for it, but you know what? Now that I'm older, I realize he did it because he loved me. I'm glad he was involved. Lillian's trying, and she might fail, but at least give her a chance."

I sighed and backed away from the door. "Whatever. I just hope I don't have to tell you I told you so."

I stomped back to the bedroom and Portia followed. "Are you going to let me help with your hair or not?"

"Do what you want. Just don't embarrass me."

She went to work with curling irons and sprays and things I didn't know anything about. I kept my eyes closed most of the time, scared of what I'd look like when she finished.

"All done. What do you think?" she asked a while later.

I opened my eyes and blinked. "Is that really my hair?"

"Do you like it?" she whispered.

"I love it. I was afraid I'd look all poufy, but I don't." I leaned closer to the mirror. "Wow! My hair has never been shiny before . . . thanks."

"My pleasure. I have a little sister and I used to do her hair all the time. It's been a while since someone let me. Can I help with your makeup?"

I didn't usually wear a lot of makeup, but after taking another look at my hair, all doubts washed away. "Absolutely."

Chapter 7

Mom didn't come back to the apartment until twenty minutes before Daniel was supposed to come get me. I glared at her the second she stepped through the door. "Are you happy now? Did he pass your test? Am I allowed to go on the date?" I asked.

My attitude didn't faze her. "Uh huh. He seems like a great guy. You have my permission."

"Good. That's the first time in my entire life I've had to have *your* permission to . . . never mind." I breathed out slowly, deciding to stop trying to push her away and just live with the idea that she might actually be trying. "What was Uncle Charlie like? Have you been talking to him? Is that why you were there so long?"

"Whoa. One question at a time." Mom put her hands up. "No. I didn't actually get to meet him. He's not home right now. I've just been talking to Daniel this whole time. He's really friendly."

"Congratulations. I think you've talked to him longer than I have. Any deep, dark secrets I should know about before I leave?"

"Nope. He's clean," she said with a smile. "By the way, you look great Jamesie."

"It's all Portia's doing."

Mom looked at Portia with raised eyebrows. "Impressive."

The front door opened again and Steven and Myles stepped through. I frowned automatically. Steven I could handle. Myles? Not so much.

Steven walked into the kitchen and pulled a glass out of the cupboard, but Myles stopped and did a double take, looking me up and down as if he were inspecting me. I shuddered and instinctively stepped behind Portia.

"Find anything interesting today?" Steven asked.

"Mostly just more unanswered questions. You?" Mom said.

"We—"

I have no idea what Steven answered. A knock came at the door right then and I bolted from behind Portia. "See ya!" I said as I flew by Mom. I managed to open the door, step into the hall, and shut the door behind myself all in one quick motion.

Daniel's face registered about six different emotions when I burst through the door, ending in bewilderment. "Uhh . . . hi."

"Hello."

"I've never met a girl so eager to go on a date before," he teased.

My mouth opened, but no words came out. An all-too-familiar warmth spread to my cheeks.

"Don't worry about it," Daniel said quickly, coming to my rescue. "You look great, by the way." When he looked at me, it didn't creep me out the same way it did with Myles.

"Thanks."

Daniel pulled his arm from behind his back and thrust it toward me. "These are for you."

I gaped at the colorful bouquet of flowers in his hand. "For me? Really?" No guy had ever given me flowers before.

"Yeah. I didn't know what kind of flowers you like. Or what your favorite color is. So . . . I got one of each."

I grinned. "They're perfect. I'm not the kind of girl that plays favorites. Thank you."

"Do you want to put them in water before we leave?"

"Uhh . . ." The idea of introducing Daniel to everyone else in the apartment, especially Myles, didn't exactly appeal to me. "I'll just have my mom take care of them."

I opened the door just wide enough to poke my head through. "Mom!" I called. Her face appeared next to mine a moment later. "Can you put these in water for me? Thanks!" I shoved the bouquet through the crack and shut the door again. "Ready to go?" I said as I turned back to Daniel.

"Yes. I'm ready. Let's go before you implode."

"Where are we going anyway?" I asked as we walked toward the elevator

"Don't laugh, but I thought maybe we could go to a museum."

"Why would I laugh at that?"

"I don't know. It's probably not the most exciting place you've been on a date. Most dates seem to involve movies and stuff like that. If we're sitting in a movie theater, we can't even talk to each other."

"Believe me. I'm more at home in museums than in movie theaters anyway. I kind of have a thing for history." *If you only knew how close I've been to history.*

"Good. Have you ever been to the Boston Tea Party Ships and Museum?"

I shook my head.

"Good. Neither have I. They're having late hours tonight so I thought we could go check it out."

Okay. Daniel was too good to be true. He looked great, his manners were impeccable, he planned to take me to a museum, and the smell of whatever cologne he happened to be wearing that night made me want to sigh with happiness. There had to be something wrong with him and even if it took me all night, I'd figure out what it was.

"I called for a cab. That's ours in front of the office," Daniel said as we exited the apartment complex.

He opened the door for me and I climbed in and put my seatbelt on while he circled around to get in the other side. I tried to touch as little of the car as possible. I hated cabs almost as bad as public transportation.

"306 Congress Street," Daniel instructed the driver before turning his attention back to me. "So . . . your mom seems nice."

"I'm so sorry about her showing up unannounced. I had no idea she was going over to see you. She purposely waited until I got in the shower so I wouldn't tie her to a chair or something."

Daniel raised his eyebrows. "You'd tie your own mother to a chair? Remind me never to get on your bad side."

"Please tell me she didn't say anything too embarrassing while she was at your house."

"Define embarrassing."

"Oh. My. Gosh." I dropped my head into my hands, hiding my face.

Daniel reached over and pulled my hands down. "I'm just kidding."

My entire body tingled when his hand touched mine. The surprise must have shown on my face because—much to my disappointment—he quickly pulled his hand away. "I like your mom. She spent most of the time talking about how great you are."

"How great I am? She barely knows me."

Daniel raised his eyebrows in surprise. "It didn't seem that way. She said you're an 'A' student. You read books like there's no tomorrow. You're a deep thinker and like things to be proved to you before you accept them." He counted down his fingers, pausing between each one. "Let's see, what else . . . oh yeah, you're a loyal friend, you're responsible, you're mature for your age—"

"Okay, stop. Now *you're* the one embarrassing me." I paused. "I didn't know she knew some of that stuff about me."

"She did say she's glad you're staying with her this summer because she wants to be closer to you."

"She didn't hold anything back." The conversation left me feeling chafed, as if a layer of skin had just been scraped off and I lay exposed to the world. I had to find a way to shift the attention to Daniel instead. "Mom said she wanted to meet your uncle but he wasn't there. Was he at work?"

"He works a couple of jobs so he's not home a lot. He knew I had a date tonight, but he didn't mention what time he'd be home. I guess I could have called him."

The taxi pulled to the curb. "We're here," Daniel said as he reached across me and opened the door.

The museum sat right at the edge of the water and I could see a replica of a colonial ship docked nearby. Daniel paid the driver while I waited on the sidewalk.

"Two for the student price," Daniel told the lady sitting in the ticket booth. Her blue dress looked like it had come straight from the 1700s and she wore a white shawl and cap with it.

"Here are your tickets, young sir. The next tour begins in ten minutes." The lady handed him our tickets and we made our way to a bench to wait.

Daniel stretched his legs out in front of himself. "I've heard that the tours of this museum are different than most places. We're all supposed to act like we're from colonial times. Sounds interesting."

"Act? I hate to tell you this, but I'm not much of an actress." *This date is going to end horribly.*

"I'm sure you'll be fine. It'll probably be the kids getting into it anyway."

A man—also dressed in period clothing—approached the waiting crowd. "Hear ye, hear ye. All who are attending tonight's meeting with Samuel Adams gather round."

We followed the rest of the group into a building set up to look like an old meeting house with rows of pews and a podium up front. Each of us was given a feather pen and a paper describing someone from colonial days. Daniel leaned over and whispered, "See, you're supposed to act like the person on that paper."

I read the paper in my hand. "I'm Rachel Staunton and I'm eighteen years old. Who are you supposed to be?"

Daniel stared thoughtfully at his paper. "You can call me Abraham tonight. I'm a silversmith."

"Intriguing. What kind of silver masterpieces do you smith? Are you going to make me some jewelry?"

He reached over and picked up my hand. Every time he touched me, my heart raced. If he continued to do that, no matter how casual and meaningless his actions, I might have a heart attack before the date ended. Daniel pretended to closely examine my fingers. In a fake-accented voice, he said, "I do believe madam wears a size six ring. Am I correct?"

I grinned. "Sure. Whatever you say. I'll expect it to be studded with diamonds and emeralds, too."

Daniel dropped my hand and threw his arms up in mock disgust. "Sorry. I'll have to pass. I only work with silver."

The 'meeting' started and an actor portraying Samuel Adams began an oration at the front podium. We learned the history of the times and why the colonial citizens were incited to act out against the British.

"Who can name someone involved in the Boston Tea Party?" one of the actors called out.

Daniel, who'd kept me laughing by totally getting into character during the 'meeting', shouted "Paul Revere!"

I tugged on his arm and whispered, "I think you're confused. He's not the tea party guy. He's the one who made the famous ride.

Remember? One if by land, two if by—"

"Correct!" The man in front yelled before I could finish.

Daniel turned and grinned at me. "What was that you were saying, Miss Staunton?"

I shrugged. "Lucky guess."

"Who else?" the man up front yelled again.

Everyone on the tour looked at each other, but no one said anything. Daniel called out again in his Abraham voice. "The four Bradlee brothers and their sister, Sarah!"

"Correct again! We have a true patriot in our midst," the actor called.

"How do you know all this?" I whispered.

"You said you like history. Well, so do I." One corner of Daniel's lips curled up in a sly grin. "And there's a strong possibility that I did a report on it for history class last year."

"So you cheated. You studied before we came. I could have memorized a list of names, too, if you'd given me fair warning," I teased.

"Sorry. The next time we go on a date, there will be full disclosure."

Conversation came easily to us—a fact that didn't go unnoticed. Our interests were so similar, I felt as if I'd known him for far longer than two or three days. *What about Peter, Jamie?* I asked myself, wondering if I should be feeling guilty. At first, I had. But by that point, almost all the guilt had vanished.

The group moved outside again where we were given a tour of the ship we'd spied earlier. Quarters were close and my hip pressed against Daniel. Concentrating on what the actors were saying with him standing so close proved difficult.

"December 16, 1773, was a day that has had an effect on millions and millions of people over the last few hundred years. People on *both* sides of the big pond," the tour guide explained. After more explanation and cheers and yells from the crowd, we each took a turn hurling crates of 'tea' off the edge of the ship and into the water.

I giggled as I watched each of the floating parcels bob up and down in the water. The entire museum was overdramatized, but I loved it.

"Way to help compromise American business," Daniel yelled to me above the cheering crowd.

"What did you say?"

"The ships the Sons of Liberty attacked were American."

"Really?"

Daniel nodded. "Yeah. I learned that while doing my report. The tea came from Britain, but the ships were American."

"I'm guessing the owners of the ships weren't very happy about that night."

Daniel grinned. "I can only imagine."

The next part of our tour took us inside where lifelike holograms told us stories and talking pictures conversed. The animations were so advanced, the holographic women looked real enough to touch.

The last stop let us see one of the actual tea chests recovered from the Boston Tea Party, one of only two known chests left in existence.

"I love being this close to things that were important to our history," I said as I peered at the chest.

Daniel rested his hand lightly on the glass case to get a closer look. "I agree."

In that moment I figured out exactly why I liked Daniel so much. It wasn't that he and Peter were different. It was that they were almost the same person. Both were kind, thoughtful, loyal friends, and both absolutely loved history. Peter, the son of archaeologists, spouted off history facts just as much as Daniel.

Maybe I'm not falling for Daniel. Maybe I'm just missing Peter.

Agh! Why does dating have to be so hard?

"Are you hungry?" Daniel asked when the tour ended and the crowd dispersed. "Ironically enough, there's a *tea* room and gift shop here."

"Sure. I could eat." Truthfully, my stomach had been growling for an hour.

Daniel escorted me to Abigail's Tea Room where we were seated at a table with a flower-filled teapot as a centerpiece. Tall windows lined the walls of the room and light from an almost full moon streamed in along with the lights of the city. "This is fun. It's a happy little place," I said.

"Good. I didn't know what to expect." He looked at the menu and then at me. "Obviously, this place is known for its teas, but they also have sandwiches and soups. What sounds good to you?"

I hesitated, not wanting to disappoint him. "Honestly? I'm not much of a tea person."

A slow smile spread across his face. "Me neither."

We both drank water with sandwiches and bowls of clam chowder. Starving, I dug into my food as soon as it arrived. Daniel ate more slowly, nibbling at his sandwich between conversation. I tried to slow down and match his pace, but the food tasted too good and I finished all of it before Daniel was even halfway through.

I set my napkin next to my empty chowder bowl. "I feel like a pig."

"What do you mean?" Daniel asked.

I nodded toward his half full bowl of soup and picked-at sandwich. "Either you're the world's slowest eater, or I'm a pig."

Daniel looked down at his food and frowned. "I have to admit, I didn't eat lunch until four o'clock. And I ate a lot. I guess I'm not really that hungry yet."

"I'll forgive you." *I finally found a difference between Daniel and Peter! No matter how recently he's eaten, Peter wouldn't leave a meal unfinished. Maybe I should make a list of their similarities and differences . . .*

Our 1700s waitress offered to box up Daniel's sandwich for him, but he declined and we stood to leave. "Want to look through the gift shop before we go?" Daniel asked.

"Sure."

We browsed through stacks of books, t-shirts, mugs, key chains, and little boxes of tea—the usual gift shop offerings—before Daniel walked to the register.

"What are you getting?" I asked.

"It's a surprise." He winked.

The cab ride home went too fast and I found myself frowning when the elevator door opened near both our apartments. I didn't want the evening to end. "Thanks for tonight. I really had a good time," I told Daniel at my door.

He reached down and picked up my hand, placing something on my palm as the familiar thrill of his touch spread over me. "This is to remember our first date. Good night."

Before I could look at what he'd placed in my palm, he turned around and entered his apartment. I smiled when I looked at what I held. On my palm was a size 6 silver ring with *Boston* engraved on the outside. "Thanks, Abraham," I said out loud before opening my apartment door and closing it behind myself.

Chapter 8

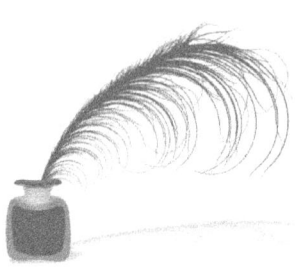

I didn't sleep well again, but it had nothing to do with the unfamiliar and uncomfortable couch. Untangling my feelings for Daniel and Peter could take the blame that time. I finally gave up on sleep at 7:30 a.m. and got up to eat breakfast.

Mom heard me and came out. "How was your date?"

"It was fun."

"What did you do?"

"We went to a museum."

"He mentioned he might take you to one. I told him you'd probably like the idea."

I laughed. "Really? So he knew before he even asked that I'd like it? Funny guy."

My right hand rested on the table and Mom reached over and picked it up. "Have you always worn this silver band? I've never noticed it before."

My cheeks flushed. If I had a way to stop that from happening all the time, I'd be one very happy girl. "Daniel gave it to me. It's just a cheap souvenir."

"Are you sure? I think it's real silver."

I took a closer look at my hand. "Are you sure?"

"Believe me, I know jewelry." She let go of my hand and stepped into the kitchen to pour herself a glass of milk. "That boy must really like you."

"Great."

She looked at me in surprise. "You don't sound excited. I thought you liked him. Did something happen?"

"I do like him. A lot. That's the problem. I'm only going to be in Boston for a few weeks. If I date Daniel while I'm here, can I go back to Marion and date Peter again as if nothing ever happened? Or should I just be friends with Peter when I go home. Or maybe I shouldn't date Daniel and wait until I get back to Marion to see how things go with Peter." I dropped my head into my hands. "I'm so confused."

Mom picked up her glass of milk and joined me at the table. "You're worrying about this way too much. Everything will work out how it's supposed to. You're only fifteen. You shouldn't be worried about being with one guy anyway."

"I'll be sixteen right after school starts, you know. And everyone always says I'm mature for my age."

Mom sighed. "Do you remember what we talked about the day I found out you knew about ghosts?"

"Remind me."

"I told you not to forget to live. You throw yourself into everything entirely. That's good, but sometimes it's okay to take a step back from things and just live in the moment. If dating Daniel feels right while you're here, then go for it. When you get back to Marion, everything will work out the way it should."

I blew out my breath. "I'll try. You might need to remind me of that once in a while, though." I rinsed my cereal bowl and put it in the dishwasher. "What are the plans for today? Did you confront Myles last night?"

69

Mom nodded. "Yeah. Portia's the calmest of the three of us so we let her take the lead. Myles admitted to being deceiving about some of his past. He never would say what happened to his mom, though. He just kept insisting that if it weren't for his dad, he and his family would be unblemished. He pointed out for the millionth time that his family has been in America since colonial times and his great-whatever grandfathers fought in the Revolutionary War and we should respect him for that and blah, blah, blah . . . We told him we were taking twenty-four hours to decide what to do about his case. After the twenty-four hours are up, we'll meet again and decide whether he wants to be honest or whether we even want to keep helping him. I don't know what's going to happen."

"Good for you guys. I'm glad you took a stand."

"That leaves us with an entire day with nothing to do. That's a rare thing for us. Do you have anything you want to do?"

"Is there a library near here? I haven't read anything in a while."

Mom threw her head back and laughed. "Oh Jamie, you haven't changed as much as I thought. I'm going to go get showered and dressed. We can go to the library if you want, but if you think of anything more exciting, let me know."

She left the room and I returned to the couch to fold up my blankets. I tucked them behind the couch with my pillow so they weren't in the way in case anyone happened to stop by. A text from my dad came in on my cell phone.

"How are things going?" Dad texted.

"Things are good." I texted back.

"Are you and Lillian getting along?"

"Yep. Surprised?"

"A little."

"Do you miss me?"

"Of course. The house has never been so still."

"You can come visit, you know."

70

"No. You need this time with your mom. Besides, I have another business trip in a few days."

"Where to this time?"

"Providence. I know it's not far, but it's a two day conference. Since you're not here, I'll just get a hotel room for the night."

"Sounds fun."

"I'm headed to work. Have a good day."

Mom took forever getting ready and Portia and I managed to play four games of Uno before she emerged from the bedroom, primped and prepped.

"Where's Steven?" Mom asked.

"He said he was going outside to paint," I answered. "Did you know he painted?"

Portia nodded toward the living room. "Who do you think painted the pictures we hung on the walls the day we moved in?"

"Really? He did all of them?"

Mom and Portia looked at each other and shrugged. "Yes," they said in unison.

I stood and took a closer look at the framed art on the walls. Sure enough, Steven's initials were carefully painted in the corner of each canvas. "I had no idea. He's really good," I said. "I've heard him mention college. Did he major in art or something like that?"

"Actually, he majored in history," Portia said. "His knowledge helps our extrication investigations."

"If Steven paints, what do you guys do on your days off?" I gathered the Uno cards and stuck them back in their case.

"We try to change it up," Mom said. "Sometimes we try new restaurants, sometimes we get manicures, sometimes we explore wherever it is we happen to be living. It all depends on our mood that day."

"I majored in University Studies during college because I couldn't narrow down my options. Can you tell?" Portia laughed. "I don't

71

make up my mind very well and I don't like to be stuck doing the same thing all the time."

"Mom and I are going to the library today. You can come with us. Unless you have a better idea," I said.

Portia creased her brows, deep in concentration.

"*Please* think of something else," Mom joked.

My cell phone beeped and I looked down at the screen. I couldn't stop the smile from spreading across my face. Mom turned to Portia. "I'll bet you ten dollars that's Daniel. The smile for Peter is slightly different."

Portia shook her head. "No way. That's a bet I'd lose."

"Leave me alone," I said, pretending to be mad as I carried my phone to the couch in an effort to get away from the two of them.

"Were we right? Is it Daniel?" Mom called after me.

I didn't answer.

"We're totally right," Portia whispered right before I turned my back to them.

"*Good morning,*" the text read.

"*Same to you,*" I answered.

"*Got any plans for the day?*"

"*Not yet.*"

"*Are you up for another history lesson?*"

"*What did you have in mind?*"

"*A walking tour. Leave at 11:00?*"

I turned to Mom. "How would you feel if I ditched you two today?"

Mom smiled. "Go. Have fun. Be a real teenager."

"Thanks."

I texted Daniel again. "*11:00 sounds great.*"

We rode a bus into the city and disembarked at Boston Common. "Have you ever done The Freedom Trail tour?" Daniel said.

I shook my head.

"It's a two-and-a-half mile walk past some of the most historical places in Boston."

"I've heard of it and I've seen some of the places on school field trips, but it's been awhile."

"Same here. The trail has sixteen stops. I'm not sure if I've been to all of them either."

"Are we doing all of them today?"

Daniel shrugged. "We'll see how far we get before we get tired … or bored. Boston Common is the first stop." He pulled a pamphlet out of his backpack and began to read on the first page. "Boston Common was home to 1000 soldiers while they occupied Boston at the start of the Revolutionary War. It was from here that they marched to Lexington and Concord."

"A thousand British troops camped here and it's a *celebrated* place?"

"That wasn't all it's known for." Daniel held the booklet open so I could see. "It was also where the city celebrated the repeal of the Stamp Act and the end of the war. The Pope came here in the 1970s. And then there were the witch hangings."

I paled, for once not turning red. "*Witch* hangings?" I asked quietly. Haven's extrication was still fresh on my mind and I didn't want to discuss witches with Daniel who knew nothing about the *real* summer I'd been having up to that point.

"Yeah. In the 1600s. I think most of them were before the Salem Witch Trials even took place. This says they hung them from a tree known as The Great Elm."

I turned in a circle, wanting—yet not wanting—to see the tree. After she was extricated, I had nightmares about Haven hanging by her neck from a tree. I swallowed hard. "Which tree is it?"

73

Peter eyed me curiously. "It's not here anymore."

I sighed in relief. "Good. That's really creepy. And kind of sad. Let's not talk about witches."

He laughed. "No kidding. I can't believe people thought they were real."

If you only knew what I know . . .

We wandered around the common for a while longer, reading signs and talking about historical events, before Daniel suggested we move to the next stop: the Massachusetts State House.

"According to this," Daniel waved the pamphlet, "the State House was built on John Hancock's cow pasture."

"The guy that signed his name really big on the Declaration of Independence?" I asked.

"Uh huh. He lived here and apparently had a lot of money."

"Cool."

Daniel closed the pamphlet and looked up at the building. "Paul Revere made the copper plating for the dome."

"Wait . . . the same Paul Revere that participated in the Boston Tea Party and the memorable ride?"

"The same one."

"I'm learning all kinds of stuff this week." *Peter would love this. I wonder if he's ever been on this tour. Maybe I should call him.*

The next stop on the tour was the Park Street Church. "The steeple is 217-feet high," Daniel read. "*My Country 'Tis of Thee* was sung for the first time here." We didn't bother to go inside. It still functioned as an operational church building. I didn't come from an overly religious family and I never knew quite how to act in places like that anyway.

We continued our walk, following a red line painted on the sidewalks. "What's next?" I asked.

"Granary Burying Ground."

"A cemetery?" Ghosts liked to hang out at cemeteries. I could only imagine what would happen if we went to the cemetery and a ghost suddenly decided I was their soul saver. Daniel would finally know I was a freak of nature.

Daniel zipped the pamphlet back into his backpack and expertly navigated through the rows of weathered headstones. "Tons of famous people are buried here."

"I get the feeling you know exactly where you're going. Just how many times have you done this walking tour?"

Daniel shrugged. "School classes come every year. It's interesting, isn't it?"

I grinned. "Fascinating. Whose grave are you headed to?"

"Well, Sam Adams, John Hancock and Ben Franklin's parents are all buried here, but there's someone else kind of special."

"Let me guess, Paul Revere?"

"Nailed it," Daniel said with a giant grin. "I visited his grave last year while I was working on my huge project. I liked learning about the guy. Let's take a picture by his headstone."

I didn't like having my picture taken, but when Daniel put his arm around my shoulder and held his cell phone out to take a selfie, a genuine smile covered my face.

"Do you want one?" he asked.

"Sure." His arms had a much longer reach so I handed my cell to him and leaned in.

I texted the picture to Camille while we walked to the next stop on the tour.

"*HOLY HOTNESS!!!*" she texted back in all caps. I hid the screen from Daniel's view and crossed my fingers that she wouldn't decide to mention the picture to Peter.

After leaving Paul Revere's grave, we walked by the King's Chapel and Burying Grounds. We didn't actually stop, but Daniel kept the brochure close and mentioned that the first woman to get off the Mayflower was buried there. We also passed a large statue of

75

Benjamin Franklin and the Boston Latin School.

"You're looking at the oldest public school in America," Daniel said as we went by. "Ben Franklin dropped out of school here."

I raised my eyebrows. "Why is there a statue of him nearby? Doesn't that give kids an excuse to use on their parents? 'If Ben Franklin dropped out of school and did just fine, so can I.'"

Daniel grabbed my hand. "That's exactly what I've always thought. Pretty ironic."

He didn't let go of my hand.

Nope. He just kept holding it, even after we turned away from the building to continue our walk.

I closed my eyes and took a deep breath, trying to calm my pounding heart. *Relax, Jamie, he's just holding your hand. It's not a big deal.* Daniel spouted more trivia from the booklet as we walked and I forced myself to concentrate on his words instead of the fact that we were holding hands.

"... bookstore. You like to read, right?" Daniel asked.

I wished I'd caught the first half of the question. "I love to read." My eyes lit up when I saw the historical plaque outside the door of the building we'd stopped in front of. "The Old Corner Bookstore," I read. "Oh wow! Listen to the people that were published here. Ralph Waldo Emerson, Henry Wadsworth Longfellow, Nathaniel Hawthorne, Oliver Wendell Holmes. Ooo!" I squealed. "Even Louisa May Alcott!"

Daniel tilted his head and looked at me. "I didn't know you could be so animated."

"Can we go inside this one?"

"Uhh . . . sure. You did hear me when I said it's not a bookstore anymore though . . . right? It's a restaurant now."

So that's what I missed. "I guess that explains where the aromas are coming from. I thought I smelled hot dogs."

"Actually, that's from the cart over there." Daniel pointed to a hot dog stand just down the road from where we stood. "Want some lunch?"

"Sure, but it's my treat this time," I insisted. I purchased two hot dogs with all the fixings and handed one to Daniel.

"Thanks. We can keep walking while we eat."

I followed Daniel to the next stop. "The Old South Meeting House. This is where the *real* meeting led by Samuel Adams took place on the night of the Boston Tea Party," Daniel explained, pamphlet in one hand, hot dog in the other.

"Do you want to go inside?" I asked.

Daniel crinkled his brow and stared at the building for a moment before answering. "No. Let's just keep going."

I finished my hot dog and Daniel took the wrapper from me. "I'll throw that away for you," he offered.

He walked to a curbside garbage can and tossed my wrapper in along with his own half-eaten hot dog. *He didn't finish his hot dog? Again, definitely not Peter.* We stopped briefly at the Old State House, the place where the Declaration of Independence was read for the first time, before moving on to the site of the Boston Massacre.

"What exactly happened during the massacre?" I asked Daniel. "I mean besides a lot of people getting . . . massacred."

He unzipped his backpack and pulled out the thick pamphlet again. "It sounds bloodier than it was. According to this, only five people died from their wounds. Here, you can read about it."

I took the pages from his outstretched hand and read about the incident. "Can you imagine living at the time all of this was going on?" I asked.

Daniel shook his head. "I can't even begin to think what it would have been like."

We past Faneuil Hall, barely even stopping to take a look. I wondered what Daniel's sudden rush was all about until I saw the next stop on the tour.

"We finally made it," Daniel said.

"The Paul Revere House. I should have known you were leading me to somewhere extremely important," I said sarcastically.

Daniel grinned and took my hand again. "Let's take a real tour of this one."

We paid for our admissions and began to walk through the carefully preserved home. Some of the artifacts were authentic and some were replicas, but all were appropriate for the time period. "Paul Revere had sixteen kids from two different wives," Daniel whispered as we stared into the kitchen.

"Sixteen?" I gasped.

Daniel nodded. "Crazy, huh?"

"That's more than crazy. That's insane. I can't even imagine having one sibling?"

"People had big families back then, I guess. It's weird."

We spent almost an entire hour at the home, browsing through every room. Some of the items on display were made by Paul Revere who, at the time, was known for his silversmithing far more than for his famous ride. Daniel looked in awe at each item. "Isn't it amazing that things can last for so long?"

I nodded. I didn't want to turn away from him. Watching him as he peered at each piece was like watching a little kid on Christmas morning. *Or like watching Peter show me the carefully preserved artifacts his parents collect and display at their home.* "I've lost track of how many stops we've made. Are we getting close to the end?" I asked after we emerged from the home.

"It's getting kind of late. Maybe we should call it a day. I should check in with my uncle anyway."

My feet hurt and my legs were stiff, but I didn't want to admit that to Daniel. He reached up and tucked a stray hair behind my ear, causing me to suck in my breath sharply.

He smiled mischievously. "You see, if we stop now, it will give me an excuse to ask you out again, you know, to finish the rest of the walking tour."

He's trying to flirt with me! "Name the time and day and I'll be here."

We took the subway and a bus to get home from where we were. By the time we spilled out of the elevator it was 5:30 and exhaustion had overcome me. "Thanks for today," I said. "I learned a ton."

"I'm glad you came. Not many girls would do it," Daniel said, taking a step closer to me. He took both of my hands in his and gently pulled me toward him.

Is he going to kiss me? I stared at his lips, my heart beating so hard I could feel it in my throat. If he kissed me, there was a good chance I would melt into a puddle right there in the hallway.

He didn't kiss me.

The elevator door opened again and Myles Westing stepped through. If it were possible to kill a ghost again, I would have done it in that moment. I expected him to make some inappropriate comment or something, but he didn't say a word. Instead, he stared at Daniel as if he hated him. I started to say something, thinking I should introduce him to Daniel before things became too awkward, but when I saw Daniel's face, I stopped. His expression matched Myles'.

Daniel let go of my hands. "I'll see you later." He closed himself inside his apartment before I had a chance to respond.

I followed Myles through the door of my own apartment. He marched in as if he owned the place and plopped right down on the sofa. "What kind of a scam are you guys running here?" he demanded.

Steven, Portia, and Mom were all seated at the table. They looked up in surprise at our sudden entrance. Steven jumped up. "Excuse me?" He narrowed his eyes and his nostrils flared. "It seems

79

to me that you're the one trying to scam us, although for the life of me I can't figure out why."

Myles ignored Steven and looked directly at my mom. "You're not even trying to help me extricate, are you?"

Mom crossed her arms over her chest. "I thought we discussed all of this last night. We *were* trying until you *lied* to us."

"This has nothing to do with things I have or haven't told you," Myles snapped. "Your daughter doesn't like me, Lillian. That's obvious. But she and her boyfriend are trying to deprive me of what should be mine."

Mom stared at him, open mouthed. When she didn't say anything, I jumped in. "You're psycho. First of all, he's not my boyfriend. And second of all, we just met each other. I have *no* idea what you're talking about."

Myles stood and walked toward me. Although my brain told me to move out of his path, I held my ground. "When I signed a contract with your mother and her friends, it clearly said I would be the recipient of all their attention." He pointed a long finger at me. "Why am I just now finding out that their focus isn't completely on me?"

"Don't you think you should explain yourself so you don't come off like a babbling idiot," I hissed.

"Jamie!" Mom snapped.

A smug smile crossed Myles' face and he looked from me to mom and then to Portia and Steven. We all stared back. He returned to the couch and sat down, folding his arms behind his head and stretching his legs out in front of himself. "Are you trying to tell me you don't know? I hadn't considered that possibility."

Whatever piece of information he had was dying to get out.

"Obviously not," I said through clenched teeth.

"Allow me to enlighten you. Your new boyfriend is a ghost."

Chapter 9

I heard the words, but I couldn't wrap my brain around them. *Daniel . . . a ghost?* "You're lying," I whispered.

"Lying? Me?" Myles said, gloating in his revelation.

"Everything you say is a lie. You can't even tell the truth to these guys when they're trying to help you." I motioned to Mom, Steven, and Portia who stood in shock around the kitchen table. I stepped dangerously close to Myles. "Get out," I hissed.

He dropped his hands and leaned forward. Our faces were just inches apart. "I'm not going anywhere, missy. You need to face the facts. That boy over there is the one that's been lying to you, not me."

I shook my head back and forth as I clenched and unclenched my fists at my side.

"Think about it. The only people who can see ghosts for what they really are, are other ghosts. I'm the only one here that knows his deepest, darkest, secret."

My stomach churned and I knew if I stood there any longer I'd puke the hot dog I'd eaten outside the Old Corner Bookstore all over

81

the living room carpet. Not wanting anyone to see me cry, I turned on my heel and ran down the hall to Mom and Portia's bedroom. I slammed the door shut right before I threw myself onto Mom's bed. I clutched at my stomach and squeezed my eyes shut as I tried to keep the tears from falling.

I wasn't successful.

Giant tears cascaded down my face and body-shaking sobs escaped my throat. *Daniel is a ghost. Daniel is a ghost. Daniel is a ghost.*

The revelation hurt like nothing else I'd ever felt. As much as I didn't want to believe it, I knew that Myles told the truth. A dozen things had pointed toward it, but I'd been so caught up with my feelings for Daniel I didn't notice any of them. His extreme knowledge of history, his impeccable manners, his inability to finish a meal—everything tastes like cardboard to ghosts—and most importantly, the look on his face when he laid eyes on Myles outside the apartment. They both knew each other's secret the moment they saw each other. Ghosts have an aura of sorts that can only be seen by other ghosts. They can know each other's true identity, but as long as they're in their body form, a living soul can't discern them from others who are still alive.

A knock came at the door. "Go away," I called.

The door opened anyway and Mom stepped through, quietly shutting it behind herself. "Honey, you okay?"

"He lied."

She sat on the edge of the bed. I hoped she didn't care about sleeping on a wet pillow because I had seriously soaked it with my tears. "Who lied? Myles?" she asked.

"Daniel."

"What did he lie about?"

"Myles is right. I know it. Daniel's a ghost."

"Did you specifically ask Daniel if he was a ghost?" Mom asked quietly.

"Why would I ask him that?" I snapped.

"Did you tell him you were a soul saver?"

I didn't answer for a long time. "It never came up."

"Then he didn't lie, Jamesie."

I sat up and wiped the tears from my face. I could only imagine what I must look like with mascara trails all down my cheeks. Mom reached a hand toward me—I think she wanted to comfort me in some way—but she stopped short and pulled her hand back.

I took a deep breath. "I'm going to confront him."

"Go easy on him, will ya?" Mom smiled. "I have a feeling he's one of the good ghosts."

I climbed off the bed and padded down the hall in my bare feet. I didn't really care how I looked in front of Daniel anymore. When I passed through the kitchen and dining area I avoided eye contact with everyone else. If I looked at Myles right then, I might do something I regretted. Instead, I headed straight for the door and stepped through it quickly. I closed the space between our apartment and Daniel's in one giant step and pounded on the door before I lost courage.

Daniel opened the door a few seconds later. "Jamie? Are you okay? Where are you shoes? Are you crying?"

I pushed past Daniel into his apartment. "Is your uncle here?"

"No. He's still gone." He looked around in confusion. "J, what's wrong?"

I turned away from him and took a deep breath. Looking at him when I said it would be too hard. "Why didn't you tell me you're a ghost?"

"Whoa." Silence filled the apartment for several moments before Daniel finally spoke. "That guy in the hall. He told you."

"*You* should have been the one to tell me." My voice cracked and I bit my lip to keep from crying again.

83

"Look at me, Jamie."

I hesitated, but gave in and pivoted around to face him.

Daniel reached for my hand, but I stepped back, just out of reach. "Will you please just sit down?" he said.

I looked around and chose a straight-backed chair to sit on. I wanted somewhere Daniel couldn't sit next to me. He collapsed onto a dark leather sofa, dropping his head into his hands.. "That guy. The one in the hallway. He told you?" Daniel asked again in a muffled voice.

I nodded.

"How are you connected to him?"

"My mom and her roommates are trying to help him with his extrication."

"Wow. You even know the terminology. I take it this isn't your first encounter with . . . people like me?"

I shook my head.

"How long have you known about ghosts? I've never met a living person who knew the truth about us before."

"I found out a couple of months ago. I'm a soul saver."

Daniel cocked his head to the side and looked at me. "Are you being serious?"

"Yes."

"I was beginning to think soul savers were a myth."

"I assure you, I'm real."

Daniel looked at me with pain in his eyes. "Is that why I feel so close to you?" he whispered.

I moved my head up and down. "I think so."

"You're . . . my soul saver? *I,* of all people, have a soul saver?" His shocked expression spoke volumes.

I lifted one shoulder and dropped it again. "In the past, with the other ghosts I've helped, I felt really close to them—almost immediately. It's like this . . . this urge I have. To be by them and help

84

them and . . ." I didn't know what else to say.

"That's why I felt so drawn to you. J, I felt something the moment I saw you moving in. I thought it was because you were pretty."

"Pretty?"

"Well . . . yeah."

"You think I'm pretty?"

Daniel threw his head back and laughed. "Of course. I can't be the first person to tell you that."

"Actually . . ." Disappointment hit. Finding out the guy I'd started falling for liked me only because of some inborn instinct didn't exactly boost my confidence.

"It's never occurred to me that *I* might have a soul saver. Are you sure about this?"

"I didn't realize it at first, but yeah. I'm pretty sure. I feel the same way I felt with the other ghosts I've helped."

Daniel exhaled. "This is all so unexpected. How does the soul saver thing work? I mean, am I supposed to do something now?"

"We examine your life and search for things you might not have finished before you died. If anything seems important, we look at it more closely." I sat up straight, wanting to appear as 'professional' as possible. Just looking at him sent waves of disappointment across me. *If only Myles had stepped out of the elevator five minutes later .*

"I'm nervous," Daniel admitted. He crossed and uncrossed his arms.

"Nervous to tell me about your life or nervous about leaving this life?"

"Both."

I tilted my head and stared at him for a few moments. "You lived during colonial times, didn't you?"

Daniel smiled and twisted his hands in his lap. "Was it that obvious?"

"Kind of. I mean, not at first, but now that I look back over the last couple of days it seems pretty obvious. What sixteen-year-old boy is that fascinated with historical sites?" *Okay, Peter is.*

Daniel groaned. "We had fun though, didn't we?"

I grinned. "Yeah. It was fun. *Are* you sixteen? I mean, is that how old you were when you died?"

Daniel nodded. "I'm probably the oldest teenager you've ever met."

"Except for Haven."

"Who?"

"Haven Mills. She's the last ghost I helped extricate. She died in 1692. They hung her in Salem."

"I guess that's why you seemed uncomfortable when we were talking about witches at Boston Common today."

I frowned and looked down at my bare feet. "Her extrication is still fresh on my mind. When a ghost is extricated, it's like they die all over again. Those of us who get to know them are left to mourn alone."

Daniel didn't say anything to that.

I cleared my throat. "So tell me, when did you die?"

Daniel's face took on a more serious expression, one I hadn't seen before. "I died in August of 1775."

"1775? During the Revolutionary War?"

"Sort of. The war had barely started when I died. Things were just beginning. I witnessed some amazing events during my life, though."

"Such as?"

"I didn't lie when I said I did a school report on Paul Revere. I like to stay in human form as much as possible. To keep suspicions down, I have to go to school. I've done countless reports on him over the decades, but I've never had to do any actual research."

My jaw dropped open. "Are you telling me *you* are Paul Revere?"

Daniel's eyes about popped out of his head. "*What?* No. Definitely no. I worked for him, kind of like an apprentice."

My chest burned, something that happened every time I learned important things about the ghosts I helped. I couldn't believe how close to history I was about to become. *History-loving Peter should be here for this. Maybe I should call him. Or maybe not.*

"So . . . when do I tell my story?" Daniel asked when I didn't respond.

I looked around. "That depends. Is there really an Uncle Charlie? Is he going to suddenly appear?"

Daniel scrunched up his lips. "Sort of. Charlie's a ghost friend. He helps me out by pretending to live here occasionally. Sometimes I need someone who looks like a parental authority. Charlie prefers to be in ghost form so he's not around all that often."

The story seemed realistic enough. Sophia, the first ghost I helped, lived with a ghost couple before she extricated. They had the same arrangement as Daniel and Charlie. I stayed in contact with her so-called parents, Jack and Rita. Partly for their connection to Sophia, who I missed dearly, and partly because they were just fun to be with.

Daniel cleared his throat. "Before I explain everything, who exactly was that other ghost in your apartment?"

I rolled my eyes. "My mom's a soul saver, too, except she isn't always drawn to her ghosts like me. After the first ghost she helped, she became obsessed with the idea of helping others. She walked out on my dad and me when I was six to pursue ghosts. Somewhere along the way, she met up with Steven and Portia. They're her roommates. The three of them started a ghost extrication business."

Daniel laughed. "A what?"

"Believe me. I was just as surprised as you when I found out." I sighed. "Anyway, ghosts who can't find a soul saver come to them and they do what they can to help them extricate. In exchange, they receive all of the ghost's assets when they're gone."

A smile spread across Daniel's face. "What an ingenious idea. I doubt they have a lack of willing participants."

"I don't know that it's as exciting as it sounds. Myles, he's the ghost you saw in the hall, is a complete jerk. Not everyone is as friendly as you."

"Why are they helping him then?"

I shrugged.

"What's his story?"

"That's just it. We don't really know his story. We know he lived in the early twentieth century and we've found records to prove that. We also know he had a prison record, and a missing mother, and an absent father who had a secret second family. Anyway, Myles keeps lying to my mom and her friends and leaving out important details of his life. He claims to want their help, but he keeps leading them on wild goose chases. They're over there deciding what to do right now. Maybe it's a good thing I'm over here. I really don't like the guy."

"He sounds like a real winner. If you want, I can talk to him. Or better yet, I can ask other ghosts if they know him. Maybe I can get a feel for what he's really like."

"That would be awesome. My mom would love you for it."

Daniel looked down at his hands. "I'm not super wealthy, but I've invested money through the years and I'm doing all right. A hundred years ago, sixteen-year-olds could work and get paid a decent wage without raising too many eyebrows. Minimum wage doesn't cut it now. You're welcome to have everything of mine when I'm gone." He paused. "That is, *if* I go."

I laughed. "I didn't mean to imply earlier that I'd only help you if you paid me."

"I know," Daniel said quickly. "I didn't take it that way. But, the money's got to go somewhere. It might as well go to you."

"You could donate it to charity."

Daniel leaned back against the cushions of the couch. "I'll let you make that call."

Sophia left me all her money when she extricated, too. It happened before I ever knew about my mom and her 'job.' Peter and Camille were the only two people who knew about the bank account with forty grand in it. I didn't even dare tell my mom. I wanted the money to be there for an emergency. An emergency of *my* choosing.

I stood and walked through Daniel's apartment, trying to get a feel for the kind of person he'd been, wondering how much of his personality from his real life still survived in his ghost life. Daniel stayed on the sofa and remained silent as I walked around. A bookcase sat in one corner of the living room and I read some of the titles on the covers. I pulled a particularly large book off the shelf and held it in my hands.

"You like biographies of historical figures," I said. "No surprise there."

"I don't read them for the same reason as most people. To me, they're often humorous more than anything. For the most part they get their basic facts correct, but when the author starts trying to describe personalities or the way others perceived the person . . . well, let's just say the books suddenly turn into comedies."

I jumped in surprise when I realized Daniel had left his seat. I could sense him standing next to me in a way I couldn't begin to describe. It scared me. In a good way.

"What's your real name?" I asked.

"It really is Daniel. Daniel Avery."

"Daniel Avery," I whispered the name. It felt unnaturally familiar on my lips but I didn't know why. "Were you famous for anything?"

He snorted at the question. "Believe me. You won't find my name in any books. At least, not any I've ever read. No, I wasn't one of the elite colonists. I never even made it into any battles."

"You were a soldier then?"

"Not exactly."

"Not exactly? That doesn't explain very much."

"It's complicated. If I started at the beginning everything would make a lot more sense."

"Okay. Start at the beginning then." I placed the book back on the shelf.

Daniel grabbed my hand. "It's going to be a long story. You might want to be sitting down for it."

I let him lead me back to the sofa and sat down next to him, but I made sure we had plenty of space between us.

"Can I get you anything before I start? I sometimes forget the living need to eat."

"I'm fine." My stomach still churned from the evening's excitement. "I want to know what you meant when you said you weren't exactly a soldier."

Daniel took a deep breath. "I wasn't a soldier. I was a spy. I worked for General Washington."

Chapter 10

MARCH 5, 1775
BOSTON, MASSACHUSETTS

Mama! Daniel's home at last!" Isabella yelled as she skipped across the floor of their little home.

Daniel Avery shut the heavy wooden door behind himself quickly, hoping to let in as little of the cold air as possible. His mother worked hard to keep the home warm and he hated to waste her efforts. He pulled the three-cornered tricorn hat from his head and hung it on a peg next to the door before sweeping seven-year-old Isabella up into the air. She squealed in delight as he swung her around in a circle three times before setting her back down.

"Good evening, Mama." Daniel stepped from behind the tiny woman standing next to the stove and gave her a quick kiss on the cheek.

She took a step back and waved a ladle at him. "Daniel Isaac Avery, you only did that to make me cold. I declare your nose is as frigid as an icicle."

At barely five feet tall, Annie Avery was hardly a threat to her tall son. Her children loved to tease and harass her just to see the sparks in her eyes. Strands of orange hair always escaped her cap, adding to the fiery effect. Despite the odds, all five of her children managed to avoid what she referred to as the Irish curse. Their hair resembled that of their late father in varying shades of brown.

Daniel unbuttoned his overcoat and hung it on the peg next to his hat. "You know I love you, Mama, but sometimes I just can't help myself." Annie tried to maintain her mock anger, but the site of her son's innocent, pleading eyes did her in and she laughed out loud before quickly covering her mouth and turning back to the pot over the hearth. "Did you remember to wash up before coming in?" She ladled a spoonful of soup from the pot and put it to her lips.

"Why do you think my nose was so cold? I do believe the wash basin outside had a layer of ice on it."

"Mama, is it ever going to be summer again?" Five-year-old Johanna creased her brow and looked toward the home's only window. She'd been carefully placing bowls and spoons on the table next to the hearth. Fitting all six Avery family members around the small table was a chore all by itself.

"I'm beginning to wonder that myself," Annie answered with a shake of her head.

Daniel's eyes scanned the room. Twelve-year-old Marta sat in the corner, quietly darning a pair of socks, but his only brother remained to be seen. "Where's Jacob?" he asked.

"Still outside gathering eggs." Annie started to lug the heavy pot to the table, but Daniel jumped in and took it from her.

"Let me get that." He easily lifted the pot and deposited it in the middle of the table. "It smells wonderful, Mama."

"It smells the same way it does every night. With all the compliments you've been throwing around since you walked in that door a few minutes ago, a mother might think you were after something." Annie raised her eyebrows and waited for her son to respond.

"I can never keep anything from you, Mama. And, you are right again. I will not be around after dinner. Paul has invited me to accompany him tonight."

Annie's eyes narrowed, revealing deep creases in her forehead. "Paul the younger or Paul the older?"

"Paul senior, Mama." Daniel took a deep breath, knowing his next words would bring anger or sadness or maybe both. "I am accompanying him to the Green Dragon."

"Have you lost your senses?" She slammed her tiny hand on the table and Daniel had to suppress a laugh as all the spoons bounced off the wooden surface. "This is not a laughing matter," Annie continued. "You will end up exactly like your father. Mark my words." There was that ladle again, waving around in front of his face.

"I trust Paul and so did Papa. You know he wanted freedom for the colonies. It is my duty as his son to carry on his work."

"Do you even know what the significance of today is? I have already sacrificed my husband to the cause. Is that not enough?" Tears welled up in Annie's eyes as she looked at her firstborn.

"You will still have me, Mama," a voice spoke behind them. "*I* have not lost my head like my brother."

Daniel whirled around at the sound of fourteen-year-old Jacob's voice. The timbre of his voice seemed to change daily as he left his youth behind. Jacob worked hard and never shirked his duties.

Daniel ignored the glares from his younger brother and turned his attention back to his mother. "I know what today marks and I *will* be careful. Paul has given me, our family, a great honor by asking me to work for him. I would not want to be ungrateful for his generosity by refusing an innocent invitation. Besides, you know as well as I do that those fighting for the freedom of the colonies are in the right.

Making sacrifices for the greater good might not be preferred, but it *is* right."

Annie looked deep into her son's eyes before turning away. "We best sit down to eat before it gets cold." She let the subject drop without any further comment on the matter, but Daniel knew the conversation was far from over.

Daniel tilted his hat forward and ducked his head as he walked into the bitter cold wind. If Boston didn't start warming up soon, planting season would be pushed back, which in turn would delay the harvest. Late harvests risked the wrath of early winter storms. It was a vicious cycle. Despite the weather, Daniel wouldn't trade his Boston home for anything. His family had been residents of Boston for three generations. It was the only life he or his father had known.

Isaac Avery passed on a year before and not a day went by that Daniel didn't think of and miss the jolly man he called Papa. Ever the patriot, Isaac fought in the French and Indian War before meeting and marrying the fiery Irish seamstress, Annie Blake. When Daniel joined their family less than a year later, Annie assumed Isaac's allegiances would be to his family, but he couldn't seem to give up his causes.

Daniel knew the significance of the day, as Annie had mentioned before dinner. It had been exactly five years since the event that had become known as the Boston Massacre. A mob of protestors—Isaac Avery among them—gathered outside the Customs House to heckle the ever-present British redcoats. The unruly crowd threw snowballs at the soldiers. Upon being hit in the face, one fired his weapon. In the chaos, other soldiers fired. When the smoke of that fateful night cleared, several men lay dead in the street. Isaac was among the wounded.

Daniel remembered vividly the night he woke to his mother's screams. He came down from his loft bed to see his father, pale even in the flickering candlelight, standing in the doorway of the home, unable to lift his leg high enough to step over the doorframe. The snow outside had turned red from the blood dripping from the wound in his thigh. At eleven years old, the idea that he might soon become the man of the house had been a terrifying prospect for Daniel.

Fortunately, Isaac recovered from the wound, but his health never completely returned. Walking with the aid of a cane, Isaac continued to meet with the others who called themselves Sons of Liberty. Isaac's close friend, Paul Revere, made an engraving of the night of the massacre and copies of it traveled through the colonies. Although exaggerated, the depiction on the engraving left its mark and many colonists joined the other rebels who desired freedom from what they perceived to be tyranny on the part of the British.

Daniel smiled to himself as he thought of his stubborn father arguing with his stubborn mother about his continued support of the Sons of Liberty. His father and Paul were among the men who raided the tea ships in December of 1773, throwing their expensive cargo into the harbor. Daniel watched as his father left that night, dressed as he normally would, but returned with his face painted as if he were one of the Indians on the edge of town. The evening had been brisk and his father struggled to get out of bed the next morning, suffering from a terrible cough. His health never returned and he passed only a few weeks later. That little tea party in the harbor had been the death of him.

Paul Revere, saddened by the death of his friend and perhaps feeling a little responsible for it, came to Annie with a proposition the following summer. Even though he had sons of his own—including Paul Jr., a mere year younger than Daniel—Paul wished for Daniel to work as his assistant, an apprentice of sorts. Learning a trade hadn't seemed possible to Daniel before that and after talking it through with Annie, they readily accepted Revere's offer. Young Jacob became the man of the house with Daniel gone from sun up to sun down every day. Jacob filled the shoes of his father far better than Daniel felt he would have been able to anyway.

The light coming from the windows of the Green Dragon Tavern promised warmth and Daniel stepped up his pace as he approached the building. When he pushed through the door, the heat from the fire and the gathered men reached him immediately.

"Avery, over here young man." Paul Revere's voice was unmistakable even amongst the din of other voices and the clanking of tin cups on the tables.

"Would you like a drink tonight?" Paul asked as Daniel sat down in the chair offered. Paul motioned toward the serving girl. "Lydia, Daniel here is ready for a drink."

Daniel knew the girl to be Lydia Canterman. She'd been four years ahead of him in school. "Thank you for the offer, but I fear I wouldn't be of much help to you on the morrow if I drank tonight, sir."

Lydia walked away and Paul clapped Daniel on the back. "You are young, but I know you have a strong head on your shoulders. That is why I have invited you to join us tonight." Revere motioned to the others sitting around the large table.

"Us, sir?"

"We call ourselves the Mechanics." Paul lowered his voice as he looked to the other men at the table. They all gave slight nods of their heads.

"But . . . I thought you were the Sons of Liberty," Daniel said in surprise.

"Think of this as an organization within an organization. We have come together to keep watch on our fine city. We each have parts to play and we need one another to help keep an eye on the devils in red." Paul paused. His voice became even quieter. "Are you in?"

Daniel's heart beat rapidly in his chest. He had wrongly assumed the evening was nothing more than a social gathering of friends. The work these men planned to do could be potentially dangerous. He looked carefully at each of the faces gathered around the table and knew without a doubt that every one of them would give their lives for their cause if necessary. If he accepted their offer to join them, he would be expected to make the same sacrifice under dire circumstances.

A man Daniel didn't recognize demanded a response. "What is your answer, young man?"

Daniel swallowed hard, but spoke steadily. "I will join you."

The man on Daniel's left patted him on the shoulder. "You have made a wise choice. We need all the young men of this city to be as willing to step up and help as you are." Daniel recognized the man as Dr. Benjamin Church. He came to their house the night his father was shot. Dr. Church also attended those who died that night.

Paul produced a tattered bible from the satchel around his neck and placed it on the table. They took turns passing the book around the circle of men, each in turn placing his hand on the bible and swearing allegiance to the group. When the book came to Daniel, he pledged in a strong, clear voice despite the fear he secretly held.

The men discussed the movements of the British troops within Boston for the next two hours. They exchanged names of people they believed to be Tories, sympathetic to the cause of the British crown, and whispered angered words about the injustices pressed upon the colonies. Many of the sentiments expressed were ones Daniel already embraced. Years of sitting around the dinner table, listening to his father's rants about unfair taxes had sunk in deeply and he knew that he wanted a free America just as much as the other men who met that night.

"You know my mother will let you have it if she learns of the real purpose of this meeting, right?" Daniel asked Paul as they stepped outside the tavern at the conclusion of the meeting.

"I am not afraid of your mother. Now, if she were to team up with my Rachel, I'd be shaking in my boots." Paul turned and grasped Daniel's shoulders firmly. "Good night, Daniel. I am glad you will be with us. Your father would be proud of the decision you made tonight."

Daniel watched as Paul walked away in the opposite direction. *My father . . . proud of me?* Making his father proud had been his only desire in life. And perhaps Paul was right. Perhaps his father watched from heaven and knew the choices he made. Daniel held his head high, despite the wind, all the way back home.

Chapter 11

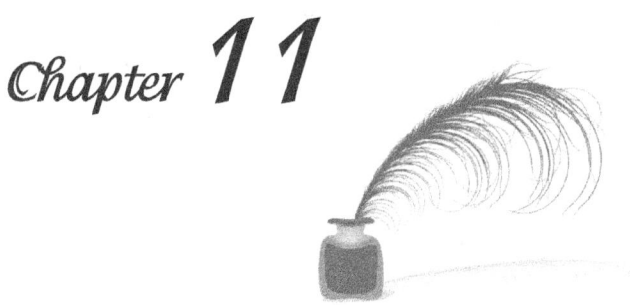

MARCH 23, 1775
BOSTON, MASSACHUSETTS

Daniel stepped through the Revere's door and deposited a bundle of mended clothing on their kitchen table. "Good morning, Rachel. Mama sent this for you." His mother and Marta spent their days mending and sewing for others to make ends meet. Daniel knew Rachel was more than capable of doing her own mending and sewing and suspected she sent things to Annie out of kindness.

Rachel was Paul's second wife. His first wife, Sarah, died shortly after giving birth to their daughter Isannah. The baby died, too. Daniel remembered Paul's sadness through that time and his returned happiness when he met Rachel. The two were married not long before the night the Sons of Liberty gathered to throw tea into the harbor, and they already had a son together. With seven children in the household, the Revere home was even more of a beehive than the Avery's home. Daniel admired Rachel for taking over the mothering of the six Revere kids when she joined the family.

A faint cry turned Daniel's attention to the tiny bassinet near the stove. Rachel set down the silver she was polishing and wiped her hands on a rag.

Daniel beat her to the bassinet. "May I?" he asked.

Rachel smiled warmly. "Of course. He won't let Paul Jr. pick him up, but I suspect little Joshua would take to you.

Daniel bent over and picked up the little bundle. All that could be seen amid the masses of swaddling blankets were two eyes, a pink nose, and two rosy cheeks. He held the bundle close to his chest, marveling at the tiny life that looked back at him. The baby stopped crying and closed his little eyes again.

"I knew you had a gentle heart," Rachel said.

The front door burst open and two figures spilled into the room. "Give it back!" Deborah Revere yelled as she chased her younger brother Paul around the table. "I swear I will—" She stopped short when she saw Daniel standing next to the stove, holding the baby carefully out of the way of his racing siblings.

Paul held one arm behind his back, concealing whatever Deborah wanted back. "You swear you will what?"

"Never mind," Deborah said quietly.

"Oh, I see," Paul continued to tease. "You cannot say because you do not wish to embarrass yourself in front of your beau."

Deborah's jaw dropped and Daniel's face turned red. Rachel stepped in just in time. She stuck a hand out toward Paul. "Give it to me immediately and do not ever treat your sister that way again."

Paul Jr. reluctantly pulled his arm from behind his back and deposited his loot in Rachel's hand. "Her diary?" Rachel gasped. "You ought to be whipped for this. Go on and help your father before he comes looking for you." She handed the diary back to Deborah and whispered, "I suggest you find a better hiding spot for this."

"I better get to the shop, too," Daniel said. He carefully passed little Joshua into Rachel's waiting arms and joined Paul Jr. as he walked back outside.

"It is true, you know," Paul said, nudging Daniel with his shoulder.

"What is true?"

"Deborah is sweet on you. I read it in her diary."

"You are a menace, you know that?" Daniel turned to his companion. "Race you to the shop?"

"You're on!"

The two boys took off at full speed and Daniel grinned, grateful that he'd avoided a continuance of the awkward conversation. He'd suspected that Deborah had feelings for him. And if he were honest with himself, thirteen-year-old Sarah probably felt the same way as her older sister. Daniel felt some guilt over the situation with the two Revere sisters. Although he thought of them as friends, his feelings for them ended there.

Paul Sr. stood with hands on his hips next to his anvil inside his silversmith shop. "It is about time the two of you decided to join me. I thought for sure you must be on your death beds, about to take your last breaths. Otherwise, there would be no excuse for you to be so late."

"I apologize, sir. You are right, I do not have an acceptable excuse." Daniel bowed his head and faced his friend and teacher.

"Not I, Father. I have a wonderful excuse. I was accosted by a crazy lass. She looked to be about seventeen-years-old. She was screeching and running around while flapping her arms." Paul Jr. demonstrated by flapping his own arms as he pranced around the shop. He had to stop to catch his breath before he finished his outrageous tale. "I do believe her name was Deborah. Yes, that is it for sure. Deborah Revere."

"Your harassment of your sister needs to stop. You are both too old to be acting like silly schoolchildren," Paul Sr. said with a stern expression aimed at his son. As he turned his attention back to the anvil, he winked at Daniel.

Daniel couldn't imagine spending his days anywhere other than Revere's shop. Although he'd been there less than a year, his skills had improved and Paul Sr. noticed. He no longer existed just as an errand boy and his duties included work with the precious metals.

"Avery, fetch my snips," Revere called over the pounding of his hammer on the anvil. Daniel grabbed them from the workbench and moved quickly to place them in the master's hand. "Son," Revere directed his attention at Paul Jr., "the piece for the Branath family is ready to be delivered. It is sitting on the front workbench. Please take it to them immediately and do not dawdle on the way."

Paul Jr. did as commanded, although he didn't move quite as fast as his father's slightly older assistant. Daniel lingered behind Revere, waiting for his next assignment, but the senior Revere said nothing until his son bundled the Branath's purchase and left to make the delivery.

"Daniel," Revere began as soon as the door shut.

"Yes, sir."

"You know the Mechanics have been keeping a closer watch on the devils this last fortnight, correct?"

"Yes, sir." Daniel had attended two more meetings of the Mechanics in the past month. He had not yet received an assignment, but he wholly supported the other members as they took turns observing and following every move the British made.

"Most of the other men have other obligations and assignments tonight. You will have a turn as watchman."

Daniel's heart pounded in his chest. "Tonight, sir?"

"Unless you are unwilling?" Revere briefly raised one eyebrow in Daniel's direction before returning his full attention to the metal in his hands.

"I am more than willing, sir."

"You will relieve Dr. Church of his watch at sundown. He will need to attend to other matters so you must not be late. You will be relieved by William Dawes at sunrise. Do you feel you are capable of this?"

"I can fulfill your request, sir."

"Good. Now get to work on this piece. It was commissioned by Lady Lennox so it must be perfect." Revere handed Daniel the bowl he'd been working on. "I want to be able to see myself in it after you have polished it."

Daniel went to work, polishing and buffing the silver. He tried to focus on the task at hand, but his mind continuously wandered to the evening assignment he'd been given. Finally, he had been proven trustworthy to help in their cause.

Daniel pulled the collar of his coat up past his ears until it almost touched the edges of his tricorn. The weather had warmed up significantly over the past two weeks, but he thought it best to let his dark clothing block as much of his face as possible. He hugged the edges of the buildings, trying to stay in the shadows and away from the pools of light reflected from the full moon.

It didn't take him long to reach the rendezvous point. He moved stealthily to the grove of trees at the edge of the Commons and rapped three times on the trunk of a large tree.

"State your business," a whispered voice came immediately.

"The crow has gone to bed," Daniel repeated the code words given him by Paul Sr.

A dark figure stepped from behind a tree and approached cautiously. "Daniel?" Dr. Benjamin Church said in surprise. "I expected Paul tonight."

"He had other matters to attend to this evening and has sent me, sir."

"Well, I am sure you are just as worthy. There have been no alarming movements tonight. That is, unless you count the brawl that broke out between a couple of them over a game of dice," Dr. Church spoke in hushed tones.

"Sounds like an eventful few hours."

"Drunken devils," Church muttered under his breath. "Keep an eye on them, boy. If any of their movements seem suspicious, or if there is an organized gathering, report it."

"Yes, sir."

The doctor tipped his hat toward Daniel as they bid farewell. As soon as he'd left, Daniel sunk down against a tree trunk. The grove of trees sat slightly higher than the Commons and from his vantage point, he could see across the tents of the British officers. Earlier in the day, Paul Sr. had sent him home to inform Annie that he would be busy on a project and would therefore be sleeping in the loft of Revere's shop for the night. It hadn't all been a lie. Upon his return from the visit to Annie, Paul Sr. insisted he take a nap in the loft so he wouldn't fall asleep during his all night watch. Daniel had tried to sleep, but it never came. With the noises coming from the shop below and the ever-present thoughts of his assignment filling his head, sleep had not been an option.

At first, he turned to every sound of the night—a squirrel bounding in the branches of the trees overheard, a bird swooping down from the sky to land in its nest, the raucous laughter coming from the tents spread out in front of him. But, as the evening wore on, and the Regulars turned in for the night, he found himself nodding off.

"Stay awake, stay awake," he mumbled to himself. When it became evident that sleep would come if he didn't do something desperate, he stood and slowly paced back and forth between the trees. He had almost fallen asleep standing up when the snap of a twig brought him fully awake in one sharp heartbeat. He soundlessly ducked behind a tree and held his breath as a figure stumbled up the slope in front of him. The figure came alone, but that didn't mean much to the unarmed Daniel. He braced his feet against the trunk and lowered himself to a slight crouch, ready to pounce like a waiting cat. But the man's stumbling gave him away. He could barely walk and fell to his knees, vomiting all over himself and the ground before finally rising and stumbling back down the slope.

"Church was right . . . drunken devils," Daniel whispered in the dark. He had never been as grateful as he was when William Dawes showed up just before sunrise to relieve him.

"Anything to report, son?" Dawes asked after giving the code words and revealing himself to Daniel.

"Absolutely nothing. They have been quiet for hours. I suspect they will be rising for the day soon."

"Good, young man. I am sure we will cross paths again soon."

"I look forward to it. Good day, sir."

Daniel hurried back to the silversmith shop as fast as he could without drawing attention to himself. All around him, households were beginning to stir. Candles could be seen in windows and smoke poured from chimneys. Instead of returning to his own home, he crawled up into the loft of the shop and collapsed on the straw, falling asleep instantly. At least an hour of sleep would be helpful.

Chapter 12

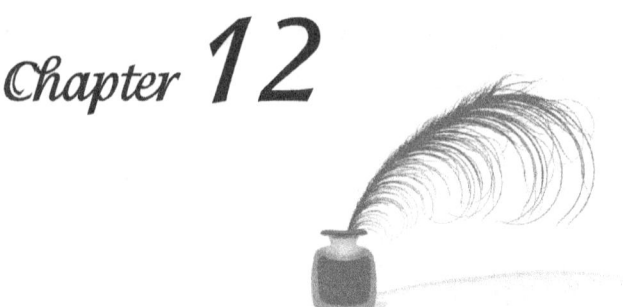

APRIL 18, 1775
BOSTON, MASSACHUSETTS

From that night on, Daniel slept in the loft of the silversmith shop. At least twice a week he took a turn keeping watch over the Regulars either on the Commons or elsewhere. He knew his mother and siblings missed him terribly, but he couldn't risk going home too often. The fewer people who knew the details of the Mechanics and Sons of Liberty operations, the better.

"You know, Daniel," Paul Jr. began on the morning of April 18th, "you used to move a lot faster. I do believe your old age is already slowing you down. You even have dark circles under your eyes. If I did not know any better, I would think you were spending your evenings at the Green Dragon instead of asleep up there in that loft." Paul pointed at the area above his head.

Daniel exchanged glances with Paul Sr. who was busy hammering on a piece of silver on the other side of the room. "Now why would I do something like that? I value my sleep. If I have dark circles under my eyes, it is certainly not because I have been spending time at the

106

tavern, but because of the snores I hear coming from your bedroom window every night. The noise is loud enough to wake the dead all the way over at Copp's Hill."

Paul Jr. picked up a pair of snips and tossed them at Daniel who dodged the flying tool just in time.

"Boys, as much as you might want it to, the work is not going to do itself this morning," the senior Revere called. The hint of amusement in his voice betrayed his effort to be serious.

Not long after, Paul sent his son on another delivery. Paul Jr. took his time getting out of the shop, but the moment he shut the door behind himself, Revere left his tools and stepped quickly to Daniel's side. "Daniel, as you know, Dr. Joseph Warren and I have established a plan to warn Sam Adams and John Hancock if the Regulars are on the move. Two nights ago, when you were not on duty, the soldiers seemed to be readying their longboats down in the harbor. We fear their march to Lexington and Concord is imminent. If we do not get there to warn the towns, they will not be ready and their arms supplies will be seized. We need to strengthen our watch. Can you handle yet another night down on the Commons tonight?"

Daniel looked into Paul's eyes. Worry and fear looked back at him. "Yes, sir. I will do as you ask."

"Many more of us will be keeping watch tonight. We must be fully alert."

When Paul Jr. returned a while later, he burst through the door with a frown. "Father, why are the Regulars out in so much force today?"

Paul Sr. whirled around and faced his son. "Explain yourself."

"There are more troops out in the streets. They are dressed as if ready for battle. I saw ten men dressed that way just in the little time I was away."

Paul gave a short nod in Daniel's direction. "I'm sure they are just conducting training exercises and perhaps practicing drills down on the Commons. Get back to your work, son."

The day seemed to drag as the feeling that something important was about to happen continued to build in the pit of Daniel's stomach. Concentrating on his work was an impossible undertaking. The other two in the shop seemed to be dealing with the same struggle. Finally, at six o'clock, Revere called it a day and ordered the boys to the house for dinner.

"Father is gone every night now," Paul Jr. said as the boys scrubbed at the washbasin outside the front door of the home.

"I am sure he is a busy man," Daniel said.

"I cannot wait until I am older so he will let me in on his secrets. I am not so much younger than you, but I know he tells you things he does not tell me."

"Perhaps," Daniel said. "Perhaps the things he tells me are musings about you. Things you would not want to know about yourself." He knew if he teased Paul, he would forget what the conversation had originally been about.

Rachel Revere set a lovely meal out for her family and their assistant, but Daniel could barely fit anything into his stomach as worry continued to gnaw at him. The family, including Paul Jr., turned in for the night, but Paul Sr. made excuses for himself and Daniel and they both slipped back out into the night. Daniel made the short trek to the usual observation position near the Commons, not knowing where Revere planned to be.

"Dr. Warren has been here already tonight," the current watchman told him. "He has sent William Dawes out across the Boston neck to let Hancock and Adams know of the devils' movements. They are not acting as they usually do tonight. I have heard from the watchman closer to the water that they appear to be readying their boats by the harbor."

Daniel gazed out on the Commons. Everything the watchman said was true. Instead of men milling about, laughing and drinking and carrying on, they were mostly quiet. Every movement seemed to be deliberate.

"Good luck tonight. I have no doubt you will have an exciting evening," the watchman said before disappearing into the dark night.

"An exciting evening," Daniel mumbled to himself. His nerves were too tense to sit down that night so he paced from tree to tree instead. Before long, barked commands from the Commons travelled up the slope to his waiting ears. He watched as row after row of British Regulars lined up below him. He inched his way closer to the edge of the trees, watching intently as the soldiers fell into position. "General Gage has ordered them to muster," he whispered to himself. He breathed hard even though he'd been standing still. "I must give warning." Without another thought, he turned and ran, carefully jumping over sticks and stones in his path as he pushed through the trees. The shouts from the Commons muted his retreat. His lungs burned as he ran behind buildings, ducking in and out of the shadows. He knew Dr. Warren would be waiting at the Green Dragon and he burst through the door without giving it a second thought. Joseph Warren looked up in surprise at the disheveled young man in front of him. "It is time," Daniel panted. "They muster."

Joseph Warren jumped to his feet. "You know this for sure?"

"General Gage has them lined up and ready to march." Daniel still struggled to catch his breath.

"I knew it. I've been watching their movements for days. They are going to cross the Charles River and move to Lexington. If they leave now, they will be there by sunrise and no one will be prepared. The citizens will be completely disarmed. Daniel, you must warn Revere. Tell him this is not a false alarm. Make haste!"

Daniel didn't need to be told twice. He bolted from the tavern and ran toward the familiarity of the Revere home. "Please let him be there," he whispered as he neared the house. "And forgive me Rachel for waking your family."

Daniel threw the door open and sighed in relief when he saw Revere standing near the hearth, fully dressed, with Rachel by his side.

"Sir, it is time. They go by sea," Daniel wheezed.

Revere jumped out of his chair and grabbed for his coat near the door. "I shall return, I promise," he whispered to Rachel. Daniel turned away as he kissed her goodbye.

"What can I do to help?" Daniel asked as the two stood outside in the dark.

"I have an agreement with the sexton of the Old North Church. Tell him the same thing you have told me. I will go and secure a rowboat for a crossing. I know a man on the other side who will lend me a horse. Warren told me earlier that Dawes has already gone ahead by land. After I reach Samuel Adams and John Hancock I will alert the countryside of the Regulars' arrival." He spoke quickly and then turned to leave, but stopped in his tracks. "You are like a son to me, Daniel. Your father would be proud of you, especially tonight. May God be with you."

"Thank you, sir. Godspeed."

It is a good thing I spend so much time racing Paul Jr., Daniel thought as he ran toward the Old North Church. His lungs had never before burned like they did that night, but the excitement of the evening kept him going and kept him from feeling the pain.

The steeple of the Old North Church could easily be seen across the river in Charlestown. Daniel had no doubt that the plan Revere set up with sexton Robert Newman must involve the steeple of the church in some way. He pounded on the door of the sexton's quarters, not bothering to be courteous. A man in his early twenties yanked the door open and glared at Daniel. "Aye, who are you and what is wanted so late?"

"I have been sent by Paul Revere. The Regulars are moving."

Newman's expression changed. "Come, we must go to the top of the church." He grabbed two lanterns from next to the door and handed one to Daniel. "Can you carry this while you climb?"

"Yes, sir."

"Tell me, how do the devils move?"

"By sea, sir. They are readying the boats now."

"Aye, I thought they would. We are smarter than them, though. They will be surprised when they find the countryside ready for their arrival." A devilish grin spread across the man's face.

The journey to the top of the steeple was just as hard as the run across town had been. By the time the pair reached the top of the fourteen story steeple, Daniel's legs burned as much as his lungs.

"General Gage himself attends church here." Robert Newman laughed and it almost sounded like a cackle. "Won't that devil be surprised to find out we used his beloved building against him." Newman clearly enjoyed his role in the night's escapades.

At the top of the steeple, Daniel and Newman knelt on the floor as they lit the two lanterns. "Are you ready for this?" Newman asked. "When the Regulars see the light, they'll no doubt know it is a warning. They will come for us."

Daniel gulped. "I am ready."

They both stood at the same time and lifted the lanterns high in the air. The view from the top of the steeple could not be matched anywhere in the city. Daniel had never been up there before and he wished it were under different circumstances. Seeing the water below, he said a silent prayer, wishing his dear friend a safe passage across the river.

"That is enough, young man," Newman said after barely two minutes of holding the light aloft. "We best get down before there is no hope for us."

They blew out the lanterns and began to descend the many stairs

111

back to ground level. The stairs were treacherous in the dark and Daniel caught himself from falling more than once. As they neared the ground, shouts could be heard outside. The pair hoped to make it through the door, but it burst open and three redcoats ran in just as the pair reached the last step. "This way!" Newman grabbed Daniel's collar and yanked. Daniel followed him as they ran to the back of the church and threw open a window. He scrambled over the sill and then reached up to help Newman out the same way.

"Good luck, Daniel. It was a pleasure giving warning with you," Newman said with a final salute before running off into the night. Daniel bolted in the opposite direction just as the soldiers arrived at the window. They shouted for him to stop, but he never turned around as he ran toward the cemetery surrounding the back of the church. He jumped and hopped as he tried to avoid tripping over the headstones in the dark, but he failed twice and had to pull himself back up to continue his run. He made it all the way back to Revere's shop before he dared look over his shoulder. Nobody followed him. He had made it.

He shut himself inside the building and crawled to the top of the loft. As he sat on the straw mat, trying to calm his pounding heart, he replayed the events of the evening in his mind. He worried about his friend and wondered how long it would be before they knew of his fate.

Godspeed, Paul.

He removed his coat and tugged his boots off. Exhaustion took over the second he lay down and he drifted off into a dream-filled slumber.

Chapter 13

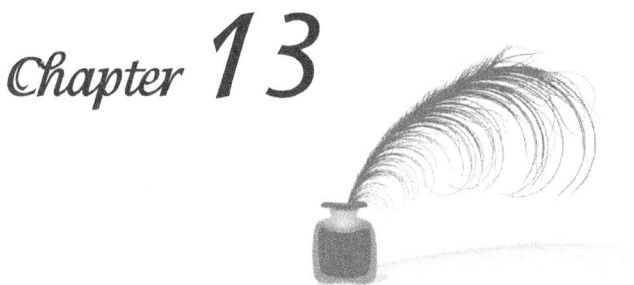

JUNE 23, 1775
BOSTON, MASSACHUSETTS

Daniel stretched his legs and arms, stiff from lying on the matted straw in the loft. He hoped one day to have time to fix his sleeping conditions. Two months had passed since the night he helped light the lanterns in the Old North Church. Paul successfully alerted the towns on the other side of the harbor that night and they were ready and armed when the redcoats arrived at dawn the next day. The British pressed through the militiamen in Lexington, but were stopped in Concord and pushed back all the way to Boston.

It had been surprising to all parties involved that their little militia withstood the advances of seven hundred British troops. Nevertheless, it served to encourage the redcoats efforts. Since that day, Boston had been under siege of the British army. Much care had to be taken when traveling around the city and strict curfews were in place. The night watches of the Mechanics and Sons of Liberty had become twice as dangerous.

113

Forcing himself out of bed, Daniel pulled his boots on and swung his legs over the edge of the loft, descending the ladder just as the shop's door opened.

"Good morning, Daniel," Paul Sr. said. The wrinkles on his face betrayed the stress he'd been under the past couple of months.

"Good morning, sir. You are here early this morning."

He sighed and dropped into a chair near his workbench. Fatigue and sorrow filled his voice as he spoke. "I have just come from the mass grave the devils dug after the battle over at Bunker's Hill a few days ago."

Daniel bowed his head. "I am sure that was a difficult thing to witness."

"I identified one of the men killed." Paul's head came up and he looked straight at Daniel. "I am afraid Joseph Warren is no longer with us."

Daniel's mouth dropped open in shock. "The rumors are true then? He perished?"

Revere nodded.

"Can this week bring any more sadness?" Daniel too sunk into a chair.

"I bring other news. Perhaps it is better. I will let you be the judge of that. The second continental congress has met in Philadelphia. They have chosen a commander in chief of our continental army."

"And who is the unlucky fellow tasked with such a job?"

"His name is General George Washington."

Daniel tilted his head. "Is he the same that served in the French and Indian War?"

Revere nodded again. "It is the same. He fought with the British then, but he has now sided with those of us fighting for freedom in the colonies. I hear he is preparing to leave Philadelphia this very day to come here."

"To Boston? Will our city be freed then?"

"Only time will tell. They will make camp in Cambridge. We best be ready for whatever may come next."

July 3, 1775 – Boston, Massachusetts

"General Washington arrived in Cambridge yesterday," Daniel said as he sat around the breakfast table with Annie, Marta, Jacob, Isabella, and Johanna. It was the first time he'd eaten with the family in weeks and it felt good to finally have everyone he loved so dearly sitting next to him.

"I am scared Mama," little Johanna said. "I don't want any more fighting. It scares me when I hear the guns."

"No need to worry, dear. The fighting will not be near our home. You are safe as long as you stay close to where you know you are supposed to be." Annie's words were intended to comfort Johanna, but her message was clearly directed at her oldest son.

"Paul has asked me to take a message to General Washington today," Daniel admitted.

"By yourself?" Annie spat.

Daniel laughed. "Mama, I am sixteen. I am almost a man. Do not worry about me so much."

"Exactly," she said with a frown. "You are *almost* a man. Why does he not go himself?"

"He has other matters to attend to. I will not meet any harm just by carrying a simple letter."

"Please be careful. I am sure there are regulars hiding out in every corner of this city."

"I am taking a delivery to someone at the edge of town. If I am stopped, I can show them what I carry. When I leave the delivery, I will just keep going. It will not be a problem. I promise."

Annie stood on tiptoes and placed her hands on her son's cheeks.

115

"I cannot bear to lose anyone else."

Daniel wrapped his arms around his tiny mother. "I will return, Mama. I love you." He placed his hat on his head an slipped out the door.

"Are you ready, my boy?" Revere asked when he arrived at the shop not much later.

Daniel gave a firm nod.

"I do not need to tell you how important it is that this correspondence be seen only by General Washington's eyes, correct?"

"Yes, sir."

Paul carefully wrapped a small teapot and two tiny cups in strips of linen. "These pieces are for the Martin Jacobsen family. Do you know where their home is?"

Daniel nodded again.

"Good. After you deliver these, follow the hillside behind their home until you get to a small stream. Cross that stream and walk south until you see a dirt path leading through the trees to a small shack. Tell the man inside you are on an errand for me and he will ferry you across the river at a narrow point. He knows where the Regulars are lax on their watches. Do you have any questions for me?"

"No, sir. Thank you for trusting me."

Daniel tucked the letter, sealed with Revere's signet, carefully inside his coat and followed the instructions he'd been given. On the way to the Jacobsen farm he passed half a dozen redcoats. When he smiled and nodded in their direction, they let him pass without a word. The Jacobsen family insisted he stay for a bite to eat before continuing on his way. He obliged, not knowing what the afternoon would hold.

With a full stomach, he set off again, following the hillside behind their home and finding a stream just as Revere had instructed. The

116

path through the woods proved harder to find, and he had to retrace his steps twice. Once he noticed the faint trail he quickly found the shack.

Daniel rapped loudly on the wooden door. "Hello?" he called.

A man in his seventies opened the door just enough to peek out. "What is needed?"

"I am sent by Paul Revere. I desire you to ferry me across the river," Daniel said.

"Revere, you say?"

Daniel nodded and the man opened the door and ushered him into the tiny home.

"What is that scoundrel Revere up to now?" the man asked.

At first, the man's tone alarmed Daniel, but then he saw the laughter in his eyes.

"He desires to send correspondence to General Washington."

"Aye, I thought it must be so. I seen 'em arriving just yesterday. All pomp with these armies, I say. No matter. I'll take y'cross. Do you have my fee?"

Daniel produced the three coins Revere gave him and placed them in the old man's palm.

"Looks right. Let's be on our way before those devils in red start snooping around."

Daniel followed the man down to the bank of the river. From under a pile of branches and leaves, he produced a hidden rowboat. The boat was small and old, but free from holes. Good thing, for he did not swim well. The pair didn't speak as they crossed the river. Tall brush lined the water on both sides and it was not hard to hide once on the bank.

"I'll be back for ya at first nightfall. I don't plan on waiting fer ya. You aren't here, I leave."

"I will be here. Thank you." Daniel used the tall weeds lining the edge of the water to pull himself up the side of the riverbank. It was easy to find the main road from the flat land above. Almost immediately he saw militiamen roaming about. Their uniforms weren't as fancy and organized as those of the British regulars. In fact, some of the men did not even have uniforms.

"Hello there," Daniel called to one soldier walking past. "Can you tell me where I might find General Washington?"

The soldier laughed and continued his pace, never looking in Daniel's direction. "Be on your way, boy. The general does not have time for gawkers."

Daniel jogged to keep up with the man. "I must speak with him, sir."

The man stopped and turned to Daniel. "Fine. I do not have time for this either. I will let those keeping watch over his headquarters be the ones to send you away." The soldier turned and pointed in the opposite direction. "General Washington is headquartered at the Vassall mansion. Good luck, boy."

Daniel gazed in the direction the man pointed. A stately two-story home surrounded by tall trees stood at the end of the block. "Thank you, sir," he called to the soldier who had already continued down the road.

Six soldiers flanked the path leading to the front door of the rebels' headquarters. Each stood at attention with their muskets at the reach. Daniel watched them from across the street for a short time, but just as he was about to step into the road, a commotion up the street caught his attention.

A large man, appearing to be drunk, stood over a young boy. The boy must have fallen because a basket of dry goods lay scattered all over the side of the road. "Get up so I can knock you down again," the man yelled, his words slurring together. "How dare you step in front of me when I am walking."

The boy, maybe age eight, tried to stand, but the man kicked him in the side and the boy fell back down, clutching his stomach. "I was just walking, sir. You stepped in front of me. I could not move in time," the boy said in a ragged, pain-filled voice.

"And now you are talking back to me? Let me teach you a lesson about how to treat your elders." The man grabbed the boy by the collar and hauled him up to a standing position. The boy trembled and ducked his head as the man drew his arm back. Daniel could no longer stand by without intervening. With only a moment's thought, he jumped forward and grabbed the man's arm, holding it back firmly. The man let go of the boy and whirled around to meet Daniel face to face.

"How dare you," the man hissed. "This boy needs to be taught a lesson."

The man stood half a foot taller than Daniel and weighed at least a hundred pounds more, but Daniel held his ground. "The boy did nothing wrong, sir. It is you who needs to let it go."

The man's face contorted and twisted with fury. He pulled his arm back and swung it forward, but Daniel easily side-stepped the blow and planted himself between the man and the young boy. Laughter erupted from the crowds who had gathered to watch the exchange.

The man breathed hard, as if the little effort he'd made had completely winded him. "Yer not worth my time." He spat on the ground and flapped his hand in Daniel's direction as if dismissing him. Daniel held his position until the man had gone half a block and disappeared into a building.

"Are you okay?" Daniel asked the young boy standing behind him.

He nodded shyly and spoke in a quiet voice. "Thank you."

"It was nothing. Someday you will be as tall as that man and you can stand up for someone else. Deal?"

The boy grinned. "Yes. I can't wait." Daniel bent down and helped him retrieve the contents of his basket, carefully packing them in once more. He tousled the boy's hair before saying, "Run along. And watch where you are stepping."

The incident helped remove Daniel's anxiety about meeting General Washington, and he returned to the walk in front of the Vassall mansion.

"Halt!" An armed soldier dropped his weapon from his shoulder, aiming it at Daniel. "Keep on moving."

"I have business with General Washington, sir."

"Business with the general? Oh, are you the king now, boy?" the soldier teased. "Be on your way."

"I *must* speak with him," Daniel demanded.

The man's expression changed to anger. "I said, be on your way." He bent toward Daniel and opened his mouth to say something else, but a voice called from an upper window of the home, interrupting him.

"Let the boy in!" the voice called.

Everyone on the front walk, including Daniel, gazed up at the man in the window. He was tall and wore an officer's uniform. His hands were clasped behind his back and a stern look covered his face.

The soldier immediately stood up straight and rested his weapon back on his shoulder. "Yes sir, General Washington, sir."

Chapter 14

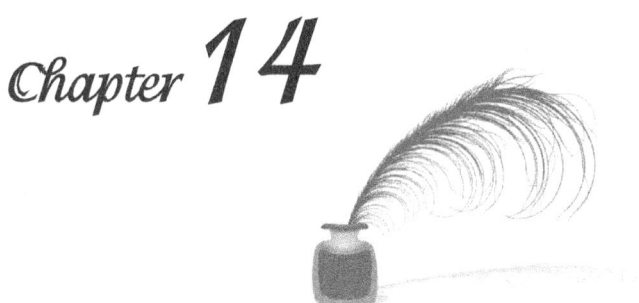

Daniel took a deep breath and marched past the six soldiers guarding the path to the front porch. One of the soldiers opened the heavy doors and he stepped across the threshold. Tapestries and ornate furnishings filled the beautiful home. If he wasn't on important business, Daniel would have liked to spend more time experiencing the beauty within the walls of the mansion.

A man in his early twenties hurried out of a doorway in the hallway in front of Daniel. "Come, come. Sit in the parlor. General Washington will meet with you shortly."

"Thank you," Daniel said.

The man ushered him through another door and then rushed out again. Daniel clasped and unclasped his hands behind his back as he scanned the room. He wondered if he should sit on the fancy silk-covered settee or continue to stand. A beautiful desk with an ornately carved chair that matched the etchings in the wood took up one end of the room. Shelves lined with volumes of books lined another wall. The settee and a matching chair filled the remaining portion of the room. Daniel finally made the decision to sit and did so right before he heard footsteps on the stairs outside the parlor door. He jumped back up when the door burst open and the man he'd seen in the upstairs window stepped through. An aide closed the door behind him.

"I am General Washington. You claim to have business with me?" the imposing man said.

Daniel made a conscious effort to stand straighter. "Yes, sir. My name is Daniel Avery. I have come with a message from Paul Revere, sir."

Washington crossed the room in two giant steps and reached a hand out to Daniel. Daniel shook his hand, noting the firm grasp of his handshake. "Revere, you say?" Washington began. "Is this the same Revere I have heard tale of? The one who alerted the countryside that the Regulars were on the march?"

Daniel nodded. "Yes, sir. It is the same man."

"What is the message?"

Daniel pulled Revere's letter from his waistcoat and handed it to Washington.

General Washington stepped behind the large desk and sat down in the chair. "Please, have a seat."

Daniel bounced his knee up and down as he sat on the edge of the settee. The presence of the commander in chief of the continental army made him nervous. Daniel tried to read Washington's emotions as he read the correspondence from Revere, but his stoic expression gave nothing away. Daniel didn't know if the letter contained something of great importance, or was merely a congratulatory letter on his appointment as head of the army. When Washington finished reading the letter, he tucked it inside a desk drawer before looking up.

"Now, what of you, my boy?" Washington said, turning his full attention to Daniel.

"Excuse me, sir?" Daniel said.

"Are you a messenger for Revere, a friend of his, or what? What is your business with him?"

"My father—God rest his soul—and Paul Revere were close friends. I am now serving as an assistant to Revere."

"Were you aware of his ride in April before it happened?"

"Yes, sir." Daniel said. He then told Washington of his role on the night the British marched to Lexington and Concord.

"That is good," Washington said at the end of the story. "And are you happy working for Revere?"

"It is good work, sir."

"Are you happy?" Washington repeated.

Daniel took a deep breath and held it before answering. "I believe so, sir."

Much to his surprise, the general threw his head back and laughed, finally showing an emotion other than pure seriousness. "You believe so, do you? Well, I will not make you answer differently. Tell me about your family."

Daniel briefly told Washington about his siblings, his mother, and his deceased father. He kept the details to a minimum, trying not to ramble, but unsure of why the general was so interested in him.

Washington nodded throughout the conversation but didn't respond until Daniel ceased talking. "It sounds like you have a lovely family. But, I do have a proposal for you."

Daniel's heart raced as Washington rested his elbows on the desk and leaned forward. His expression returned to the serious one he'd maintained for most of their meeting. "Tell me, Daniel. Why did you help the boy outside my window before you came to the door?"

"Because, sir, it was the right thing to do. The man may have been an elder to the boy, but the boy did nothing wrong and he was too small to protect himself."

"The man was bigger than you, too. In fact, I think he would have been bigger than me."

Daniel didn't doubt that fact. "Size is not important when dealing with right and wrong, sir."

A small smile played on Washington's lips. "Do you realize of all the people on the road watching the events unfold, you were the only one who had the courage to step in and remedy the problem?"

Daniel didn't say anything. He felt Washington was still leading up to something.

"It is hard to find men who have courage like you. I need men on my side who have integrity in all circumstances. Would you be willing to put your assistantship at risk while we fight for the freedom of the colonies?"

Daniel's heart pounded so hard he could hear its steady beat in his ears. "What do you want me to do?" he whispered.

"I need someone who can infiltrate General Gage's camp and apprise me of their operations. I've been searching for someone trustworthy, someone who could blend in. I doubt anyone would suspect a boy your age of being a deceiver. I think you would be a perfect fit for this assignment."

"You want me to *spy* on General Gage's camp?" Daniel's words rushed out.

General Washington gave one firm nod of his head.

Daniel blew his breath out slowly. "My father served in the French and Indian War. He was wounded in the massacre in Boston a few years ago. He died while trying to make a difference. I want nothing more in life than to make him proud. I *will* do as you ask."

"How are your theatrical skills?"

Daniel lifted his eyebrows. "My . . . theatrical skills, sir?"

"Do you think you can convince Gage that you want to spy for him? I want you to make him think you are nothing more than a messenger boy who wants to share secrets with him about our

124

operations here. You can feed him false information with a little bit of the truth mixed in to keep him interested. All the while, you will be observing the movements of his camp and reporting back to me."

Although the idea of doing what Washington described absolutely terrified Daniel, he found himself nodding in agreement. "I will do my best, sir."

"You are not the only one I have given this assignment to. You are the last of five men whom I have chosen. Are you familiar with the bible, Daniel?"

"I faithfully attend my church meetings sir."

"I give new meaning to a scripture found in Matthew. Let not thy left hand know what thy right hand doeth, Matthew wrote. Daniel, you are the last of five people I have chosen to act as my eyes in General Gage's territory. None of you will know the names of the others. If one of you were to be captured, you would not be tempted or even able to give up the names of the others. Do you understand?"

"Yes, sir."

"Good. Now let's make a plan for you." The general spent the next hour discussing possible scenarios and believable lies with Daniel. His incredible strategy planning impressed Daniel more than anything else ever had. Finally, Washington stood and walked to the parlor door. "I will begin by sending a letter back with you addressed to General Gage."

He opened the door and called to the man waiting outside. "I need a scribe, immediately."

Within seconds a skinny man with a powdered wig sitting slightly askew atop his head hurried through the room, inkwell and paper in hand. He set the inkwell on the corner of the desk and sat in the chair next to the settee. "Ready, sir."

Washington clasped his hands behind his back and paced the room as he dictated the letter. "Sir, I understand that the officers engaged in the cause of liberty, who by the fortune of war, have fallen into your hands have been thrown indiscriminately into a common jail appropriated for felons. My duty now makes it necessary to apprize you that for the future I shall regulate my conduct towards those gentlemen who are or may be in our possession, exactly by the rule which you shall observe towards those of ours who may be in your custody. If severity and hardship mark the line of *your* conduct, painful as it may be to me, your prisoners *will* feel its effects. But if kindness and humanity are shown to ours, I shall with pleasure consider those in our hands only as unfortunate and they shall receive the treatment to which the unfortunate are ever entitled. I beg to be favored with an answer as soon as possible and am, Sir, your most obedient and very humble servant."

Daniel almost couldn't breathe as he listened to Washington dictate the message to his scribe. His words were cordial, but his manner and tone of delivery showed he meant every word of what he said. He did not seem the type of man who would tolerate someone failing their duties.

The scribe sealed the letter and handed it to the general, who passed it to Daniel. "You remember what we discussed?" he said.

"Yes, sir," Daniel answered. He took the letter from Washington's hands and carefully tucked it inside his waistcoat.

"Remember, let no one, not even your dearest friends and family, know what you are doing."

Daniel gulped and nodded. General Washington turned and exited the room without another word. "Good day," the scribe said as he held the door open for Daniel. Once outside the headquarters, Daniel felt like he could finally breathe correctly again. His legs trembled as he walked past the same soldiers on the walkway and followed the road down to the river. Thankfully, the man who had originally ferried him across waited in the brush along the banks.

"I thought you'd decided to enlist, gone so long were ya," the man said gruffly.

"Sorry to keep you waiting," Daniel apologized.

"Makes no difference to an old man like me. Get in."

The return trip across the river passed in a blur. Just like the first time, there was very little conversation and Daniel bid the man farewell with hardly a second glance. As he returned to downtown Boston, staying in the shadows since night had fallen, he could barely pull his mind from the assignment he'd been given by the highest ranking officer in the continental army.

Daniel sighed in relief as he came within sight of Revere's silversmith shop. He let himself in and crossed the dark room to the ladder leading to the loft. Sleep beckoned.

"You have returned."

Daniel whirled around at the sound of the voice in time to see a candle flicker to life near one of the workbenches. The shadow of Paul Revere bounced on the wall behind him.

"I did not see you there, sir." Daniel grinned.

"I figured there was no sense in alerting anyone who happened to pass by at this hour that I had not yet retired for the evening. You were gone much longer than I expected. Did you have trouble?"

The fact that Paul stayed up, concerned for his assistant's safety, made Daniel like the father figure even more. "No, sir. Washington was otherwise occupied when I arrived and I waited for him to be free so I could personally deliver your letter to him." The truth was only slightly exaggerated.

"Is he as impressive of a man as rumor says?"

"More impressive, sir."

Paul laughed. "Did he send any correspondence for me?"

Daniel reached into his waistcoat and pulled out the reply Washington had written to Revere. He made sure the letter intended for General Gage remained carefully concealed away from Paul's eyes as he did so. "This is for you, sir."

Paul took the letter from Daniel's hand and stood, candle in hand. He didn't open the letter in front of Daniel. "I will let you sleep now, boy. Perhaps you can have a late start on the morrow. Dine with your family in the morning and then come to work. I suspect Annie wonders about your safety."

"I will do that, sir. Thank you."

Revere left the shop, leaving Daniel alone in the dark with nothing but his never-ending thoughts.

Weary as he was, Daniel could not find the peace of sleep that night. He rose before dawn, knowing the inevitable task awaited him. He dressed quickly and slipped out of the silversmith shop before smoke had even begun to rise from the Revere's chimney. He slipped past homes and buildings as he made his way down to the Commons, stopping only long enough to tell his brother Jacob, who had already begun his outdoor chores, that he had returned and would be unavailable for a time.

The Commons buzzed with activity even at that early hour. It surprised Daniel that he did not draw more attention from the Regulars walking about. No one said a word to him until he stood in front of the building where General Gage lived and worked.

"I am a messenger hired to deliver a letter for General Gage. I bring correspondence from General Washington in Cambridge," Daniel told one of the men guarding the entrance.

The guard gave a short nod and stuck out his hand. "Give me the letter. I will see that the general receives it."

"I am afraid I am under strict command to deliver it only to the general himself."

The soldier looked Daniel up and down and must have decided

he didn't pose a threat because he rapped solidly on the door without another word. Another man dressed in the uniform of a Regular opened the door and ushered Daniel into a large room. A long table filled most of the empty space in the room. General Gage sat at one end of the table, still breakfasting. Daniel recognized General Gage immediately, having seen him around town on his watches with the Mechanics. At the sight of the elaborate spread of food, Daniel's stomach growled, reminding him he hadn't eaten since the previous afternoon. He willed it to remain quiet.

The general remained seated. "What correspondence do you bring at this early hour?" He seemed friendly enough to Daniel. Perhaps the assignment given him by Washington wouldn't be as difficult as he imagined.

Daniel reached inside his waistcoat and pulled out Washington's letter. "I am but a silversmith's apprentice, sir. I made a delivery yesterday and was stopped by General Washington's troops. They paid me greatly to deliver this letter to you, sir."

General Gage set his fork on the table and gazed more closely at Daniel. "How old are you, boy?"

"I am sixteen years, sir."

"You expect me to believe that the commander-in-chief of the continental army let a boy of only sixteen make a delivery for him?"

Daniel's hands trembled and he clasped them behind his back, hoping the general and the Regulars who flanked the table wouldn't notice. "A pair of rebel soldiers stopped me in the road, sir. They are the ones who asked me to bring it to you." Daniel paused and took a deep breath. Speaking quietly, as if sharing a great secret, he said, "I overheard them as I was leaving. They were discussing Washington's plans, sir."

General Gage raised his eyebrows at Daniel, but didn't say anything. He looked amused.

Hoping for the best, Daniel continued with his lie. "Sir, my father

129

has always been a loyal subject of the king. He sailed to Boston with his father when he was my age, but he has raised us to be obedient subjects of King George. I feel it is my duty as a loyal subject to apprise you of what I heard."

A smile crept across the general's face. "I do believe we've found ourselves a spy? What do you think men?" he glanced at the two soldiers on either side of him, but didn't respond to their mumbled answers.

"Faye!" he called and clapped his hands once. A woman in a servant's uniform rushed in from the doorway leading to a kitchen. "Fetch this boy some breakfast. He will be joining us this morning."

Chapter 15

AUGUST 1775
BOSTON, MASSACHUSETTS

Daniel forced himself not to run as he left the presence of General Gage that morning. The man, under different circumstances, would have been fine company. But lying to a man of his caliber had been torture on Daniel's nerves. His story had been simple. The two men representing Washington had given the letter for Daniel to deliver so they could spend time at a local tavern before their absence was noticed. As they walked away, Daniel overheard them discussing where some of the munitions were being stored. Of course, the location did not really exist, but General Gage did not know that. And even if he never intended to do anything with the information, Daniel had proved to him that he could deliver. Before leaving Gage's presence, Daniel promised to watch for any new information and bring it immediately to headquarters. He had successfully infiltrated the redcoats.

"Ah. I see you have decided to join us," Paul Revere said when

Daniel walked back into the shop. "When I told you to breakfast with your family this morning, I did not know it would turn into such a long event." The twinkle in his eye proved he wasn't really angry with Daniel.

"I am sorry for my tardiness, sir." Daniel hated deceiving his dear friend, worthy cause or not.

"I think I will be late tomorrow, Father," Paul Jr. teased as he hammered at a piece of metal. "We are taking turns, right Daniel?"

Daniel grinned. "Sure, Paul." It felt good to be back in the comfort of the silversmith shop where friendships were genuine and honest work waited.

The days passed rapidly over the next two weeks. Daniel spent as much time in the Commons as possible, listening and observing, and took every opportunity he could find to be in General Gage's presence. Three times in those two weeks he was ferried across the river by British Regulars who dropped him at the opposite side, believing he would be spying for them. On each trip, General Gage would send meaningless correspondence and Washington would respond in kind. The subject matter of the letters was not important. What *was* important was the information Daniel provided to Washington about General Gage's plans and the fake information he fed Gage about Washington. At times, he had to remind himself what was truth and what was fiction.

The hardest part of the ordeal were the lies he told his mother, siblings, and the Revere family. He didn't want to hurt his friends and family, but they couldn't know the truth. After running out of excuses, he told Annie he would be away on business with Paul for a fortnight, hoping to save himself the burden of concocting more lies. He told Revere Annie was not well, and needed him at home. Being the friend that he was, Revere gave Daniel a two week leave from his job.

He got the break he needed. With nowhere else to stay, Daniel

132

reported to General Gage and asked for a berth. Gage obliged and gave him space in a building next to the general's headquarters. Being that close to the army at all times proved an effective way of gathering information. Especially when General Gage let something slip during a dinner Daniel had been invited to.

"If we can find enough of the king's loyal subjects to help us, we will have this war finished in no time," General Gage said to the officer seated next to him, Major General William Howe.

Howe led the troops into battle at Bunker's Hill. Britain lost over a thousand men that day. If the colonists hadn't run out of ammunition, it would have been worse and they would have been victorious. Daniel kept his head down, sipping his soup, but keeping an ear on the conversation at the head of the table.

"We have confirmed the new information The Healer brought us. Everything was exactly as he said again," Howe said.

"That is good. I hoped that would be your answer."

Major General Howe continued, talking through a bite of bread. "He is well-known among Bostonians, sir. They believe he is fighting their cause with them. Fools." He laughed and some of the bread fell from his mouth. "One of our men will be meeting him again tonight. Let us hope he has the information we have been looking for."

"Bring any correspondence to me as soon as you receive it."

"I will, General."

Daniel felt his face turn red and hoped no one else at the table noticed. *What are they talking about? Who is The Healer they speak of?* Daniel couldn't think of any of the Sons of Liberty or the Mechanics that might be traitorous enough to feed real information to General Gage. It had to be someone he didn't know. If he could discover the identity of The Healer, it might make a difference to Washington's continental army and their fight for liberty. Finding the identity of the traitor would become his new goal.

"How is your meal, young Avery?" General Gage called down the table.

Daniel glanced up at the sound of his name. Swallowing hard, he answered, "It is wonderful, sir. My compliments to your kitchen staff."

"I have some of the finest chefs in England working for me. I do not lack good food." Daniel held his breath while General Gage's eyes lingered on him. He felt as if the man peered into his very soul. Gage spoke again. "Have you any new information for me? Everyone at this table is trusted. You can speak freely."

"No, sir. I have nothing new yet. I thought to return to Washington's camp tomorrow. Would you like to send correspondence?"

"I will think on it tonight. Come to me before you leave on the morrow."

The meal ended without any further conversation. Daniel could barely force the food down, sick from hearing Gage and Howe's conversation at the other end of the table. As soon as the guests were excused, Daniel hurried outside, sucking in the fresh night air as hard as he could in an attempt to calm his nerves and stomach. "I have to figure this out tonight," Daniel whispered to himself as he walked to the building with his berth. Instead of entering, though, he slipped quietly around the back and crouched in the shadows. From there, he could see the entrance to Gage's headquarters. He sat for a full hour, barely daring to blink as he kept watch. The sun had long since fallen before Major General Howe came through the door of the headquarters. He looked back and forth before stepping out into the street.

Daniel waited for a moment before darting out of the shadows and around the side of the building. He watched from the corner of the headquarters as Howe walked north before turning left and rapping sharply on the door of a small home. Only a small amount of light slipped from the doorway, but Daniel could see a man dressed in the uniform of an officer standing next to Howe. Unable to hear their conversation from his vantage point, Daniel slipped behind a tree in front of the house next door. His foot kicked a rock as he ran and it bounced and rolled. Both Howe and the man he spoke to at the door turned to the sound of the noise. Daniel stayed behind the tree, not even daring to breath. When they resumed their conversation without leaving their positions, Daniel sighed in relief.

From his new vantage point, Daniel heard a few words.

"Meet . . . soon . . . deliver . . . rebels . . ."

"Come on, give me something to work with," Daniel whispered.

Daniel peeked at the men from behind the tree. After a few more words, Howe stepped off the porch and walked back in the direction he had come. Daniel pressed himself up against the tree and turned his head to the side, trying to make himself as inconspicuous as possible. As soon as Howe passed his hiding place and disappeared from his sight, he emerged from behind the tree. He hurried to catch up to the other officer headed in the opposite direction. Daniel ran behind headquarters and then behind two other buildings in an attempt to catch up without being seen.

"Where did he go?" Daniel whispered as he came out from behind the buildings to check his progress. The man had vanished. A small tavern was the only place he could have gone, but it wasn't open at that late hour. He had to try. Carefully looking in all directions, Daniel stepped to the front window and peered in. No light or sound came from the building. A scrape of a boot on a rock caught his attention and he ducked, laying completely flat behind a bush that flanked the front of the tavern.

"Do you have it?"

Daniel raised his head and turned his ear to the sound of the voice. He recognized it as the same voice he'd heard moments earlier. It was the man Major General Howe met with.

"No greeting tonight? You are all business this evening. Surely my offerings deserve at least a word of welcome," a different voice responded. Something about that second voice triggered a recognition that pulsed through Daniel. He'd heard the voice before, of that he was certain. But where? He only had one option: leave his hiding place and risk getting caught. If spotted, he could run, but the officer would quickly raise an alarm and Daniel would be caught long before he slipped away from the areas controlled by the Regulars.

Acutely aware of every move he made, Daniel managed to turn himself around and rise to his knees. He crawled to the edge of the tavern and peered around the corner. The two men stood on the side of the building. The British officer blocked Daniel's view of the other man and he silently cursed. He had to see who the voice belonged to.

"I do have the information General Gage requested. He will be surprised by this one," the unknown voice said.

The officer reached out and took something from the hands of the other man. As he brought his arm back, Daniel clearly saw a folded letter. The officer tucked it inside his coat.

"Thank you," the officer said. "We will send word when your help is needed again." He turned and strode away without another word. With the way cleared, Daniel got a full view of the man who had just betrayed his fellow colonists.

Dr. Benjamin Church. The Healer.

Daniel stuffed his fist in his mouth and bit hard in an effort to keep from yelling out loud. So fierce was his anger, he tasted blood. It couldn't be true. Dr. Church was a friend of Paul Revere and Daniel knew him well, too. He had been present at all the meetings of the Mechanics and had been with the Sons of Liberty for years. He had come to Daniel's house the night of the massacre to help his father. Anger boiled up inside Daniel at the lives that could be lost because of the information Church relayed.

Breathing hard, he clenched his fists and stood, determined to teach the doctor a lesson. But then he stopped. Taking his anger out on that one man wouldn't stop the information from getting into the hands of General Gage. It took every ounce of control Daniel could dig up to stay put while Dr. Church slipped into the shadows behind the buildings and disappeared into the night.

"I have to stop the officer," Daniel whispered. He searched for anything that could be used as a weapon and grabbed a large rock before hurrying off in the direction the officer had gone. "Hello!" he called as he neared the soldier in the road. No time for secrecy.

The soldier stopped. "Who's there?"

Daniel stepped into his view. "General Howe asked me to retrieve the letter given to you."

"Who are you, boy? I do not know what letter you speak of."

"I work for General Gage. I have been sent to retrieve the letter Dr. Church entrusted to you."

"Liar."

"I speak the truth, sir."

"You have erred. I have never heard the name you speak of. If you are referring to The Healer, you must know that he has not given his real name to anyone."

Daniel's heart fell. It would be impossible to talk his way out of the hole he'd dug.

The officer took a step closer to him. "I think you need to come with me."

He had no other choice. Without a second thought, Daniel swung his arm around with all the force he could muster. The rock he'd kept hidden in his hand collided with the officer's head with a sickening thud and the man crumpled to the ground. Daniel had never purposely caused harm to anyone before and his stomach threatened to spill its contents all over the ground as he looked at the man's blood-soaked face. The man moaned and Daniel sighed in relief, grateful the officer would live.

But he had to hurry.

Daniel dropped to his knees and slipped his hand inside the man's red waistcoat. A door slammed shut nearby just as his fingers curled around the letter. Daniel grabbed it and ran into the night, darting in and out of shadows, around trees, and behind homes, desperate to separate himself from what he'd just done.

He ran all the way until he reached the Jacobsen farm. Finding his way around to the shack of the old man who had ferried him across the river the day he met Washington was nearly impossible at night, but Daniel didn't have a choice. He searched and searched until he found it.

"Hello! This is urgent! Hello!" Daniel yelled as he pounded on the door of the little shack. No other homes were anywhere near and he didn't worry about being heard.

The old man answered the door in a nightshirt with a sword in his hand. "What are ya doin' at this hour, boy? Tryin' to wake the dead?"

"Sir, I must have immediate passage across the river. You are the only one who can help me."

The man narrowed his eyes as he looked at Daniel. "I charge extra for nighttime trips."

Daniel spoke calmly and with pleading in his voice. "Sir, I have nothing. I can get the money, but I do not have it now. Please, if you have any care about the freedom of Massachusetts and the other colonies, you must help me."

"Just what are you doing, boy?"

"I cannot say, sir."

"Does it involve stopping the devils?"

"Yes."

"Let's go."

The pair didn't dare light a candle as they launched the boat in the water. A bobbing light in the night would be sure to draw unwanted attention. The passage took longer than usual in the dark and Daniel felt a huge burden fall from his shoulders as they safely reached the other side. "Do not wait for me tonight," he told the old man.

"God be with ya, boy," the man said before slipping his oars back into the water. Daniel hurried along the familiar road, not caring if he was seen. He easily reached General Washington's headquarters before being stopped by a sentry.

"Halt!" he soldier yelled.

"I must speak with General Washington," Daniel said firmly.

"The general has gone to bed."

"It is important. Give him my name and I assure you he will see me. I am Daniel Avery."

The sentry hesitated, but rapped sharply on the front door, which was then opened by another man. After a whispered conversation, they admitted Daniel and instructed him to wait in the parlor. Daniel paced back and forth across the rug as he waited for Washington. He checked many times to make sure the letter had not fallen from his coat.

"Daniel? Why have you come at this hour?"

Daniel whirled around at the sound of Washington's stern voice. "General, sir. I have intercepted a letter. I had to harm a man to get it."

"Give me the letter," Washington commanded.

Daniel placed the letter on his palm and felt an immediate release of burden as the correspondence left his possession. He watched as Washington set the lantern he held on the desk and sat behind it. Complete silence filled the room as Washington read. Daniel tried to interpret the emotions of the man as his face flickered in the lantern's light. Concern etched itself into his face the longer he read.

When Washington finally spoke, it was with sadness. "The letter is not signed. Did you see the person who delivered it?"

Daniel swallowed hard. "Yes, sir. His name is Dr. Benjamin Church."

Washington's head came up sharply. "Church, you say?"

Daniel nodded. "I have known him for many years. It saddens me to report of his treason."

"I know the man you speak of. I would have never expected this." Washington sighed. "Were you discovered as you took this?"

"Yes, sir. The officer I took it from would recognize me if I were to report back to Gage's camp." Daniel frowned. "I am sorry, sir. I wanted to be of more help to you, but I am afraid I can no longer operate in the same capacity."

"Your acts tonight saved some valuable information from falling into the wrong hands. Your fellow countrymen owe you much for your bravery." Washington stood and walked around the side of the desk. Taking Daniel's hand firmly in his, he said, "I spoke to you the day we met about choosing five people to aid me in my watching of General Gage's movements. Do you remember?"

"Yes, sir. You said we would not know each other's identities."

"I had something made up for each of you. Something to show my gratitude. Keep it safe. I may call on you for help again sometime, but for now, I thank you for your service and release you from your obligations to me."

Daniel looked down at the object Washington placed in his palm. A gold pocket watch, still gleaming from a recent polishing, rested there. Daniel opened the clasp on the watch. Inside was a simple engraving, *Daniel Avery – 1775*. "Thank you, sir. I will treasure this always."

As he left Washington's headquarters that night, Daniel contemplated the events of the summer. His part in the revolution of the colonies couldn't possibly be over yet, could it? He dropped the watch into his pocket and disappeared into the night.

Chapter 16

PRESENT DAY
BOSTON, MASSACHUSETTS

'd changed positions multiple times in the two hours it took Daniel to tell his story, ending curled up in a ball in one corner of the couch. At one point, Daniel covered me with a blanket. But then something he said caught my attention and I jumped up. "Wait ... what did you just say?"

"Uhh . . . I've said a lot of stuff. Which part do you want to hear again?" Daniel asked.

"The part about the pocket watch Washington gave you."

"He told me he had them made for five of us as a thank you of sorts."

"Right, but what about the engraving?"

Daniel narrowed his eyes and lifted one corner of his mouth. "Really? That's the part that stood out to you? It had my name on it. And the year . . . 1775."

My heart pounded in my chest. "That's why we were drawn to each other. That's why I'm supposed to be your soul saver. As soon

141

as I learned your last name I knew I'd heard your name before, but I didn't know where." I paused to take a breath. "I have your watch."

Daniel's jaw dropped. "What? How? That's impossible. The watch was lost when I died."

"Your family had it. They just kept passing it down from one generation to another."

"My family . . . you mean . . ." I could see Daniel trying to wrap his mind around that one. "Are we related to each other?"

"No," I said quickly. "At least, I don't think so. I helped one of your descendants. Nicholas Trenton. He told me about the watch. It had been in his family for generations, but he lost track of it when he died, too. After he was extricated, I found the watch in a trunk. The watch is in my dresser back in Marion."

"Are you sure about this? I don't have any descendants. I died at sixteen, remember?"

"But—he said it came from his father who inherited it from his father or something like that."

"Did you say Trenton was the last name of the guy who told you about the watch?"

I nodded and then watched as a smile spread across Daniel's face.

"Jacob, my only brother, died in the War of 1812. He never married. My younger sisters, Isabella and Johanna, both died of a fever when they were ten and twelve. My sister Marta was the only one to ever marry. I never knew him in life, but her husband's last name was Trenton."

"Have you followed her family's history?" I asked.

Daniel lowered his head. "No. I stopped watching them about the time she got married. Mama died shortly after Marta's marriage and it was too hard to be around everyone without them knowing I was there. I desperately wanted to make myself visible, but I couldn't do it at that point. I lost track of Marta. I didn't know she had any children."

"Sounds like your family had a curse if Marta's the only one to live a normal life."

Daniel shrugged. "That's the way things were back then. People live a lot longer now with modern medicine and better living situations."

"So if you weren't stalking your family, what have you been doing all this time? You've been dead for almost two and half centuries."

"As soon as I'd been dead long enough to figure out how to become visible, I crossed the ocean. I wanted to see what I died trying to get away from."

"And? Was it as evil as you thought?"

Daniel shook his head. "No. I actually lived there for quite a few years. That's the first place I lived as a normal person again. I got a job and I rented a room in a boarding house. I saw other places, too. Every few years I moved on to a new town or a new country. Earlier I told you I'd spent my whole life in Boston. I did spend my whole life here, but I've spent most of my ghost life in other places. I mean, I've been back for a few years here and a few years there. Most recently, I've been back for about a year and a half. I don't know how long I'll stick around."

"Do you even want to be extricated?"

"Of course I do. Who would want to be here forever?"

I shrugged. "I can think of a couple ghosts who don't want to leave."

"Not me. I'd love to be done with this. Being sixteen for as long as I have is kind of boring." He grinned. "I'd like to see what seventeen feels like. Maybe even eighteen."

"Maybe we should—"

My thoughts were interrupted by a tapping on Daniel's apartment door. I jumped in surprise. Sometimes I got so caught up in the ghost world, I forgot that the living world continued to function around me.

Daniel crossed the room and looked through the peephole. "It's your mom." He turned the knob and opened the door.

"Is Jamie over here still?" I heard Mom ask.

Daniel opened the door further and stepped back so Mom could see me sitting on the couch. "I must say, I never saw this one coming," Mom said as she patted Daniel on the arm. "Even after talking to you yesterday, I would have never suspected you were a ghost."

"Ghost?" Daniel scrunched up his face. "What are you talking about?"

Mom's jaw dropped and she glanced from Daniel to me. "Jamie, I thought you were coming to talk to him. What have you been doing over here?"

Daniel couldn't hold back his laughter any longer and Mom slugged him in the arm. "Jerk. I thought I'd just blown something."

Mom pushed past Daniel and plopped down on the couch next to me. So, what's your story?" she asked Daniel.

"Uhh—"

"It took me two hours to hear it, Mom," I said, cutting in. "You'll have to get the condensed version later. He doesn't need to retell it all again right now."

Daniel didn't say anything. I took that to mean he agreed with me.

"What happened with Myles?" I asked, hoping to change the subject.

She sighed. "We told him what we learned about his life and he still tried to dodge some of the questions and make up unbelievable stories. We had to cut him from our client list."

"I'm so sorry." I *was* sorry, but maybe not for the reasons I should have been. I couldn't stand Myles and if Mom and her partners weren't helping him anymore, I wouldn't ever have to be around him. Score ten points for me.

Wait . . . if they aren't helping Myles anymore, they might leave Boston to help some other ghost. If they leave, I'll be sent back to Marion. The idea of leaving Daniel so soon after we met made me feel as if I'd been punched in the stomach. Much to my horror, tears sprung to my eyes.

Mom tilted her head and looked at me. "Jamie . . . are you okay? I thought you didn't like Myles."

"I don't. He's awful. I just . . . well . . . I feel bad that you lost a client." I lied.

"Oh, sweetie, we'll be okay. We've got a waiting list. We'll just move to the next name down."

That's what I'd been afraid of. "How soon?" I whispered.

Mom looked from me to Daniel. "Don't worry. I think we can wait awhile. We could all use a break anyway. We usually move on pretty fast, but—" Mom paused to steal a glance at Daniel. "The last woman we helped extricate paid well, if you know what I mean. We'll be okay."

I let out the breath I'd been holding. "Good. I mean, I should probably try to help Daniel."

"Steven, Portia, and I can help, too. You know, if you want us to." Mom looked a little too eager.

Daniel opened his mouth as if to say something, but I jumped in again before he could get any words out. Poor guy. "I'll let you know if I need help." If I were successful in my job as a soul saver, I wouldn't have much time with Daniel. Even knowing his true identity, I couldn't help the pull I had to him. The idea that I might not be around him for long scared me and I didn't want to share that time with my mom and her friends.

Mom yawned and I did the same thing. It didn't faze Daniel, though. Ghosts don't really sleep. They *can* put themselves in a sleep-like state. I think it's kind of like a trance. Some ghosts do it regularly to help time pass, others do it to attempt normalcy. I had no idea what Daniel's habits were, but he wouldn't be feeling the same effects of tiredness as Mom and me.

"Maybe we should call it a night. You can finish telling me your story tomorrow, when I've had some sleep," I said.

Daniel lifted his palms in the air. "I finished my story. You've heard it all."

"You never told me how you died."

"I didn't think that part was important."

"It's always important," Mom and I said in unison. We looked at each other and grinned.

Mom patted her hands on her thighs and stood up. "I'll be in the apartment. Don't be too long."

"I'll just be a minute."

Daniel shut the door behind my mom and then turned to me. "I feel like I've been released from something. Telling you my story took a huge weight off me."

I stood next to him. "Yeah? Well, thanks. Now you've put the weight on me," I joked.

Daniel's eyes widened. "I didn't mean for that. I'm sorry."

I laughed. "It's my job. Don't worry about it—'cause worrying is my job, too."

Daniel took a step closer and my palms began to sweat. "Would it be okay if I waited until tomorrow to tell you how I died? It's not a fun subject."

I nodded, unable to speak with him that close.

"Good. I'll see you tomorrow then." He leaned forward and gave me a hug. I wrapped my arms around him, returning the hug. It took every ounce of willpower I could dig up to pull my arms down and take a step back. He must have struggled too because I let go first.

"See you in the morning." I kept my eyes down as I walked into my apartment across the hall. If I saw his face one more time after that hug, I would melt all over the hallway floor.

"I hear congratulations are in order."

My head jerked up at the sound of Steven's voice as soon as I entered our apartment. I expected everyone else to be in bed, but the three of them were still sitting around the kitchen table. "Excuse me?"

He laughed. "I've never met a soul saver who can jump from ghost to ghost as fast as you. I think the rest of us could take some lessons from you."

"I don't think it has anything to do with skills. In fact, it might be a curse. What other teenage girl has ghosts following her around constantly?"

Portia leaned forward in her chair. "I would have been a blubbering mess if a ghost as cute as that one started following me around when I was your age. Your mom showed us a picture. I'm a little jealous."

My face burned. Portia was only joking, but I felt like my attraction to him flashed like a neon sign stuck to my forehead. *Get a grip, Jamie. Who falls for ghosts?* "Wait . . . how did you get a picture of him, Mom?" My eyes darted to my cell phone sitting on the kitchen counter. When I'd stormed over to Daniel's apartment earlier, I didn't think to grab it. The picture of us I'd texted to Camille was on the phone. *Did she seriously go through my phone? I'm going to kill her.*

"Yesterday. When I went to talk to him. I snapped a picture of me and him."

I shot my mom an angry look. "You are so embarrassing."

Mom threw her head back and laughed hard. "Finally! I have arrived as a mother. My daughter thinks I'm embarrassing."

147

I didn't bother to point out the fact that I'd *always* thought she was embarrassing. The mood in the apartment was light and I didn't want to be the one bringing everyone down.

"Want to play?" Steven asked. "We were just about to start a new round."

I walked closer to the table. "What are you playing?"

"Candyland," he answered with a straight face.

"We're playing Trivial Pursuit," Mom said, answering honestly. "Portia and I always lose. Steven's the trivia buff around here."

I glanced at the clock on the wall. I wanted to go to bed, but my bed was the couch. With all of them in the room laughing and talking, I wouldn't be able to fall asleep. I might as well play with them. Besides, with all the books I'd read over the years and the fact that my father pushed academics, trivia came easy to me. "Sure. I'll play."

The game lasted for an entire hour and a half. Partially from my inability to roll the colors I needed and partially from Mom and Portia spending so much time thinking of answers to their questions. I won the game in the end, but I'm pretty sure Steven purposely answered questions wrong to let me win.

One good thing about the game, it gave my mind a chance to turn off. Instead of lying awake on the couch for hours, thinking about Daniel's story, I fell asleep as soon as my head hit the pillow. Instead of falling asleep thinking about Daniel, I dreamed about him. Good dreams.

Chapter 17

I woke to my ringing cell phone the next morning. In my half-asleep state, it took a moment to realize where the sound came from. By the time I figured it out, I had to run to grab my phone off the kitchen counter before my voicemail picked up. "Hello," I said, trying to catch my breath.

"*Good morning.*"

I smiled at the sound of Peter's voice. "Thanks. You, too."

"*I was beginning to think you'd moved on.*"

Moved on? Did Camille tell him about Daniel? I'm going to kill her! "What do you mean?" I forced the words out.

"*I left two messages last night and three texts. I thought maybe you'd forgotten who I was.*"

I sensed laughter in his voice. *Good. He doesn't know yet.* "I'm sorry. I was gone until late and I accidentally left my phone in the apartment when I left." *Please don't ask where I was.*

"*It's not a big deal. What did you do yesterday?*"

"I walked around the Freedom Trail. Or, most of it, anyway."

"*I guess you can't live in Boston and not do that.*"

"True."

"*What are you doing tonight?*"

149

I hesitated. "I'm not sure yet."

"*Remember how I said my dad and I had tickets to a couple of the Red Sox games?*"

"Uh huh."

"*One of the games is tonight. Dad had a presentation come up and can't make it. Mom offered to drive me up there, but she hates baseball. Want to go with me?*"

I thought about Daniel in the apartment across the hall. I wanted to spend all my time with him, but knew my attraction to him was an illusion of sorts. Maybe hanging out with Peter for the night would help pull me back to reality—a reality where I wasn't falling for a ghost. "Sure. I can make that work."

"*Good. Give me your new address and we'll be there around six. We can grab some food at the game.*"

"Okay. Sounds good." I gave him the address and then the conversation stalled. Silence filled both sides of the line.

Peter cleared his throat. "*How are things going with the new ghost? I know you said you didn't like him very much.*"

I opened my mouth to protest, but then realized Peter referred to Myles—not Daniel. "Actually, Mom and her friends sent him packing. He couldn't figure out how to tell the truth. I'm not sorry he's gone."

"*If they're not helping someone in Boston, are you going to stay there?*"

"Yeah, for now. They're going to take a little break." *While I stay busy.*

"*Good. I better go.*" Peter paused. "*I know it's only been a few days since we've seen each other, but I'm glad I get to see you tonight.*"

"Me, too." I meant it. Seeing Peter would help bring me back down to earth.

I hung up the phone and jumped in the shower. Everyone else in the apartment continued to sleep. I guess I'd been wrong about them being morning people. Maybe that only applied when ghosts were around. When I came out of the bathroom, Mom was sitting in her bathrobe at the kitchen table. "Mornin'." She raised one hand in greeting.

"No offense, but you look like crap," I said.

"No offense taken. I feel like crap." As if to prove the truth of her statement, she sneezed and then coughed.

"Want me to get you anything?"

"Something warm. I think there's some hot cocoa mix in the cupboard."

I opened one cabinet and found plates. I opened another cabinet and found dry goods. The third door I opened held spices. "I wasn't in the kitchen when you unpacked it. Want to give me a hint as to which door the prize is hiding behind?"

Mom lifted one hand and pointed a shaking finger at the small cabinet above the fridge Her hand fell back to the counter as if the small effort drained all her energy. Before I finished making the cocoa, Portia came out of her bedroom with a box of tissues tucked under her arm. "You, too?" she said, gazing at the pile of wadded up tissues in front of my mother.

"Uh huh." Mom mumbled something else, but I couldn't understand it.

I made Portia a cup of cocoa, too. She thanked me when I set it in front of her. "Maybe it's a good thing we broke ties with Myles. I definitely don't feel like working today," she said.

"As soon as I drink this, I'm climbing right back in bed." Mom sneezed again.

"Is Steven sick, too?" I asked. I hoped the germs would die off with Mom and Portia.

"Don't know. There's a note on his door saying he went for a run. I'm guessing that means he's fine," Portia answered between coughs.

"No offense, but . . . umm . . . I don't want what the two of you have." I backed away. "I'm going over to Daniel's. And Mom? Peter's coming tonight. *Please* don't say anything about Daniel. I want to be the one to tell him—on my own terms."

She nodded and laid her head on her arms resting on the table. With any luck, she'd stay in bed all day and I wouldn't have to worry about her saying the wrong thing. I crossed the hall and tapped quietly on Daniel's door. It was already ten and I doubted he had anything going on so I didn't text him first. My heart soared when he opened the door after only a couple seconds.

"Hey."

One. Word.

That's all it took for him to make my face turn red.

Get it together, Jamie, I scolded myself. "Am I too early?"

"I never even went to bed last night."

"Too much on your mind?"

"You could say that. What do you want to do today? I assume you're here because you can't stand to be away from me."

I felt my mouth moving, but no words came out.

Daniel's lips turned up on one side in his famous half-smile. "Don't worry. I want to be with you, too."

And now I'm melting again. "I thought you could tell me about your death. You haven't done that yet." *Death should be a safe topic. I'll just think of rotting corpses.*

"Okay. But first, let's go for a walk while we talk. We can take a picnic with us. For you, I mean."

I followed Daniel's gaze into the kitchen.

"But . . . I'm afraid I'm fresh out of picnic stuff." He paused. "To tell the truth, I'm out of every kind of food."

I laughed. "What? You don't want to put things in your mouth that taste like cardboard and sawdust?"

"You describe the tastes so well."

"I've known a ghost or two." I grinned. "Come on, we'll get something from my place."

I doubted Steven had come back in the few minutes I'd been gone and Mom and Portia were going back to bed. We could go in, grab something, and be back out in a matter of a few minutes.

But I was wrong.

Mom and Portia still sat at the table and Steven stood in the kitchen guzzling a glass of water. They'd already seen me. I couldn't shut the door and pretend I hadn't just thrown the door open. Daniel followed me into the apartment and I introduced him to everyone. Portia sat up straighter and started finger combing her hair. *She's just as bad as Mom*, I thought. Daniel offered to shake her hand, but she motioned at the pile of tissues she'd accumulated and declined. Steven wiped his hands, sweaty from running, on a towel before accepting Daniel's handshake. Mom continued to stare at the wall like a zombie.

"Can ghosts get sick?" I asked Daniel, wondering if Portia's germs would have even affected him.

"Yes . . . sort of. If we stay in our human form for long periods we can get sick. If it happens, we go into ghost form and heal immediately. No big deal."

"So, Daniel, Jamie hasn't told us your story. When did you live?" Steven asked.

"I was born in 1759," Daniel answered.

Steven leaned on the counter. "You've seen a lot in your days."

Daniel smiled. "You could say that."

I made myself a quick sandwich and grabbed an apple from a bowl on the counter. "We're going for a walk. I have my phone if you need anything."

Mom gave a short nod before dropping her head back down. I'd never seen her that quiet. "That wasn't as bad as I thought it would be," I told Daniel when we were in the hall again.

"What do you mean?"

"I figured they'd all demand your entire story."

"They seem nice. I don't mind if they want to help. I mean, it's their job, right?"

"True. We'll see later if there's something they can help with." If I had it my way, I'd keep Daniel all to myself.

The sun beat down from the cloudless sky, but the humidity didn't bother me like it had before. We walked away from the apartment complex and turned right. "Are you ready to tell me about your death?" I asked. "I know it's hard for ghosts to talk about stuff like that."

Daniel swallowed and gazed up at the surrounding buildings before saying anything. "It's hard. I feel like I'm still alive when I'm in this form." He motioned toward his body. "Talking about my death reminds me that I'm not real."

"Just because you're a ghost doesn't mean you're not real. I made the mistake once of referring to the living as humans. A ghost friend gently reminded me that just because ghosts aren't always in their touchable form, they're still human, too."

Daniel smiled and slipped his hand into mine as we walked. It felt nice. "After I left General Washington's presence the night I gave him the letter from Dr. Church, I didn't know where to go. I knew that if the officer I'd hurt recognized me, he would tell General Gage. It wouldn't be that hard to track me down and I didn't want my family to know about my connections to the cause. If they didn't know about it, it couldn't hurt them, right? Anyway, I couldn't very well go back to Revere's shop. He'd given me a two week leave of absence. To get back to Boston, I had to go all the way around on land since I didn't have a boat to get across the river. It took me all night to get back to the main part of Boston. I decided to go to Dr. Church's house. You know, just to see if he were there."

"That was bold."

"I didn't plan on knocking or anything. I just wanted to see him. Anyway, as I got closer I saw that officers of the continental army were still there. They had just arrested Church and were taking him away."

"Did he put up a fight?"

Daniel shook his head. "When I saw him, he was sitting quietly in the back of the wagon. He saw me, but he didn't say anything. He just stared. I got the impression from his angry expression that he knew I was the one who ratted him out."

"Who would have told him?"

"Don't know. I never had time to find out. He was whisked away and held for trial and I was dead before that ever happened. I decided in that moment that I needed to come clean with Revere. Washington had released me from his service and he didn't mention that I still couldn't tell anyone. I walked into the silversmith shop and confessed that I'd been spying for Washington."

"I'm guessing he was surprised?" I said.

"Not as much as I'd expected. It was almost as if he already knew. He was pretty upset when I told him about Dr. Church, though. They'd been good friends for a lot of years."

"Did he let you return to work?"

Daniel shook his head. "We both agreed that it would be a good idea for me to lay low for a while. He said he had a friend, someone by the name of Samuel Taft, who lived in Uxbridge. It was a few days journey from Boston, but Revere knew he would let me stay. I thought if I waited long enough, the British occupation of Boston would pass, Gage would move his troops elsewhere, and I could return home."

"Based on the fact that you're now a ghost, I'm guessing your plan didn't work."

"Nope. I only made it to the edge of Boston before I was stopped

155

by a couple of redcoats. One of them recognized me as the boy Gage wanted brought in for questioning. They took me back to the British headquarters. Needless to say, Gage wasn't very happy."

I cringed. "What did he do?"

Daniel gripped my hand tighter. "He knocked me around a little, yelled a lot, and called me a few dirty names. I was fine with all of that. I would have been mad, too. Gage wanted me to talk, tell him everything I knew and everything I'd lied about. I just sat there and took the abuse. I didn't say a word. He locked me up in a makeshift jail they had for the night and . . . well . . . about midnight of that night, the officer who I'd punched the night before came by to positively identify me." Daniel stopped to catch his breath. The further he got in the story, the faster the words came out. "When I refused to talk to him, he pulled out his gun and stabbed me through the heart with his bayonet."

I gasped. "You didn't even get a trial?"

He shook his head.

"That's not fair! Did the officer who killed you get in trouble?"

"It might not seem fair to you, but that's how things were done back then. Keep in mind we were at war. Ethics and rules of humanity were changed."

I let go of his hand and did what felt natural. I wrapped my arms around his neck. He slid his arms around my waist and returned the hug. "I'm sorry," I whispered.

I'm not sure how long we stood like that, but we both pulled away when a cyclist passed us on the sidewalk and honked a bike horn at us.

"I guess I've given you another burden to carry, huh?" Daniel said.

"Don't worry about it."

"I thought about something last night. Is there any chance I could see my pocket watch sometime? I'd love to see it again. You know, to remind myself that my real life wasn't a dream."

"Of course. I can get one of my friends to get it out of my room and mail it to me."

"Not your dad?"

"Then I'd have too much explaining to do. If I send my friend Camille, I won't have to give as much explanation."

"I don't want it to be a bother."

"It's not a bother. Wait!" I snapped my fingers. "If I can get Camille to go in my room and get it, she can give it to Peter. He can bring it with him when he comes up here tonight."

Daniel stopped walking and let go of my hand. "Who is Peter?"

Chapter 18

My mind raced for an answer that wouldn't completely turn Daniel away from me. "Peter? He's . . . umm . . . a friend from back home."

Daniel shoved his hands in his pockets and continued walking. I had to jog to catch up. I guess he was done holding my hand. "Is he your boyfriend?"

"No. I mean, we have dated. But . . ." *How can I explain our complicated relationship to someone who hasn't been through everything with us.* "We're just really good friends."

"And he's coming *here* tonight?"

"He has tickets to a Red Sox game. He asked if I wanted to go with him. You know, as friends."

"Okay. I hope you have a good time tonight," Daniel said stiffly. He cleared his throat and changed the subject from Peter. "I love baseball. Have you been to many pro games before?"

I shook my head.

"You'll have fun. I played with the New York Knickerbockers not long after they first organized. That was a long time ago."

"I thought the Knicks were a basketball team."

158

"The Knickerbockers were the first organized baseball team. I started playing with them in the mid-1800s. It was the first time anyone wore a baseball uniform."

I stared at him, trying to judge his words. "Are you being serious?"

"About the uniforms?"

"No. About the team. Did you really play with them?"

Daniel grinned and nodded. "I'm telling the truth. I had to pass myself off as a twenty-year-old. All the guys called me Babyface Avery. There's a picture of the team. You can find it on the internet."

I laughed. "Oh my gosh! You *are* being serious."

"The game was a little different back then, but basically the same idea."

"You and Peter would get along great." It wasn't the first time I'd had that thought. I still hadn't decided if I'd tell Peter about Daniel when he got to Boston. I'd wait and see how the night progressed. If Peter knew about Daniel, he would insist on helping with the extrication. I wouldn't be able to act normal if both of the guys I had crushes on were around at the same time.

"Are you going to introduce me to Peter?" Daniel asked as he nudged me in the shoulder with his own.

"Maybe. I better call Cam if we're going to try to get your pocket watch here." I pulled out my cell and punched Cam's speed dial number into the keypad.

"*How was your date with the hottie?*" Cam skipped the hellos and got straight to a subject she cared about.

I stepped away from Daniel, afraid he might hear Camille through the speaker of my phone. "Fine. I'll tell you about it later." I cupped my hand over my mouth as I spoke.

Camille didn't say anything for a few seconds. Then she whispered, "*Are you with him right now?*"

"Maybe."

Camille squealed. *"This is sooo not like you."*

I glanced in Daniel's direction and then took another step back. "Cam, I need you to do me a huge favor."

"What? Does hottie have a cute friend who wants to double date? Remember, I don't have a boyfriend right now. Just say the word and I'll find a way to get there."

"Very funny. No, I need you to get something out of my house and take it to Peter. He's coming up here tonight to go to a game. It's really important that I get it."

"What is it?"

"A watch."

"You can't live without a watch?"

"Will you do it for me or not?"

"Yeah, I'll do it. Is your dad home?"

"No. He's at work. And it's a really long story, but I don't want him to know about the watch."

Camille didn't answer right away. *"Does this have something to do with another ghost? Are there going to be creepy ghosts floating around your house again?"*

I glanced at Daniel and knew I had to be honest with her. "It does have something to do with a ghost, but I don't have time to explain it all right now. There aren't any around my house. I promise." *And hopefully that's the truth.*

"How do I get into your house if your dad's gone?"

"There's a spare key under one of the legs of the swing on the back patio."

"Fine. I'll call when I get there."

I could have sent Peter. He'd been in my house before. He'd even been in my bedroom. But, the idea of asking him to rummage through my underwear drawer was less than appealing. I ate my lunch in a grassy park while I waited for Camille to call back. Being the only one eating felt weird. I tried to take small bites so I didn't

160

have a full mouth in case Daniel attempted conversation.

"Have you had any thoughts on what your unfinished business might be?" Maybe if I kept him talking, I could chew my sandwich.

"Not really. Well, I guess there's a couple of things I've wondered about."

I swallowed my food before responding. "Like what?"

"For starters, I've never been able to get over the whole incident with Dr. Church. I mean, what possessed him to turn on his friends? Maybe my unfinished business is to get an answer to that."

"It could be. What happened to him after you died?"

"There weren't really any laws back then about what to do with traitors and prisoners. I mean, we weren't even officially a country until almost a year later. If I remember correctly, he was taken and held in Connecticut for a while. I hadn't been dead long enough to make myself visible or believe me, I would have tracked him down and given him a piece of my mind."

I smiled at the idea of Daniel yelling at the doctor.

"I guess he got sick or something and was allowed to come back to Massachusetts, but he was basically under house arrest. He couldn't go anywhere without a guard."

"As a ghost, did you see him when he came back?"

"Here and there. Again, I couldn't do anything about it so I tried to avoid him. It made me feel better."

"Did he ever get released? From the house arrest, I mean."

"In 1778, two years after he'd come back from Connecticut. He was named in the Massachusetts Banishment Act."

"The *what?* I've never heard of that," I said.

"Basically, it was the government's way of exiling people. He had to leave the newly formed United States."

I finished eating my sandwich and sat up straighter on the bench. "So you don't know what happened to him? You don't know how he died or anything?"

161

Daniel shook his head.

"Maybe you're right. Your extrication could totally have something to do with Dr. Church."

"Really?"

I nodded just as my cell started to ring. "Hey, Cam," I answered. "Are you there now?"

"*Yeah. I'm in your backyard. Are you positive your dad isn't here? If you make me walk in on him I'm never talking to you again.*"

"You know my dad. Does he ever miss work? If it makes you feel better, knock on the door."

I heard a faint tapping noise through the phone. "*He's not answering.*"

"Maybe it's because he's not there."

"*Where did you say the key was?*"

"It's under one of the legs of the patio swing."

I heard rustling noises before Camille came back on the phone. "*Okay. I got it.*"

"That's the key that opens the patio door. Just go in."

More rustling and then, "*Okay. I'm in. You said your watch is in your bedroom, right?*"

"Uh huh. It's in the top drawer of my dresser."

"*I'm sorry to tell you this, but your house is super creepy without anyone here. I don't even care that it's the middle of the day.*"

"All the ghosts are gone. I promise."

"*You can't promise anything.*" Camille gasped. "*What was that? I heard a noise! Never mind, it's just the air conditioner kicking on.*"

I rolled my eyes. "You're fine, Cam. No one's going to jump out and get you." Daniel covered his mouth in an attempt to hold his laughter in. I'm sure only hearing my half of the conversation was entertaining.

"*Okay. I'm in your room and I'm opening your dresser.*"

"The watch is rolled up in a sock in the back of the dresser. I think

162

it's on the right side."

"Jamie, when you get back, we're taking you shopping again. Have you bought new underwear in this decade?"

"Cam!" My face burned. *Please let Daniel be deaf.*

"Sorry. Okay. I feel a lumpy sock." Camille paused in her narration. *"You didn't say it was a pocket watch you were looking for. This thing is kind of cool looking. Is it old? Oh wait, there's a date on it. 1775! Where did you get this?"*

"It came out of Jeremiah's trunk."

"Eww! And I'm touching it?"

"It didn't belong to Jeremiah. He stole it from Nick Trenton after he killed him." I saw Daniel perk up at that statement. I hadn't told him the story behind his great-grandnephew's death yet.

"Why does the name on it sound familiar?" Cam asked. I knew the moment she figured it all out because she screamed into the phone. I had to pull it away from my ear. *"Jamie! Isn't that the name of the hottie? Oh my gosh! Is he a ghost?"*

"Yes."

"Why didn't you tell me this before?"

Daniel stood and walked a few yards away, reading a plaque attached to another bench. The last thing I wanted to do was explain everything to Camille right then. "I didn't know about it before. I promise. Listen, I'll explain everything later, okay? We need the watch, though. Can you make sure Peter gets it? He's coming up here tonight and I'm not sure what time he's leaving."

"Yeah. I'll take it to him right now."

"Thanks. I owe ya. And Cam?" I lowered my voice, hoping Daniel wouldn't hear. "Please don't tell Peter about this . . . about Daniel."

"I won't, but you'll need to. He'll never forgive you if everyone knows but him."

"I know. I'll tell him. Eventually."

I hung up and walked to where Daniel still gazed at the sign. "She

163

found the watch. She's taking it to Peter right now."

"I'm excited to see it. I really had no idea where it ended up. When I died, my family claimed my body. In my distress over being dead, it didn't occur to me to keep an eye on the whereabouts of the watch . . . or anything else for that matter. It didn't say it was from General Washington so I doubt they even had a clue how significant it was."

"Who received the other four watches?"

"I never found out." Daniel shrugged. "I think about it all the time, though. I mean, I have my suspicions on some, like Paul Revere, but I don't know for sure. Wouldn't that be funny if we'd both been spying, not knowing what the other was doing?"

"If Washington was as secretive as you made him sound, that idea isn't so farfetched. Besides, if he already trusted Paul, and he knew Paul trusted you, the fact that Washington recruited you would make more sense."

"Want to go back to the house and take a closer look at the collection?" Daniel asked.

I lifted my eyebrows. "Back to the Revere House?"

He nodded.

"Right now?"

"Why not?"

I looked at my watch. I had at least four hours until I absolutely had to be back for my outing with Peter. "Let's go."

We caught a city bus and rode it across town. I texted my mom while we were en route. She must have been sleeping because she never bothered to respond. "I swear we were just here," I said as we stood in front of Paul Revere's home. "Oh wait. We were. It hasn't even been twenty-four hours. What if they recognize us?"

"They get thousands of tourists through here every year. I highly doubt they'd recognize two random teenagers."

"Who are you calling random?" I said, playfully punching him in the arm.

Daniel grinned. "Sorry. I shouldn't generalize. I wonder how many handsome ghosts they get in here."

"Probably not very many. I've never met a handsome ghost." I nudged him with my shoulder. *Am I flirting? This is totally not like me. The world might come to an end.*

Daniel caught my hand and pulled me close. My breath caught in my throat. "That's just cruel," he whispered in my ear.

I willed myself to pull away. "I'll try to be nice. Let's go."

Inside the home, the lady selling tickets peered at us intently. "Weren't you two here last night? Did you leave something? I don't think we have anything new in the lost and found but I can check if you'd like."

I suppressed a smile. So much for not being recognized. "We enjoyed ourselves so much, we decided to come again," I told the lady.

She stood up from her chair, a wide grin spreading across her face. "I love it when young people find enjoyment in history. Someone needs to appreciate it so the past is preserved. If no one remembers, things will be lost forever." She stopped talking and looked around the room. Then, she lowered her head and spoke quietly. "Since it hasn't been that long since you were in here, I'll waive your ticket fees today. Don't tell anyone. Enjoy!"

The lady sat down again and turned her attention back to the screen in front of her.

"Thanks," Daniel and I said in unison.

We took our time walking through the home. There were so many artifacts to see—some original and some replicas—I worried we might miss something as small as a pocket watch. "Maybe we should just ask the lady at the front where the watches are," I told Daniel after we'd walked through four of the rooms without seeing anything.

"We don't even know if there *is* a watch here," Daniel reminded me. "And if Paul did receive one, who knows where it would have ended up after a few hundred years."

We continued to search the rooms, not actually touching anything, but covering every inch with our eyes. Disappointment hit each time we turned away without finding anything. Finally, in an upstairs bedroom, something caught my eye. "Daniel," I whispered. "Look at the nightstand."

There, on a little table next to an old straw bed, was a gold pocket watch. I hadn't seen Daniel's watch for a long time and couldn't remember exactly what it looked like, but the one on the nightstand looked familiar.

Daniel leaned in and took a closer look. "I *think* that might be one of the watches. I never got a very good look at mine. Wow. I can't believe this. All this time, and I might be able to prove who at least one other recipient was."

I stared at the watch. "How do we know if it's one of the five?"

"There's only one way to know for sure. If it has the same kind of engraving inside as mine did, it's the real thing." Daniel reached an arm forward to pick up the watch. My eyes flicked to the ceiling and I grabbed his arm before he could touch the watch.

I nodded slightly toward the ceiling. "I don't think that's such a good idea." The red light of a security camera blinked back at us, reminding us to keep our hands off the carefully preserved possessions.

Daniel sighed. "I have to open it to know for sure."

"Can you do it in your—" I stopped talking as an elderly couple stepped into the room. I leaned closer to Daniel and he dropped his head to mine. "Can you open it while in your other form?" I whispered.

Daniel grinned. "I think so. Can you cause a distraction?"

"Sure, but—I feel so . . . evil."

Daniel chuckled and squeezed my shoulder. "J, if this is the worst thing you ever do, you'll be okay in life."

"One distraction coming right up. Follow me." I stepped out of the bedroom and into the hall. Daniel followed close behind. In the hall, I scanned the ceiling, but there weren't any cameras.

"What are you going to do?" Daniel asked.

"You just worry about yourself. I've got this."

"Yes, ma'am." Daniel saluted me and then vanished into invisibility.

"Good luck," I whispered into the air.

I entered the other upstairs bedroom and scanned the room, searching for something to focus my attention on. "Ooo!" I squealed as loud as I could. "This is so cool!" Just as I'd hoped, the couple that had been in the other bedroom hurried across the hall and into the room with me. I pointed at the tall four-poster bed with a floral canopy in the middle of the room. "Look at that bed! Isn't it neat? I've always wanted a bed like that. That's the kind of bed princesses sleep in. My bed is boring. I mean, it's just a normal bed, you know what I mean? Do you think this was Paul Revere's bed? That would be so cool if he really slept in this one. I just love history, don't you? And that Paul Revere? Wow. What a cool guy." My acting skills had never been great, so I tried to channel Camille. She could ramble on about one little thing forever. I figured as long as I kept talking, they'd feel obligated to keep listening.

"Did you know Paul Revere made the covering on the dome of the Massachusetts State House?" I continued. "I learned that when I visited there. If you haven't been there, you should go. Revere was the first one in the country to roll copper into sheets. That's what they originally put on the dome of the state house, but it's not there anymore. The dome has been gray, it's been yellow, and it even had gold leaf put on it." The couple sharing the room with me glanced around as if looking for a way to escape. If Daniel didn't hurry, I would run out of things to say. Or else run out of breath and pass out on the floor. Now *that* would cause a distraction. "Oh, yeah! Do you know what's on the very top of the dome? A pinecone! Isn't that cool? I think I read somewhere that it symbolizes the state's role in the lumber industry."

Much to my relief, Daniel came into the room right then, fully in human form. "There you are, Jamie. I didn't know where you went."

"She's been giving us a history lesson," the little old lady said. "She sure knows a lot. Oh, my."

The elderly man stepped closer to Daniel and tapped a finger to his head. "Is she all right up there?" he whispered, but not so quietly that I couldn't hear.

Daniel frowned and shook his head as if deeply saddened by something. "I'm afraid not. She fell out of a tree as a young child. She's never been the same." He grabbed my hand. "Come on, Jamie, we need to get you back to your special home."

He pulled me into the hall and down the stairs. I only made it down half a flight before bursting into laughter. "Way to throw me under the bus," I said as I slugged him in the arm.

Daniel threw his hands up defensively. "Hey, I didn't know what you'd been telling them. I thought maybe it was all part of the plan."

"I'm not sure what I was telling them, but I think they got a history lesson on the dome of the state house."

Daniel threw his head back and laughed. "Only you, J."

"Not to change the subject, but you haven't told me yet."

"Told you what?"

I rolled my eyes. "Did you see the inside of the watch?"

Daniel grinned and nodded. "If anyone looks at the security footage of that room, they'll see the watch moving all by itself. The haunting rumors will start for sure if they haven't already."

"Come on, don't leave me hanging. Was the watch the same as yours?"

Daniel stopped walking and took my hand. "It was. It said *Paul Revere – 1775*."

I blew out a long breath. "Paul Revere was one of the five spies."

Chapter 19

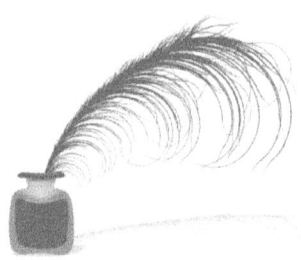

I paced the kitchen floor while waiting for Peter to arrive. Mom and Portia sat in the living room chairs, still looking like zombies. If the mound of tissues on the coffee table in front of them was any indication of how sick they were, I wouldn't be entering the same room as either of them for at least a month. They'd both changed out of their pajamas, but Mom's idea of being dressed was sweatpants and an old concert t-shirt. That's how I knew she really didn't feel good. She usually prided herself in her ability to look good at all times. I didn't get that gene from her.

Steven had taken his easel and paints and gone who knows where. Mom said he'd been gone most of the day—probably trying to avoid them. I couldn't wait to leave so I could spend the evening in the open air instead of the germ-filled apartment.

At ten minutes to six, there was a knock on the apartment door. "Peter's here," I said. "Remember, don't tell him about Daniel. I want to do it later," I instructed both of them.

"Got it," Mom mumbled.

I threw the door open, but to my surprise, Daniel stood there instead of Peter. "What are you doing here?" I hissed. I watched the elevator door down the hall, sure it would open at any moment.

170

"Don't I get to meet the guy?" Daniel asked.

"No. You don't."

Daniel raised his eyebrows. "Why not? If we're as connected as you say we are, I should know more about you. Meeting your friends would be a good start." He winked at me and a smile formed on my lips despite my attempts to stop it.

"Go away," I said, pushing him back toward his apartment door by pressing on his chest.

"I promise I won't tell him I'm a ghost. I wouldn't want to freak the guy out."

"Peter knows about ghosts."

Daniel's mouth dropped open. "He does? Then why can't you introduce me?"

"It's complicated."

"That doesn't make any sense."

"*Please*, Daniel. I can't really explain it." I couldn't explain it because I didn't know the reason myself. *Why can't I let Daniel meet Peter?*

"Okay, okay." Daniel put his hands up. "Really I came over to tell you about Dr. Church. I looked him up on the internet and you're never going to believe what I found out. Apparently he—"

Before Daniel could finish telling me about the doctor, the elevator door opened and Peter stepped out. The decision of whether or not to let Peter meet Daniel had been made for me. I dropped my hands from Daniel's chest and stepped back. "Peter!"

The smile on his face made my heart happy and I returned it with a genuine one of my own. We'd been through a lot together and I realized in that moment that my feelings for him were just as strong as they'd always been. "You found the apartment. It's good to see you." *I really, really like him. Great. Wonderful. Shoot me now.*

Peter stood close to me and eyed Daniel warily. "Hey. I'm Peter Ashby. You know Jamie?"

171

"Daniel Avery." I watched as they shook hands, wondering if Peter would notice anything odd about Daniel. He didn't say anything. "I live across from J. I came over to say hi to my new neighbors," Daniel explained. "You must be her date to the baseball game. Go Red Sox."

"It should be a good game. Have you always been a fan?" Peter asked.

"Lived here my whole life. So . . . yeah."

"My dad grew up here," Peter said. "His sister still lives here."

Daniel crossed his arms over his chest. "What do you think the chances are of the Sox going to the World Series this year?"

"If they keep playing the way they have been, I think they've got a shot at it. Have you gone to any games this season?"

"One. At the beginning. Tonight will be a better game than the one I attended. I should have gotten tickets for tonight."

"Too bad I don't have an extra one. You could come with me and Jamie."

Yeah, that would have been my dream come true. Talk about awkward.

The two boys continued to discuss the team and their favorite players for several minutes before I finally jumped in. "We better go. I'd hate to be late. Don't they sing the national anthem at the beginning?"

Peter laughed. "That's the part you're excited about?"

I shrugged and stuck my head inside my apartment door. "Peter's here! We're leaving!"

Mom nodded and waved. Even that small movement took effort.

"I'll see you around, Daniel," I said as I walked away, pulling Peter with me.

"Have fun," he called back.

I turned to give him one last look. He winked and flickered in and out of visibility. I glared, just for good measure.

"Daniel seems pretty cool," Peter said once we were both in the elevator and the door had closed.

"I guess so."

"Have you seen a lot of him since you've been here?"

"He's come over once or twice. He lives with his uncle who is gone all the time. I think he's bored."

Peter grinned. "I doubt it's because he's bored."

"What do you mean?"

Peter draped an arm around my shoulders. "It probably has something to do with the girl next door."

I rolled my eyes. "I doubt that." *We barely talked to each other in front of Peter. Is it that obvious?*

"I'm a guy. I know these things." His boyish grin made me laugh and I relaxed. "Come on, my mom's parked over here."

Mrs. Ashby dropped us off at Fenway Park and set up a place for us to meet her at the end of the game.

"There's an atmosphere at ballgames that you can't find anywhere else," Peter said. "Especially not by watching them at home."

We grabbed hot dogs, nachos, and sodas and found our seats behind third base. "Remember when we used to play baseball at recess every day in elementary school?" I asked.

"You could hit farther than anyone else back then," Peter said. "What happened to you?"

I glared at him. Actually, I *had* been good at sports at one point in my life. In elementary school I hung out with the boys more than the girls. One day, I don't even remember when, I stopped playing with them and my athletic skills had since suffered. "I don't know if I was ever that good. It was just that no one else had a clue how to play. I got lucky a few times."

"All I can remember is that when we were choosing teams, you were always picked before me."

"Really?" I laughed. I honestly didn't remember that.

We watched in silence as the Red Sox warmed up on the field.

"Aren't you going to quiz me about the team?" I asked. "Before I left Marion, you said there'd be a test." Daniel helped me memorize names and stats on the bus ride home from Paul Revere's house that afternoon. If I didn't get the information out of my head soon, it might disappear into oblivion with other facts I deemed unimportant.

"You studied?" Peter said.

"I always study for tests."

"Okay. Hmm . . . let me think of a hard question."

Peter proceeded to quiz me on the team and I answered each question correctly. "I'm impressed," he said. "I thought you were joking when you said you studied."

"You might be the history king, but don't underestimate my memorization skills."

We ate our food and chatted, making it all the way to the top of the fourth inning before I started feeling funny. Peter reached for my hand and the air around me changed, getting heavier. The tiny hairs on my arms stood on end.

Something wasn't right.

All around us people talked, yelled, or got up and down in their seats. But even though we were outdoors, something about the way the air moved made me nervous. The first ghost I ever helped taught me to recognize the feel of a ghost moving around. It took a lot of practice, but eventually I got better at it. The feeling I had at the ballpark was just that. The question was, did Daniel follow Peter and me to the game, or was another ghost floating around me?

"Did Camille come see you today?" I asked.

"Oh, yeah. I almost forgot about that. She gave me a brown paper sack and asked me to give it to you. She said I couldn't look inside. What's up with that?"

I felt the air pressing on me. It had to be Daniel. "It's not that big of a deal. Just something I didn't think to pack when I left."

One of Boston's players hit a ball into the crowd near us, catching Peter's attention. He didn't question the package further. "I need to use the restroom," I said. "I'll be back in a minute."

Peter turned his attention back to me. "Do you want me to come with you?"

"No. I can find it." I wandered through the stadium, looking for a place where Daniel could appear without being caught. Privacy was hard to come by in a place like that. I found a pillar and ducked behind it.

"Daniel!" I hissed. "If you are anywhere near here, you'd better come out right now." I thought about stomping my foot on the ground to show how mad I was, but I didn't want to go overboard. I mean, I was already standing in a corner of Fenway Stadium having a conversation with myself.

Just as I suspected, Daniel appeared within seconds. "How did you know I was here?" he asked. "Can you see me when I'm in my ghost form? Is that part of being a soul saver?"

I shook my head. "I can't see you, but I can sense you if you're moving around a lot."

"It was an exciting game. I couldn't just sit there—or float there, I guess."

"Why are you here?"

"It sounded fun?"

"Nice try. Now tell me the real reason."

"I honestly don't know. I didn't plan on doing it, but then I met Peter. Don't get me wrong. He seems like a cool guy. I could see us being friends, but then . . . never mind."

"What?"

Daniel shoved his hands in his pockets and took a few steps away, turning his back to me. "I think I got jealous."

And there goes my face again. Why is it always turning red? "I told you, Peter's not my boyfriend."

"Are you sure he knows that?" Daniel said, his back still turned.

"I'm not her boyfriend," a voice spoke behind me. "And apparently I'm not even wanted on this outing."

I whirled around at the sound of Peter's voice. "Peter! Where'd you come from?" *How long had he been standing there?*

"It's fine, Jamie. I get it. Look, why don't you and Daniel finish watching the game. I'll just call my mom and tell her it was boring and I want to leave early. I'll see you when you get back to Marion."

"Peter, stop. *Please.*" I whimpered. "You don't understand." *I don't even understand what's going on.*

He stopped walking but didn't turn around. "I'm not mad. Disappointed, sure. But I'm not mad. You and I are meant to be friends, that's all."

"Daniel's a ghost."

Peter turned around and faced me. "What did you say?"

Daniel stepped next to the two of us. "What's up?"

Peter's eyes darted from me to Daniel. "I thought you said the guy your mom was helping turned out to be a jerk and they cut him loose."

I shook my head. "That was a completely different ghost. I met Daniel when we moved in and I didn't know he was ghost at first. I'm helping him now."

"You mean you're his soul saver?" Peter asked.

I nodded.

"Why didn't you tell me this before?"

"I don't know. I was going to tell you, but . . . it's kind of nice not always having ghosts with us when we hang out."

"Ouch," Daniel said. "That was low."

"That's not what I meant!" I covered my face with my hands. "See? This is why I didn't tell you. Everything gets so complicated. I thought if I kept this to myself, you and I could see if we're still friends when there aren't ghosts pulling us together." *I'm swearing off boys until I'm forty. I can't handle this pressure.*

Daniel cleared his throat. "I followed her here. She didn't know about it. Sorry. All the talk about baseball sounded fun so I figured I'd come. I used to play."

Peter shrugged. "It's okay. I know how things are when she's saving souls. Sometimes she gets a little weird."

"Weird? What's that supposed to mean?" I crossed my arms over my chest.

"When you were helping Haven, you tried to electrocute me. Oh, and then you stabbed me," Peter said.

"You're making me look bad in front of the new ghost," I whispered.

Daniel frowned. "I think I need more explanation. Should I be worried?"

"You're dead, she can't hurt you," Peter answered.

I rolled my eyes. "You failed to mention the fact that you were possessed at the time."

"So anyway . . . you mentioned you used to play baseball, Daniel. Where did you play? High school? College?"

"I played pro—a really long time ago. It was after I died."

"When did you die?"

"1775."

Daniel gave Peter a condensed version of his story while I stood by and listened. By the end, they were laughing and chatting as if they'd been friends forever. I knew they would hit it off. They were the same guy—born in different generations.

"If you two are done with your bonding, the game just ended," I said as people streamed out of the stadium entrances.

"What?" Peter looked up in surprise. "What was the score? Who won?"

We pushed our way through the crowds until we could get a look at the scoreboard. "Red Sox pulled it off," Daniel said and high-fived Peter. I shook my head. In the future, I might have to set a female-only policy for my ghosts.

We waited for twenty minutes before Peter's mom showed up. Daniel watched with us and then went invisible as soon as her car came into sight. "How was the game?" Mrs. Ashby asked.

"Good. We won," Peter answered.

"I heard the end of the game on the radio when I was driving over from your aunt's house. And Dad texted me, too. He's sad he missed the game. What about you, Jamie? Did you have fun?"

"I did. I've never been to a game before. It was . . . eventful."

Peter and I both sat in the back seat. He reached down and picked up a paper sack. "Here's the thing Cam asked me to give you."

"Thanks for bringing it," I said. "Want to see it?"

"You mean it's not something . . . girly?"

I grinned and opened the bag. "Take a look," I whispered, trying not to draw Mrs. Ashby's attention.

Peter took the bag from my hands and looked inside. "A watch?" he mouthed.

I nodded. "Open it."

He dumped the bag upside down and picked up the pocket watch. He turned it over and around in his hands a couple of times before unhooking the clasp that held it closed. "It's Daniel's?" he whispered. "I thought you barely met him?"

I reached over and took the watch from his hands. "I did. When he told me his name, something about it seemed familiar. This is why. I found this in Jeremiah's trunk earlier in the summer. I didn't think much of it then. We think Daniel was one of Nick's ancestors."

I tried to hold the watch so that Daniel could see it if he happened to be sitting in the seat next to me, which I was pretty sure he was.

"Is there some significance with the watch or is it just an heirloom?" Peter asked.

"General Washington gave it to him," I whispered.

Peter's eyes just about popped out of his head. He reached over and grabbed the watch. "General Washington? As in *George Washington*? First President of the United States? Founding father?"

"Shh!" I hissed.

"I'm holding something George Washington touched!"

I grinned. With archaeologist parents, Peter's house was filled with interesting things. I felt bad that I'd thought about leaving him out of the loop. When we pulled into the parking lot of my apartment complex, I thanked Mrs. Ashby and Peter climbed out to walk me up to my door. I thought Daniel would reappear in the elevator, but he didn't. He must have decided to give Peter and me some privacy.

"Thanks for inviting me," I said. "Sorry I ruined your night and made you miss the game."

Peter took my hand and squeezed it. "You didn't ruin my night. You wouldn't be you without a ghost following you around. Besides, I like Daniel. He's a good guy. I'll call you soon. Maybe I can come up here again and help you with his extrication."

"That would be fun." I didn't know if I meant it or not. Seeing Peter? Yes. Helping with Daniel? Not so sure.

Daniel chose that moment to reappear. "It was nice meeting you," he said, shaking Peter's hand. "Maybe we'll see each other again sometime. And Jamie, I'll see you tomorrow." He turned as if he intended to walk into his apartment, but I stopped him.

"Don't you want to take your long lost watch with you?" I said. I pulled the watch out of my pocket and reached to hand it to Daniel. Just before our fingers touched, the elevator door opened and Mrs. Ashby stepped through. Daniel ducked and immediately went invisible. I'd already been moving my hand toward his and I let go of the watch just as he disappeared. I watched in horror as the 18th century antique slipped from my fingers and cascaded toward the tile floor of the hallway.

Chapter 20

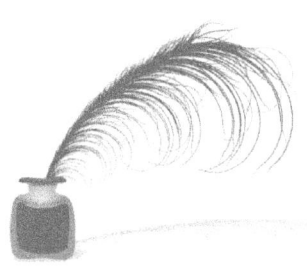

I froze, physically unable to move. The timepiece fell closer and closer toward the ground, but shock kept me from doing anything about it. Peter lunged forward, falling to his knees as he attempted to catch the falling pocket watch. I closed my eyes, not wanting to witness the horror.

Mrs. Ashby stepped out of the elevator and stepped toward us. "I didn't mean to scare you, Jamie. My word, you look as if you just saw a ghost."

I opened my eyes and peered at the floor, expecting to see a dozen broken pieces of metal scattered across the hall.

Nothing.

I sighed in relief. "You just surprised me, that's all."

"Why are you on the floor?" she asked Peter.

"I . . . uhh . . . tripped," he answered.

Mrs. Ashby narrowed her eyes at him but didn't question him further. "I know I told you I'd wait in the car, but then I decided it would be rude if we came all the way to Boston and I didn't at least say hello to Lillian."

Mr. and Mrs. Ashby were acquaintances of my dad, but I wondered if Mrs. Ashby had ever even met my mom. Saying hello to my mom might just be her excuse to meet the lady who abandoned me as a child.

"I'll see if she's still awake. She hasn't been feeling good today so she might already be in bed." I pulled out my key and unlocked the apartment door. All the interior lights were off. The faint ticking of the clock on the living room wall was the only sound that could be heard. "I'm sorry," I said to Mrs. Ashby. "She must be asleep already."

"Oh, that's fine. Will you tell her I said hi?"

I nodded.

"Thanks." She turned to her son. "We better get going. It's a long drive back to Marion."

"I'll call you sometime," Peter said. He brushed my fingers with his hand, sending confusing emotions racing through my body. When I realized what his true intentions were, my fingers grasped the watch he passed to me.

"Thanks for saving it," I whispered.

"How was the baseball game last night?" Steven asked while I nibbled on a piece of toast the next morning. "It was good. The Red Sox won." *Honestly? I don't remember anything about the actual game.*

Steven poured himself a glass of milk from the carton in the fridge. "I caught part of the game on TV. I had dinner at a sports bar downtown, you know, trying to get away from the sickos in this apartment." Steven motioned toward Portia as she emerged from her bedroom. "You feeling any better?" he asked her.

"The headache is gone. I'm still really stuffed up, though," she answered. She didn't need to tell us that. I could barely hold my laughter in while listening to her attempts at pronouncing words with a plugged nose. Judging by the expression on Steven's face, he felt the same way I did. Portia plopped down on a stool by the counter. "This is ridiculous. Who gets wiped out by a cold in the middle of the summer? I thought they didn't even exist until at least November."

"Is my mom awake yet?" I asked. "How is she feeling?"

Portia rolled her eyes. "She's snoring like a freight train in there. That's the only reason I'm out of bed right now. Judging by the unnatural sounds coming from her, she's not any better. She doesn't usually make any noise when she sleeps. And I should now because we've been sharing bedrooms for years."

"Looks like I have another free day on my hands," Steven said. "Do you need help with anything, Jamie? I'm a great researcher. Especially if it gets me out of this apartment and away from Portia and Lillian."

"Ha. Ha. Just wait until it catches up with *you*." Portia pointed a finger at him and tried to look threatening, but lapsed into a coughing fit instead. "I'm going back to bed. Maybe if I cover my head with my pillow I can drown out the noise. Or maybe I'll just pass out. That will be even better."

I watched Portia pad down the hall in her fuzzy purple socks. As soon as the bedroom door closed, Steven leaned toward me. "*Please* let me help you. Don't leave me here alone with those things."

I put my hands up. "Okay, okay. You win. I don't even know where to begin looking, though. Daniel spied for General Washington and we want to see—"

"General Washington? As in *President* Washington?" Steven interrupted.

"That's the one."

Steven scooted closer to me. "You have my complete attention.

183

I'm in. Whatever you want me to do, I'll do it."

I raised my eyebrows. "That's all it takes? A little name dropping?"

Steven folded his hands on the counter in front of himself. "The first ghost I ever helped once I hooked up with your mom and Portia, the one who made me an official soul saver, had a connection to Washington. I spent a lot of time researching the president back then. Of course, this was a long time ago, and the connection to Washington ended up not having anything to do with my ghost's extrication, but I've been fascinated with the man ever since."

"Tell me then, what do you know about his use of spies?"

"I know that some experts say that's why the colonists won their independence. I mean, think about it. The British had trained armies and weapons and ammunition. The rebels had thrown-together groups of armed farmers and hardly any supplies. They had to find advantages in other ways."

I nodded along with him as he spoke. "Keep going."

"Washington utilized spies almost from the beginning. A lot has been discovered about it as historians have done research over the last few centuries and as documents have been made available. I talked to a guy once who said he believed there were countless other spies who would never be known because no one documented their activities and the men, or maybe even women, took the secret to their graves," Steven said. "What's Daniel's last name?"

"Avery."

Steven squinted his eyes, creasing his forehead into little lines. "I don't remember reading or hearing that name."

I crossed my arms over my chest and leaned back in my chair. "He said no one knew about it. He'd only been spying for a few weeks before he got caught. And then he was killed before he had a chance to tell his family."

"That's rough."

"No kidding. At the time, Washington told Daniel he was one of five official spies working in Boston. We found out who one of them was, but the other three remain a mystery. That's just one of the leads I thought we should look into. There're others, too."

"What's the name of the one you know?"

I smiled. "Ever heard of Paul Revere?"

"You're kidding."

"Nope."

Steven let out a low whistle. "Jamie, you could find out information that changes history."

"Way to add pressure to me."

"I do what I can." He smiled. "It sounds like you've got a lot to work with already, but if you want, I'll go down to the library and see what I can find out about known spies while you and Daniel follow another lead."

In the beginning, I'd wanted to do the extrication work all by myself so I didn't have to share my time with Daniel. But, if Steven was at the library, I'd still get Daniel to myself and I'd get research material, too. "Thanks. I'd really appreciate that," I answered.

A knock on the apartment door brought my attention back to the real world. I opened the door and gazed into Daniel's incredibly handsome face. "Good morning."

"Morning. Am I too early?"

"Nope. I was just explaining to him what our goals are." I motioned to Steven sitting at the table. "He offered to try to find more spy leads for us."

Daniel grinned. "Thanks. I'll take any help I can get."

"I still have your watch." I walked across the room and retrieved it from the coffee table where I'd set it the night before.

"Remind me to tell Peter that was an impressive catch last night when you dropped it," Daniel said.

"You're hilarious. I wouldn't have dropped it if you wouldn't have

185

vanished."

"Peter's mom doesn't know who I am or that I went to the game with you two. Did you want her to see me?"

"No."

"I rest my case." Daniel's eyes sparkled. When he took the watch from my hands, he took his time, letting his hand rest on mine for a moment. I pulled away, not wanting my face to turn red while Steven watched.

"That watch looks old." Steven leaned toward Daniel. "Is it from when you were alive?"

Daniel walked back to the table. "General Washington gave it to me many, many years ago."

Steven's jaw dropped. "Really? Can I . . . touch it?"

Daniel stretched his arm out to hand the pocket watch to Steven, but history repeated itself. Just like the night before, the watch slipped from his fingers and started to fall. Moving quickly, Steven grabbed the watch just before it hit the ground.

"What was that you were saying about me dropping it a minute ago?" I patted Daniel on the back as I walked behind Steven, looking over his shoulder as he unclasped the watch and opened the case.

"It's beautiful," Steven whispered. He gently traced the etchings on the case with his fingers. "Have you tried to get it working again?"

Daniel shook his head. "I haven't had it in my possession since before I died. Long story short, Jamie found it in a trunk and had her friend bring it up from Marion last night. We think that's why we're connected in the first place."

Steven nodded without looking up. "That would make sense." He set the watch on the table and stood. "I guess if I'm going to spend the day at the library, I better get going. Your mom has my number, Jamie. Call if you need me to do anything else for you."

"I will. Thanks."

Daniel took Steven's empty seat at the table. "He seems like a good guy."

"You now know him about as well as I do. My mom has been working with him for years, though."

I twirled the watch in my fingers. "Do you think we could get it working? That would be cool."

Daniel took the watch from me and stared at it. "We'd have to take it to a professional. I wouldn't dare take it apart on my own. These things are pretty intricate. It's not like we can just replace a battery."

"True."

Daniel set the watch down and looked at me. "Are you ready to hear what I found out?"

"Found out?"

"Last night, before Peter arrived and interrupted us, I was about to tell you what I found out about Dr. Church."

I'd forgotten Daniel had something to tell me. The awkwardness of introducing Peter to Daniel washed all thoughts of it from my mind. "Right. What did you find out?"

"After Dr. Church was named in the Massachusetts Banishment Act, he boarded a ship for Martinico—"

"A ship to *where?*"

"Martinico. It's an island in the Caribbean. Nowadays, it's known as Martinique, but back in the day it was known as Martinico. It was occupied by the French. In fact, I think it's still run by France."

"So this Church guy tries to give classified information to the enemy, becomes a traitor, and then is *punished* by getting shipped off to some island in the Caribbean? How is that possibly a punishment?"

Daniel shrugged. "I have to admit, that thought crossed my mind. But, the story gets even better." He paused for affect. "Dr. Church never arrived in Martinico."

I narrowed my eyes. "What do you mean?"

"I mean, he never arrived. He was seen boarding the boat that would take him there, but the boat disappeared, presumed lost at sea."

A sharp twinge of something I couldn't explain grabbed at my insides. It was as if all my muscles tensed at once and then released. My heart pounded out a hard rhythm in my chest. I'd felt the feeling before. More than once. Every time I'd had that odd feeling, the information I learned had something to do with my ghost's extrication. I blew out a slow breath. "Daniel," I said, my voice quiet. "We have to find out what happened to Dr. Church. He's the key to your extrication."

Daniel tilted his head sharply. "Are you sure?"

"Pretty sure." I rubbed my fingers across the pocket watch. "Call it my soul saver sense or whatever, but I know we need to figure out what happened to him."

"How are we going to do that?"

"I have absolutely no idea."

"Great. This should be really easy then." Daniel reached over and laced his fingers through mine. "I'm really glad I met you. And not just because you're helping me. You're a good friend, J."

My brain told me to pull away. Going down that road would only cause pain when Daniel eventually extricated. I couldn't seem to get the message from my brain to coordinate with my fingers and my hand stayed put, carefully knotted with Daniel's. "Let's make a list of everyone who might have known Dr. Church. We can visit their graves and see if anyone happened to survive as a ghost. If they did, we can ask them if there were any rumors about the good doctor. You know, like maybe he survived the shipwreck, if there really was one, and he showed up in the United States again."

I unwillingly pulled my hand out of Daniel's and went in search of paper and a pen. While Daniel wrote names and approximate ages on the paper, I searched burial site websites for the same names, hoping we could find the final resting places of his once friends.

"Any chance Paul Revere became a ghost?" I asked as I read through the names of those buried in the same cemetery as him.

Daniel laughed. "No. Sorry. That one I did look into. He's really dead."

"Wait . . . where are *you* buried?"

Daniel shrugged. "I have no idea."

"How can you not know?"

"I didn't follow my body to the grave. I know, it's strange for ghosts not to do that, but . . . I just couldn't watch. Unfortunately, my family never mentioned the burial ground when I happened to be spying on them."

"You need a headstone. *Everyone* needs a headstone."

"I told you before, J. I'm a nobody, completely forgotten in history. There's no proof I ever existed. It's okay."

"I'm going to find a way to make you remembered. No one deserves to be forgotten."

Daniel shrugged. "Thanks for the thought, but . . ." His words trailed off. I didn't say anything so he motioned to the paper in front of us. "We've got a few names now. Let's go see if we can track down some ghosts."

Chapter 21

"Which cemetery should we go to first?" I stared at the cemeteries listed on the paper in front of me. We'd identified three in the Boston area where people who knew both Daniel and Dr. Church were buried. It was a long shot, but we had nothing else to try.

Daniel tapped his pen on the table as he looked at my laptop screen. "How about Forest Hills? It looks nice."

"You're choosing our next move by looks?"

"What's wrong with basing things on looks? That's how I chose my soul saver." He reached over and tucked a strand of hair that had escaped my ponytail behind my ear. His blatant flirting made it hard to concentrate.

I turned away from him and cleared my throat. "Forest Hills it is."

"Good. I'll call a cab."

Forest Hills Cemetery was located in the Jamaica Plain neighborhood of Boston. History seeped from all areas of that district. I gawked out the window like a tourist as we pulled in front of the cemetery's chapel. Daniel paid the driver and we hopped out.

"First stop, the grave of General Joseph Warren," Daniel said as we walked through the gate.

"He's the one who died at Bunker Hill, right?"

Daniel nodded. "Good memory. He was very vocal about his feelings and causes. He got involved in a lot of ways, including with the Sons of Liberty."

"You'll tell me if you see any ghosts, right?" I knew all too well that ghosts liked to stay near their bodies. There could have been any number of invisible ghosts floating around the cemetery.

"All clear so far."

We followed the cemetery map until we reached a headstone bearing General Warren's name and some of his relatives. I brushed fallen leaves away from the headstone so I could read all of it. "I found on the internet that his body was moved a couple of times. This cemetery didn't exist until the 1800s. When I die, I hope they just leave me in one place."

Daniel stepped closer and slipped his hand in mine. "What if you become a ghost?" he asked. "What happens if you die before you save all the souls you're supposed to help?"

The thought that *I* might become a ghost had never entered my mind. The pain and misery of living an endless life I couldn't fully participate in made my heart race, or maybe it was the feel of Daniel's hand in mine. Either way, I didn't want to think about it. "I guess I'll cross that road when I get to it. Now do you see anyone?"

Daniel turned in a full circle. He shook his head. "Not a soul. That's not normal. I would have thought there'd be more ghosts around. Maybe it's because this cemetery has so many older burials. Newer cemeteries have far more spirits hanging around. Who else is buried here?"

I looked at the list in my hand. "William Dawes."

Daniel smiled. "Good guy. You remember him from my life, right?"

I nodded. "He used to do night watches with you. He was also the guy who rode ahead of Paul Revere the night you put the lanterns in the Old North Church."

Daniel grinned. "Wow. You do listen."

"I like facts." I looked down at my notes. "He might not be buried here. There's some debate over whether he's buried here or over at King's Chapel. Some think his body was moved here, others don't know for sure."

We crossed the cemetery to the place where William Dawes *might* be buried. "Do you see any kind of grave marker with his name?" I asked.

"Not right here. We can ask the lady standing by the tree, though."

I turned in the direction he pointed, but saw nothing. I took a deep breath and blew it out again. It sounded shaky. "There's no one there, Daniel."

"No one *you* can see."

I always got nervous when meeting new ghosts. If they were in human form, I didn't have a problem, but knowing that they were around me and I couldn't see them always set my nerves on edge.

We walked closer to the tree, Daniel pulling me along.

"Wait!" Daniel suddenly yelled. "I just want to ask you a question. She knows about us. It's okay."

I swallowed hard as I looked in the direction he spoke. If anyone else were to witness the exchange, they'd think he was having a conversation with the large leafy tree. I knew what was there—and it gave me the creeps. I squeezed Daniel's hand tighter when a woman, who looked to be near forty, suddenly appeared in front of the tree. Being a ghost had its perks. There were times when I would have loved to come and go as I pleased without anyone knowing of my presence. The woman had long blonde hair that cascaded down her back. She stayed close to the tree with her hands wrapped around the trunk.

"I know what you want. And the answer is no. He's not a ghost anymore. Or if he is, he hasn't been back to see his body in decades," the woman spoke softly, never taking her eyes from mine. I couldn't have blinked even if I wanted to. Graveyard ghosts tended to be nervous around living souls and this woman was no exception to the rule.

"Who's not a ghost anymore?" Daniel asked.

"The man you're looking for."

"Which man? Do you mean William Dawes or Joseph Warren?"

The woman shrugged and Daniel tensed beside me. I decided to take over the questioning. "It's really important that you tell us everything you know. It could help with his extrication." I nodded toward Daniel.

The woman finally tore her eyes away from mine and looked sharply at Daniel. "Extrication? You're going to be extricated?"

"I hope to be. Someday," he answered.

"I'll never leave. I'm here forever." She dropped her eyes to the ground. I couldn't tell by her emotionless tone if she wanted to be extricated and had given up hope, or if she *wanted* to exist forever. "The man you said, Dawes, he used to come around a lot. I talked to him a few times. I haven't seen him in at least a hundred years, though. I think he's gone now."

"What about the other man, Joseph Warren?" I asked.

"I've never met anyone by that name."

My heart fell. Dawes could have been Daniel's connection, but we were too late—by quite a while. "Did Dawes mention anything about his life when he was here?"

The woman seemed to relax a little. "He said he'd helped during the war for independence."

"Did he happen to say *how* he helped?" I asked.

"Something about him and Paul Revere and that famous ride. I don't really remember the details. Sorry."

193

"It's okay."

"I don't think he was a spy. He probably would have mentioned it."

Daniel stepped closer to the woman and she took a step back. "Why would you say that?" If he wasn't careful his eagerness would chase her off.

The lady's eyes widened. "I thought that's why you were asking about him. That's what the others have asked."

"*What* others?" Daniel said firmly.

By this point, the woman looked like she might bolt at any second. I tugged on Daniel's arm, trying to rein him in. He took a breath and asked more gently, "Have others asked you about Dawes?"

She hesitated, but then nodded.

"And they asked if he was a spy?" I continued.

Another nod.

"Do you know how long it's been since someone else asked?"

"Five years, give or take a year."

"Did they give their names?" I held my breath while waiting for an answer.

"One man told me his name was Chapel. Something Chapel. That's all I remember."

I frowned. The information told me nothing. "Thanks for your help."

The woman nodded and disappeared.

"Have a nice day," Daniel called into the air before turning toward the cemetery entrance and pulling me with him. We'd only walked a few paces before the woman ghost suddenly appeared in front of me, just inches from my face. I gasped, but managed to stifle a scream. She reached out and put one of her bony hands on my shoulder. If Daniel wouldn't have been with me, I probably would have punched her. On the creepy scale, she was a ten.

The woman stared at me for a few torturous seconds before whispering, "I was wrong. The man wasn't named Chapel. His name was Church."

Back in his apartment, Daniel sat next to me on his couch. "I can't believe the traitor is still alive." Anger slipped out with his words.

"If you want to get technical, he's not alive. He's dead," I said, trying to cheer him up. It didn't work. "I'm not surprised at all. It would make sense that he's your unfinished business. I mean, he's the reason you died, right?"

Daniel raised his shoulders and then dropped them. "So what am I supposed to do? Track him down and tell him I don't like the way he acted when he was alive and hope I'm immediately zapped to the next life?"

"Why the anger? I'm trying to help."

Daniel sighed and dropped his head into his hands. "I'm sorry. I just don't like the idea that I'm going to have to see him again. I put that part of my life behind me. I don't want to think about it, why would I want to relive it?"

"The first ghost I helped extricate had to get revenge on the people who wronged her in life. Sort of. Maybe that's your unfinished business, too."

Daniel raised his eyebrows. "Revenge? That's not really how I work."

"Okay, maybe not revenge then. Maybe you have to get an apology from him. Or maybe you just need closure on why he did what he did. It could be anything."

"How do you propose we track him down?"

"That's where we need all the help we can get. My mom and her partners offered to help so we can use them. We need to contact all our friends in the ghost world and find out if anyone has ever met someone by the name of Dr. Benjamin Church. We might get lucky and find someone who has a connection."

"I'll start by looking for Charlie. He's pretty observant and he's been in Boston for a long time."

"Charlie your fake uncle?"

Daniel nodded. "He doesn't always have his phone with him so I'll probably have to leave a message and hope that he checks it sooner rather than later."

"Should we bother visiting the other cemeteries on the list?"

Daniel lifted his head. "I don't know. What do you think?"

"I think our time would be better spent trying to find Dr. Church. If we run out of leads with him, we can always return to the cemeteries."

We crossed the hall to my apartment. Mom and Portia were both sitting in the living room. Portia had a book open in front of her and Mom typed on her laptop.

"Is Steven back yet?" I asked as soon as we entered the room.

Mom looked up from her screen. "Hello to you, too." She giggled. *Yep. Definitely feeling better.* "I haven't seen him since last night. Do you know where he is, Portia?"

Portia set her book in her lap. "He's still at the library doing research for you. At least he was when I texted him thirty minutes ago." Portia tilted her head and narrowed her eyes as she looked from me to Daniel. "You guys found a clue, didn't you? I recognize that look."

I grinned. "Actually, we have more than one lead." I sat down on the couch next to my mom, and Daniel sat on the rug with his legs stretched out in front of himself. The patio door was open to the screen and a light breeze blew through the room, rustling the newspaper sitting on the coffee table. "Remember when we told you

196

about Dr. Benjamin Church?"

Mom and Portia moved their heads up and down in unison. "That's the guy who Daniel caught spying for the British, right?" Mom asked.

"Uh huh," I nodded.

"We think he's still around," Daniel announced.

I spent the next thirty minutes explaining about the watch, the five spies, and the missing doctor. By the time we finished discussing the subject, we had three notebook pages filled from top to bottom with possible scenarios—including the conclusion we'd come to that Church must have been one of the five spies. Daniel specifically remembered Gage referring to The Healer as a double agent. How else would he have gotten all of his information?

My throat was dry from the unusual—for me, at least—amount of talking so I stepped into the kitchen for a glass of water. As soon as I turned back around, I caught a glimpse of someone staring back at me from the patio window. I gasped and dropped the cup I held. Water splashed up around me as the plastic cup bounced across the floor.

"J?" Daniel asked from his position on the rug. "You okay?"

"Someone's on the patio," I whispered.

Mom and Portia jumped up and turned to the door. "Where?" Portia said. "And how?"

I pointed at the empty balcony. "I know I saw someone. I think it was a ghost."

Daniel jumped up and raced to the window. He threw the door open and stepped out onto the balcony. "Are you sure?"

Am I sure? "I . . . I think so."

"What did they look like? Male? Female? Hair color? Height?"

"It was a man. He was tall and . . ." The glimpse had been fleeting, but I suddenly knew why the face triggered feelings of recognition. "It was Myles."

197

"Myles? As in Myles Westing?" Mom's mouth gaped open.

"I'm pretty sure. I only saw him for a split second. Sorry."

Daniel stepped back into the room with us. "Whoever it was, he's gone now. I can't see him anywhere."

"Maybe I'm just losing my mind," I said.

"I doubt that. This Myles guy, he's the one who told you I was a ghost, right?" Daniel asked.

I nodded.

"And you guys told him you didn't want to help him anymore?" Daniel asked Mom and Portia.

"He wouldn't be honest with us," Mom said. "We didn't have a choice."

"Any ideas why he'd want to come back? Did you keep something of his maybe?"

Mom shrugged. "I can't think of anything."

"Maybe he's just curious as to why you're around," I told Daniel.

"Maybe. If any of you see him lurking around again, let me know. I want to talk to the guy."

The front door flew open and I whirled around, half expecting to see Myles standing there, but it was Steven who burst through the entrance.

"You're never going to believe what I found!" he yelled.

Chapter 22

We scurried over to the table to hear what Steven found out. Daniel stood guard at the patio door, watching for uninvited eavesdropping ghosts.

"As soon as I got to the library, I gathered all the books they had on Washington," Steven began. "A few of them were strictly about him and his spies. I started by scanning them for names so I could have a list of people to research further." Steven opened his laptop and showed us a document. The page had been divided into three columns and each column contained at least thirty names.

My heart sunk. Daniel's extrication might never happen. "All of those names are spies?" I asked.

"Not necessarily," Steven answered. "The ones with asterisks are ones where we know for sure that there's some sort of written proof about their espionage."

"Only a few have asterisks," Portia said. "Who are all the other people?"

"The others are acquaintances, friends, assistants, leaders, etc. I'm sure this list is only the tip of the iceberg, but it's a good jumping off point, right? I mean, no offense Daniel, but would anyone have ever expected you to be involved with spying for General Washington?"

"No way." Daniel shook his head.

"Exactly. And I assume you weren't the only one that he chose because of the non-connection."

"So now what? We divide the list amongst ourselves and start researching?" I asked.

"I haven't even gotten to the exciting part yet," Steven said. "One of the books that the reference computer listed as being about Washington turned out to be a family history of sorts. It was titled, *Generations of Freedom* and it documented one family's genealogy from the time they came to the continent in the 1600s until the book was written in the forties."

I crossed my arms over my chest and tapped my foot on the ground, convinced I'd be a ghost myself by the time Steven got around to telling us what he discovered.

"I briefly scanned the book to see why the reference computer listed it as having a connection to George Washington," Steven continued. "Some of the ancestors lived in Cambridge at the time of the war. The book quoted a journal entry from someone named Matthew Heinrichsen. He wrote about seeing General Washington the day he arrived in Cambridge after becoming head of the army. Matthew wrote about how important and dignified Washington looked as he rode his horse down the street into town."

I drummed my fingers on my arm and bit my tongue to keep from yelling at Steven to spit it out.

"I couldn't find any other reference to Washington in the book so I figured it wasn't important and added it to the pile that needed to be reshelved. Apparently I don't balance things very well because after I added the book to the pile, the entire stack toppled. I bent to pick them up, and saw that *Generations of Freedom* had fallen open to this page." Steven reached into his bag and pulled out an old hardback book with a boring tan cover. I would never have picked up a book like that on my own. He flipped to a certain page and then set the book on the table in front of us before leaning back in his chair, a giant grin on his face.

Mom, Portia, and I leaned in to get a closer look and Daniel left his guard duty at the window to see what had produced so much excitement out of Steven.

On the page, a black and white photo of an old writing desk took up a quarter of the left page. It wasn't the desk that brought smiles to the group, but the pocket watch sitting on the desk. Underneath the photo were the words, *Desk (circa 1789) and Watch (circa 1775) belongings of Matthew Heinrichsen.*

I looked to Daniel expectantly. "Is that the same kind of watch as yours?"

Daniel pulled his own watch from the pocket of his jeans and set it next to the book. "It looks like they could be the same or at least similar. It's hard to tell. The photo isn't very big and it's in black and white."

"I already took care of that problem," Steven said as he reached into his bag again. "I used the library's copy machine to blow up the picture." He set a piece of paper on the counter. The image was blurry, but clear enough to see that there was a name next to the year 1775 engraved into the inner casing. The style and size of the engraving and casing matched Daniel's exactly.

"Well, that's four of the five spies known, now to find the fifth," I said.

"Wait . . . four? Did I miss one?" Mom asked.

"There's Daniel, and this Matthew Heinrichsen guy, and Paul Revere, and we can assume Benjamin Church was one of the five since he is apparently trying to locate other spies."

"Paul Revere was one?" Portia asked with raised eyebrows.

"Didn't we tell you that? We found his watch in his house

201

museum."

Mom turned to Portia. "I think we missed a lot while we were sick."

"I haven't been sick and I think I missed something," Steven said. "Jamie, what was that you just said about Church trying to find Daniel?"

"Oh yeah. You weren't here earlier. By the way, the doctor became a ghost and he's looking for other spies. Meaning, he's most likely looking for Daniel."

After catching everyone up on all the case details, we decided to take a break from looking for the fifth spy and focus our efforts on finding Dr. Church. More importantly, we wanted to know why he wanted the same answers about Washington's spies as we did.

I texted Jack and Rita. They were ghost friends of mine who lived in Marion. No one would ever believe they were ghosts because they acted like humans in every way. Jack had a full-time job and Rita stayed home and took care of the house. She even grocery shopped to keep up appearances even though they rarely ate. Every time I visited, she insisted on cooking for me. I'm ashamed to say it, but until I found out my mom was a soul saver and that was the reason she'd abandoned me and Dad, part of me wished Rita could be my mom. Anyway, Jack and Rita were a long shot. They'd only been in Massachusetts for a short time and they hung out with the living more than the dead.

My phone beeped. *"Sorry, sweetie. I don't think I've ever heard of anyone by the name of Benjamin Church. Are you soul saving again already?"* Rita texted.

I smiled to myself. *"I'm attempting to."*

"Should I be worried that you might accidentally extricate me

sometime?" A smiley face accompanied Rita's text.

"I'll try to keep my skills away from you."

I stuck my phone in my back pocket and turned to Daniel. "Sorry. That was my only lead in the ghost world and it's a no. They don't know Church."

"Don't worry about it. There're a lot of ghosts we can ask. I don't know what it is about this town, but I feel like there are far more ghosts here than in the average city."

"Maybe it's the town's historical culture."

"Maybe. I left a message on Charlie's voicemail, but he hasn't called back yet. With him, it could be a few days or a few hours. I'm never sure," Daniel said.

The day wore on, but we didn't get any more leads. None of the ghosts my mom and her team contacted had ever heard of Benjamin Church. Daniel called a few people, but ran into dead ends on all of them. Charlie still didn't return his call. I had a nagging feeling that I'd overlooked something important. I ran through the details of Daniel's life and death over and over in my mind a million times and wrote every detail in the notebook Daniel and I started. Nothing stood out more than anything else—except the watch.

For some reason, every time I touched the watch, I had a strong feeling that it was the key to Daniel's extrication. We knew there were five watches, and we knew four of the five owners, but that information triggered nothing. Could Daniel's extrication be as simple as figuring out who owned the fifth watch? *Why am I so drawn to the stupid watch?*

Daniel suggested we all take a break to clear our minds. We sat in my living room and watched a movie with Mom, Steven, and Portia. Exhaustion must have finally broken me because the last the thing I remember of that night was closing my eyes for just a moment during the movie. I woke up to a dark apartment. Rubbing the sleep from my eyes, I stared at the clock on the DVD player. I'd slept for three hours. Mom, Portia, and Steven had gone to bed and Daniel must have returned to his apartment because he no longer sat next to me on the couch. Someone had covered me with a blanket. I closed my eyes, determined to fall asleep again, but a shuffling sound near the dining table brought me fully awake.

Someone's in here.

Mom? Steven? Portia?

I opened my mouth, about to ask who was awake, but clamped it shut when the person came into my view. It wasn't one of my roommates.

Myles Westing.

I burrowed under the blanket until only my eyes peeked out. Myles might not have noticed me on the couch, but whether or not he knew of my presence, I for sure didn't want him to know I was awake. Myles shuffled from the dining area into the kitchen and began to quietly open and close each of the drawers and cabinets. There was some method to his madness.

What's he looking for? We have nothing of his! Can't he just leave us alone?

I thought about yelling or running across the hall to Daniel's, but Myles would disappear long before I got out the door. Or worse, he might decide to take me with him. Ghosts can harm the living if they're in their human form. It was smarter to keep quiet and try to figure out what Myles looked for rather than risk getting myself caught.

The minutes dragged on as he searched every nook and cranny. I wondered how long he'd been there before I woke up and whether or not he'd searched the back bedrooms. *Did he do something to anyone?*

Myles left the kitchen and stepped into the living room. I closed my eyes, pretending to be asleep. My heart thumped so loud in my chest I could barely concentrate on anything else. I held my breath and then let it out slowly, trying to imitate the sound of someone sleeping . . . and to calm my racing heart.

Myles hovered right above me. I could feel his breath on my forehead and I almost gagged.

Go away!

I heard him pick something up off the floor, but didn't dare open my eyes to see what it was. When I heard the familiar sound of a zipper, the mystery was answered for me. Myles had my purse.

Jerk! Get out of my stuff!

Time seemed to stand still as I waited for him to make his next move. I heard the zipper close again and he set the purse back on the floor.

Did he take something?

The more time he spent in the apartment, the closer I came to leaping off the couch to strangle him. Myles scanned the room one last time before walking to the front door and vanishing through it. Staying in his human form while he searched had been a cocky move.

The moment he disappeared through the door, I leaped off the couch and grabbed my cell phone off the table. "Mom!" I screamed at the same time I dialed. "Mom!"

Daniel answered after the first ring. "J? What's wrong? It's three in the morning."

"I know. I'm sorry. Where are you?"

"Sitting on my couch. Reading."

"Myles is back. Make sure he's not lurking in your apartment."

"What? Really?"

Steven emerged from his room first, just in time to hear the last part of my conversation with Daniel. He flipped on the kitchen light and we both blinked, trying to adjust to the sudden brightness. Mom came out of her room wearing fuzzy pink pajamas. "What's going on out here, Jamie?"

"Myles was in the apartment," I said. "He looked through all the drawers and cabinets."

Mom's jaw dropped and she stared at me as if she couldn't comprehend what I'd just told her.

Steven jumped into action and opened the kitchen drawer closest to him. "Is anything gone? Look for anything that looks out of place," he instructed as he opened another drawer.

Daniel appeared through the door before Steven got to the third drawer. "Sorry I didn't knock," he said.

I stepped next to him. "It's fine."

Shaking herself out of her stupor, mom asked, "Why does Myles keep coming back?"

"He's probably mad that we stopped helping him," Steven answered as he continued his frantic search for stolen items.

Mom shook her head in disbelief. "We stopped helping him so he decided to rob us? That's pretty childish."

"Did you see what he took?" Daniel asked me.

"The lights were off and I didn't dare move. Wait . . . he went through my purse." I raced back to the couch and grabbed my purse from the floor next to it. Nothing seemed to be missing. "My cash, my debit card, sunglasses. It's all here. He even left a gift card dad gave me sitting right on top of everything."

Portia came into the room then. "What's going on? Why are you all out of bed?"

Mom explained again what happened while she and Steven continued looking through drawers and cabinets.

Daniel watched my mom and her roommates for a moment, but didn't offer to help. When he spoke, I had to lean closer to hear him. "He wasn't here to rob you."

"What makes you so sure?" I asked.

"If he was, he would have at least taken the laptop on the table. He was looking for something specific."

Portia sat down on one of the kitchen chairs and tucked her legs up under her chin. "That doesn't make sense. He never gave us anything of his. And he barely spent any time here so he wouldn't know what valuables we had—not that we have any."

I looked at my surroundings one more time, trying to make sure Myles really left empty-handed. It had been dark when Myles was in the room and my eyes were closed half the time. He could have easily picked something up without me noticing and slipped it in his pocket. My eyes fell to the coffee table.

And then my heart fell.

I sunk to the couch and dropped my head into my hands. "He did take something."

"What?" A chorus of voices asked.

"I left the notebook with all of our case details sitting on the coffee table when we were watching the movie. It's gone now." I looked up. "And Daniel, I'm sorry, but . . . the pocket watch was sitting on top of it. It's not here."

Tears leaked from the corners of my eyes and I brushed them away with the back of my hand. "I'm so, so sorry."

Daniel crossed the room in about two strides and sat down next to me, putting an arm across my shoulders. "Hey, don't worry. We'll track him down and get the notebook back." He lifted my chin and forced me to look at him. "Look." He reached into his back pocket and pulled out the now familiar pocket watch. "I took it with me when I left last night. You were asleep and I didn't want to wake you up. Myles didn't get it."

I grabbed the watch from Daniel's hand and threw my arms around him, almost knocking him over. Then, realizing what I'd done, I dropped my arms and scooted away. "Sorry."

Daniel sighed. "Maybe it would have been better if he'd gotten my watch instead of the notebook. We had a lot of notes in there."

"True, but the watch is important to you," I said. "And to history in general. Myles would probably just pawn it once he knew where it came from and whoever eventually ended up with it wouldn't know of its significance."

"It might be important for sentimental reasons, but I can't take it with me when I leave. When I'm gone, it's yours."

"I wouldn't worry too much about the notebook either," Steven said as he sat down in one of the chair across from us. "I've got a lot of the same info backed up on my computer and you've got the main details inside your heads."

"Are you sure about that Steven?" Portia said, joining Daniel and me on the couch. "If that's the *only* thing Myles took, he must want something he knows is in there. Is there any information in that notebook that might have something to do with Myles?"

"Not that I can think of."

Mom sat down in the chair next to Steven's and leaned back against the cushions. "Maybe it's just his way of getting revenge on us for dropping him from our client list. He probably thinks by taking the notebook he's sabotaging our next case. You think you saw him on the patio yesterday when we were talking about the case. Maybe he thought he'd take all the info about it."

"But it's not even your case. It's *mine*," I snapped. All eyes were on me, but no one spoke. I took a deep breath. "Sorry. I'm really glad all of you are helping. I'm just frustrated and annoyed and angry."

"Don't let Myles get to you. You'll only give him satisfaction." Portia yawned. "Are we done here? Can I go back to bed? I'm still not feeling a hundred percent."

Mom snickered. "Tell me about it. I got winded just walking across the room."

Steven stood. "Let's all go back to bed. We'll call Myles tomorrow and see what he's up to. I doubt he'll answer, but . . ."

Mom walked into the dining area and locked the patio door. She did the same thing with the apartment door. I didn't have the heart to remind her that ghosts could walk through walls if they wanted to.

Unless they wanted a living person to know where they were, their presence was completely unknown. They could come and go as they pleased. Falling asleep on the couch again, knowing that Myles might return, seemed like an impossible task.

"Daniel?" I whispered after both bedroom doors had shut. "Do you think you could . . . umm . . . stay?"

He smiled at me, revealing a dimple I hadn't noticed before. "Actually, I was going to suggest it. And if you turned me down, I would have only pretended to leave."

"Thanks."

"I'm just going to run across the hall and grab my book. I'll use a flashlight to read and then you can keep sleeping."

"Okay." Weariness kicked in and I sunk to the couch.

Daniel opened the door to leave, but I jumped off the couch again. "Wait! Take your watch with you. I don't want to be responsible for it."

I stepped toward Daniel, but the blanket I slept with became tangled around my ankle, pulling me to an abrupt stop. The watch didn't get the memo that we were going down and it propelled forward. I had no choice but to watch in horror as it landed with a sickening thunk on the tile floor of the kitchen.

No one needed to tell me that the watch didn't survive. I heard each of the parts land separately on the hard floor.

Chapter 23

Neither Daniel nor I moved. We couldn't. Neither of us spoke either. Nothing I said, and no amount of apologizing would change the fact that I'd just shattered his more than two hundred year old watch. Part of me wanted to throw up, but part of me—and this is where it got weird—felt relief.

Here come the tears again. I'm such a baby when ghosts are involved. Stupid emotions.

I could have stayed on the ground where I'd landed for the rest of the night and been completely content, but Daniel left his position by the front door and reached toward me. "Don't worry about it. Okay? It didn't work anyway." He bent down and offered me a hand, pulling me up and wrapping his arms around me.

I lay my head on his shoulder and let the tears silently fall.

"J, *please* don't be upset. We've both almost broken the stupid thing in the last few days. It was bound to happen. I mean, the watch had a weird death wish."

"Yeah, well I would have rather you were the one to break it than me." I lifted my head from his shoulder, knowing that my tears were probably soaking through his shirt. *Embarrassing.*

210

He brushed the back of his hand across my wet cheek. "Maybe it's still fixable."

We both turned and looked at the kitchen floor. The overhead lights were still on and the little metal pieces scattered across the floor reflected the light, sending glowing beams into the air just to prove to me how much damage I'd caused. If antique-loving Peter were there, he would have passed out from the sheer horror of the carnage.

I carefully stepped around the pieces and into the kitchen to get something to collect them in. Daniel crouched down and began gathering the pieces off the tile. I knelt next to him, handing him the small bowl I'd pulled from one of the cabinets. "I can't believe how intricate the insides are. There're seriously a million pieces here," I said.

"Personally, I think today's technology is a lot more complicated than it was back when I was alive."

"Maybe, but it sure makes life easier."

Daniel shrugged. "That's your opinion."

I stopped picking up pieces and looked at him. "You don't think life is easier now?"

"Not really."

"What do you mean?"

"Technology complicates things."

"I disagree."

"That's because you didn't live when I lived."

I grinned. "Okay, Mr. I've-Been-Around-Forever. Explain yourself."

Daniel stopped searching for watch pieces and sat cross-legged on the tiles next to me. "When I was alive, we woke up, we worked, we went to bed. The next day, we repeated the process. If we had rare free time, we could read, visit friends, or play simple games. Nowadays, free time is completely consumed by electronics—you

211

know, video games, computers, TVs, phones. Because of all those things, you have to know a lot more, which means more schooling, more memorizing, and more stress. True, electricity and plumbing and all those things are nice, but we didn't know any better back then so we weren't bothered by not having them. Smaller houses meant less space to clean. Fewer food options meant less money to spend and less chance of becoming overweight." Daniel paused and grinned at me. "Do you want me to keep going?"

"No. You've made your point. My life sucks and yours was way better." I pretended to be upset and dropped my head into my hands.

"That's not what I meant. I'm sure your life is great for you." He grabbed my hand and pulled it away from my face, shaking his head when he saw me secretly smiling. He gave my shoulder a playful nudge.

I nudged him back and he tackled me to the floor in a fit of muffled giggles, pinning my arms down. I don't think either of us knew where to go from there. Flirting wasn't my forte and Daniel hesitated.

And then I saw something spark in his eyes. He let go of my hands and jumped away from me, his attention focused on the carpet at the edge of the kitchen. "J, look," he whispered.

I sat up and took the piece of watch casing he handed me. As soon as I looked down, a rush of heat and joy washed over me. "I knew it! I *knew* there was more to this watch." Engraved numbers and letters covered the piece of casing in my hand. "How did we not see this before?" I asked.

"It was all hidden underneath the watch's mechanisms."

"This is a clue to your extrication. I don't know how to describe it, but I can feel it."

Daniel took the casing back and studied it. "None of this makes any sense. The letters don't combine to make actual words."

"Didn't one of those books Steven had say something about the use of secret codes by Washington?"

Daniel's head jerked up and he looked at me sharply. "You might be on to something. Both sides used secret codes."

Daniel stared at the watch casing while he walked to the couch and sat down. I picked up the bowl with the rest of the pieces and followed him.

"Do you think . . . I mean . . . what if . . ." He couldn't seem to decide which question to ask first. "If General Washington put a code in here, did he intend for me to solve it all those years ago? Or was it intended for someone else?"

"Your name is the one engraved on there."

"Yeah, but maybe he meant for me to pass it on to someone else and I somehow missed the clue."

"He had the watches made up before he knew Church was a traitor. My guess is, he intended to use them for something special, but had to change plans last minute."

Daniel rubbed the sides of his mouth with his thumb and index finger, something he did when concentrating really hard. "I bet you're right. Instead of using them for their intended purpose, he pretended they were gifts for our services."

"Exactly."

"We know that I received mine, and Revere received his because we saw it in his house museum. And Matthew Heinrichsen must have received his watch because there's a picture of it in a book." He paused for a moment. "Do you think Church received his watch before I turned him in? I hadn't received mine before then. Maybe Church didn't either."

"If Church didn't receive it, how did he find out about them?"

"Good point. Maybe the fifth person, the one we still don't have a name for, didn't receive theirs." Daniel sighed. "I think this just became a lot more complicated."

213

"So . . . how good are you at cracking codes?"

Daniel frowned. "No experience whatsoever. You?"

"Nada."

"Maybe we can look at that code book Steven brought home in the morning."

I glanced at Steven's closed bedroom door. "Or, you could always sneak in there and get it so we can look right now."

"I'm not that kind of ghost." He leaned back against the couch cushions and put an arm around my shoulders. "Besides. You need to get some sleep. No offense, but your eyes look a little . . . glossed over. I'm not going anywhere tonight and I doubt Church will catch up to me before morning."

"Fine. You're still keeping watch for Myles though, right?"

Daniel opened his mouth to say something, but his phone buzzed.

Who calls him in the middle of the night?

He quickly pulled the phone from his pocket and looked at the screen. "It's Charlie," he whispered before answering the call and pressing the speaker button. He held the phone between us so we could both hear.

"Hey, Charlie."

"*Where are you?*" Charlie's words were crisp and direct.

"I'm visiting a friend. Did you get my message?"

"*I'm in your apartment. You need to come home right now. I need to talk to you. Privately. I don't trust these phone things.*"

Daniel started to say something else, but Charlie ended the call from his end before Daniel could respond.

"He sounds like a real winner," I said drily.

"He's great as a ghost. He's just not that comfortable pretending to be alive. Let's go."

"He said to come alone."

Daniel picked up the bowl with all the watch pieces and grabbed my hand. "He doesn't know yet that I have a soul saver. Whatever he has to say, he can say with you there."

We opened and closed the apartment door quietly, hoping not to disturb the three people sleeping in the back rooms. I thought about leaving a note, but I had my phone with me. Mom could find me easily enough if she happened to wake up again. But, judging by the way she still looked, she'd be asleep for quite some time still.

"What's going on?" Daniel said as soon as we stepped through his apartment door.

A squat man with bushy hair—who I assumed was Charlie—stood in the middle of the living room. He took one look at me with Daniel and panic set in. His eyes darted around the room and he shuffled his feet on the carpet. I thought for sure he would bolt or vanish at any second. Daniel must have sensed Charlie's impending flight, because he let go of my hand and quickly stepped toward Charlie.

"Hey, man. It's ok. Jamie's cool." Daniel's hands were up as if he were surrendering to the ghost.

Charlie stared at me without blinking. It made me a little nervous, but I slowly raised one hand and waved at him. "Hi. Nice to meet you."

His eyes finally left mine and returned to Daniel. "I thought I told you I needed to speak to you privately," he whispered.

"Jamie's my soul saver. She knows all about us. Whatever you need to say to me, you can say in front of her." Daniel ended with a reassuring nod of his head.

Charlie shrugged and turned his body away from me and toward Daniel, choosing to just ignore me. It didn't offend me at all. "On the message you left me earlier today you asked if I knew a man."

"Right," Daniel said. "Benjamin Church."

"I didn't know him. At least, not before this evening."

"You *met* him?" The words came out louder than I intended and Charlie jumped. "Sorry."

215

"Where did you meet him?" Daniel asked.

"He came by a place me and a bunch of other guys," he glanced at me and then back at Daniel, "in the same situation as you and me like to hang out."

"What did he say? How did you know it was him?"

"He came right out and introduced himself as Benjamin Church. He said he was trying to track down an old ghost friend by the name of Daniel Avery."

Daniel crossed and uncrossed his arms. "Did you tell him where I lived?"

"No. Something didn't feel right about the situation. When I heard your message later, I was glad I didn't give anything away."

"What didn't feel right about it?" I remembered to speak quietly that time and I didn't make any sudden movements.

"He was offering a cash reward for information on finding Daniel. Who would pay money to find an old friend?"

Daniel's lips twitched as he fought a smile back. "Did anyone else with you know who I was?"

Charlie looked nervous. "One guy did. I don't know his name, but I've seen him around. He talked to the Church guy privately and then they left together. I assumed that meant he knew something. I finished my card game and came straight here to talk to you."

"Thanks, Charlie. Any chance you could describe the guy who talked to Church?"

"Uhh . . . he was kind of tall. Maybe somewhere in his mid-twenties. And he had red hair."

Myles Westing.

I knew it. He'd already paid us a visit that night and he must have come to our apartment as soon as he finished talking to Church. Daniel and I exchanged looks and I knew by his expression that he'd come to the same conclusion as me.

"We know the guy," Daniel told Charlie. "I'm not surprised that he took Church up on the offer. He's kind of mad at us right now."

"And you dragged me into whatever is going on?" Charlie's mouth gaped open.

"You're not involved in this. You can leave and no one will even know you stopped by to warn me, but I'd appreciate it if you passed on anything else you hear to us."

Charlie gave a short nod and then, with one more look toward me, he vanished into the air. I watched Daniel's eyes as they slowly followed a path around the room, watching Charlie's aura leave. "Church knows I have my watch," Daniel said after returning his attention to me.

I raised my eyebrows. "What makes you so sure?"

"We know that Church sent Westing to look for me. Why did he go to your apartment rather than mine?"

I chewed on my lip. "He knew about the watch because he was on our balcony earlier in the day and heard us discussing it." I slapped my forehead. "If he'd gotten the watch, that would have been the easiest money he ever made. Talk about being in the right place at the right time."

"He might not have gotten the watch this time, but he'll be back. He's a con man who happens to be mad at your mom and her partners. If he can get revenge *and* get paid, it'll be his happiest day ever."

A thought hit me and I felt as if I'd been stabbed by a knife. "Daniel," I grabbed his arm to steady myself, "Myles might have already won. He got the notebook. If Church didn't already know who owned the other watches, he'll have the answers as soon as he reads my notes. If his extrication and your extrication both depend on finding all the watches like we suspect, you might never be extricated if he gets all of them first!"

Daniel held me by the shoulders and bent his head to mine. "We've got to find Myles. If we wait until morning, it's too late."

"How are we going to do that?"

"Do you know how to access your mom's client files? We need his address, phone number, something."

"I might be able to get the info off Steven's laptop. I don't know if it's password protected or not. But . . . you'll have to break your ghost rule and sneak into his room to get the laptop."

Daniel frowned. "I don't really have a choice. Come on."

We hurried back across the hall and silently pushed our way through the door. Daniel quickly scanned the room and assured me that Myles hadn't returned. I waited in the living room while he slipped unseen into Steven's room and brought back the computer.

"Cross your fingers," I said, following my own advice. I opened the cover of the computer and clicked on the icon with Steven's name. It went straight to his desktop. "We're in! There's no password."

I held the computer in my lap on the couch and began opening and closing files, trying to find Myles' information. Daniel sat next to me, tapping his foot on the ground. "Maybe I should go to the place where Charlie saw Church. He could be meeting Myles there."

"Charlie didn't name the place. And you can't leave me alone."

"Maybe he didn't name it out loud, but I know where he and all his ghost friends congregate. There're always a lot of them there. Think of it as an underground hideout for ghosts. And I promise I won't leave you. I'm getting anxious just sitting here."

"I found it! Myles Westing. Here's his phone number and his house number." Daniel and I both entered the information into our phones.

"Do we call him or just show up on his porch?" Daniel asked.

"I'm not calling. That will just tip him off that we're on to him and he'll disappear. Put Steven's computer back while I write a note to my mom."

"You don't think you should wake her up and tell her we're

leaving?"

"She'll want to come and then we'll have to wait for her to get ready." *And I prefer to work alone.* "Hopefully she doesn't kill me."

"If she does, we can be ghosts together."

I frowned. "Sounds fun."

By the time Daniel came back to the room from returning the laptop, I'd laced up my sneakers and pulled on a gray hoodie. "Let's go."

Myles had an apartment a few miles west of where we were. The city buses were just starting to run for the day and we managed to find a route that dropped us off near his complex. As we exited the bus, I saw the first hint of sunlight on the horizon.

"Do we knock or are you just going to poof yourself in there?" I asked as we approached his apartment. Many of the windows had bars on them and the chipped paint on the outside of the building hadn't been updated since . . . well, ever.

Daniel raised his eyebrows at me. "First of all, I don't poof." He made squiggly movements with his fingers. "Second of all, there's an unspoken rule about not invading other ghosts' privacy."

"That rule doesn't count with Myles. He invaded *my* privacy."

"J—"

I sighed. "Don't worry, I'll knock." I looked at the door. At least there wasn't a peephole. If we knocked, Myles might actually open the door out of curiosity. "Here goes nothing," I muttered as I rapped my knuckles on the door a few times. I held my breath, waiting to see if Myles had returned to his own home after he left our apartment. Another door down the hall opened and an elderly man stepped out. He crossed his arms over a battered t-shirt and stared at us. I turned my back to the busybody and knocked again.

That time, I heard the sound of shuffling feet. Someone was home. Whether or not the sounds came from Myles remained to be seen.

219

The doorknob started to turn and I grabbed Daniel's arm, bracing for the confrontation. The door opened to reveal a smirking Myles Westing.

He looked from me to Daniel. "How'd you figure it out so fast?"

Chapter 24

Where is it, you weasel?" I yelled at Myles, forgetting to be scared of him.

Daniel slipped an arm around my waist and pulled me back. "What she means is, you came to their apartment earlier and took her notebook. We came to get it back," Daniel said calmly. "If you'll return it, we'll leave you alone and you won't ever have to see us again. Deal?"

Myles threw his head back and laughed. It brought to mind pictures of him as the evil villain in one of those melodrama plays they have in old west replica towns. He stopped laughing and stared right at Daniel. "You want to make a deal? Fine. How about this? You give me your pocket watch, and I won't tell that guy that's been looking for you where you live."

"Not even close," Daniel answered, before adding, "and I have no idea what watch you're talking about."

"Don't play dumb. I heard all of you talking about it earlier. You have a watch and some guy wants it."

"If I had one, I wouldn't give it to you or anyone else. Just give us the notebook."

221

Myles stopped smiling. "I don't do anything for free."

I rolled my eyes and pulled out my wallet. "Seriously? For someone who wants to be extricated, you're not trying very hard to right your wrongs. How much do you want?" Daniel shook his head at me, but I ignored him.

"Who says I want to be extricated?" Myles said.

I shook my head. "You did! Remember? You came to my mom and her partners and asked for their help?"

Myles shrugged. "That was when I was running low on cash. Maybe I'm not in such a hurry to leave now. Let's just say your friend has offered to make my stay here on earth a little more luxurious. Whatever miserly amount you offer wouldn't begin to compare to his generosity."

"My friend?" I said.

"He means Dr. Church," Daniel said, not taking his eyes off Myles.

"He's a doctor? Didn't know that tidbit. Oh well. It doesn't matter. Now, if you don't mind, I'd like to return to what I was doing inside . . . alone." Myles started to shut his door, but Daniel stuck his arm out and caught it. He took a step toward Myles. Their faces were only a couple of inches apart and they seemed to be sizing each other up. Myles had a couple of inches on Daniel, but I didn't doubt Daniel would win any fight. He had more muscle in one arm than Myles did in his entire body.

"I said," Daniel spoke between clenched teeth. "We're not leaving without the notebook."

Myles' nostrils flared. "Then I guess you're going to be waiting for a very long time because I no longer have it." A smile crept onto his lips. "That's right. When I make a deal with someone, I deliver promptly. You know, before someone else can swoop in and steal my thunder. If I were you, I'd watch your back. I'll get your watch from you . . . one way or another." Myles pushed against the door again and that time Daniel stepped back, letting it close in our faces.

"I'm so sorry," I said. "I had no idea I shouldn't be writing everything down. My mom and her partners do so I thought I would. If Myles already gave the notebook to Church, we're too late to stop him from finding all of the watch owners."

Daniel gave me a quick hug. "If Church is that desperate to find the watches, he must know about the codes inside."

I nodded in agreement. "What if there's not a code in all of them? What if yours was the only one and that's why Church is after it?"

"I guess that's possible. Without seeing the others, we'll never know."

"Basically we need to find Dr. Church."

Daniel frowned. "Unfortunately. Let's take you home. If I'm going to track Church down, I'll have to go to the place where Charlie and all his ghost friends hang out."

"I'm coming with you."

"No way."

"Why not?"

"If I took a mortal to the immortals secret spot, I'd be the most hated ghost in all of Boston. No one would ever trust me again." We'd walked away from Myles' building and Daniel nodded toward it. "I don't think you have to worry about him anymore . . . at least not right now. He knows we're alerted and he knows we're not willingly going to give up the watch. He doesn't seem like the kind of guy that would follow through on a threat if there isn't any immediate gratification. I think he's all talk."

"I hope you're right."

We stood at the bus stop, barely talking. I was lost in my own world as I tried to sort through my thoughts. When the bus pulled up, Daniel cleared his throat and shifted his eyes away from mine. "I think we should split up right here. We can move faster if you take this bus back to your apartment while I head over to Ghostville on

223

the next bus. We've both got our phones so we can stay in touch."

By that time of day, the city was alive as everyone bustled to wherever it is busy people bustle off to every day. The sun shone down and everything seemed completely harmless in the light of day. "That's probably a good idea," I agreed. "But *please* be careful."

"I will. You, too. Call me if anything—*anything*—seems off."

I climbed onto the bus and sat down near a window that faced the sidewalk where Daniel stood. He waved as the bus started to pull away. I stuck my hand up in response. "Stop!" I screamed as a sudden thought hit me. I jumped up from my seat and pushed my way down the aisle. "You have to stop! I have to get off. It's an emergency!" All eyes were on me.

The driver glared at me through the rearview mirror, but didn't bother to turn around. "Sorry. I'm already moving. You'll have to get off at the next stop," he said curtly.

"But you haven't even completely pulled away yet." I pointed to the sidewalk outside the bus.

He pushed on the gas again and then glanced over his shoulder at me. "Now I have."

"Thanks for nothing," I muttered as I walked back to my seat. Someone had filled it in my absence and I was forced to stand instead, holding onto one of the straps hanging from the ceiling of the bus.

I could see Daniel standing on the sidewalk with his hands and shoulders raised in a questioning way as the distance between us grew. He had to have seen my run up the aisle. I pulled out my phone and called him. "Change of plans," I said as soon as I heard his voice.

"*Already?*"

"Yes. We might not have any power to stop Church from finding out that Revere was one of the spies, but we can stop him from getting Revere's watch." I kept my voice low, hoping that none of the

224

passengers on the bus were listening. Or worse, that any of the passengers were ghosts. "As soon as he reads that excerpt from my notebook, he'll send someone to get it."

"*Let me get this straight. You want me to break in and steal Paul Revere's pocket watch from a museum dedicated to him.*"

"Yes."

"*J, that's crazy!*"

"Is it? Maybe. But if you don't do it, Church will. Who do you think would take better care of the watch and give it the respect it deserves? Who would make sure it eventually got put back in the museum? You or him?" I hoped to appeal to his love for Revere.

Daniel didn't say anything.

"Listen, Daniel. We saw it there the other day which means Church hasn't figured out that Paul was one of the five yet. As soon as he reads my notebook, he's going to head straight to the museum. We're wasting time. When you're extricated, I'll make sure the museum gets the watch back." *Of course, I'll have to find a way to do it without them thinking I broke in and stole it.* "If you go now, you can be in and out of the building before it even opens for the day."

That was the clincher.

"*Alright, alright. I'm going. Pray for me.*" Daniel hung up and I smiled to myself. Soon, we might just have the upper hand on Dr. Benjamin Church.

My phone rang just as I stepped off the bus at the stop closest to my apartment complex. Caller ID told me my mom must have found my note. "Hello?" I said.

"*Jamie? Where are you? I can't believe you left in the middle of the night,*" Mom said.

"I'm standing right outside the building. I'll be up there in a

225

minute." I hung up the phone without giving her the chance to respond. Her attempts to parent me were getting on my nerves. She gave up that right when she walked out on Dad and me a decade before. I'd gained a lot of respect for her since we'd been in Boston together, but it felt more like a mutual friendship than a mother/daughter relationship. I knew I was probably in the wrong, and I needed to change my ways, but I'd save that for another day.

I rode the elevator up to the fifth floor and took a deep breath before I opened the door. Whatever she said to me, I needed to stay calm. "I'm back," I called as I entered.

Mom, Portia, and Steven sat at the table eating what looked to be omelets. Mom jumped up from the table as soon as she saw me. "Why would you leave without telling me?"

"You were asleep. And I knew you weren't feeling good," I said. "And besides that, I was with Daniel. What better bodyguard can I have against one ghost than another ghost?"

Mom's shoulders relaxed and she sat back down. "Next time, just wake me up and tell me you're leaving. I'd rather you do that than leave a note." She put another bite of eggs in her mouth.

That's it? That's all she's going to say? Maybe she doesn't care.

Steven cleared his throat. "Did you find Myles?"

"Uh huh."

"Any luck with him?"

"He'd already delivered the notebook to Church before we got to his apartment. By now, Church knows everything we know about Daniel and the watches."

"Speaking of Daniel," Portia said. "Where is he?"

I sat on one of the barstools and explained everything that happened to the rest of the group, ending with an explanation of why I returned alone.

"Poor Daniel," Portia said. "He's not the kind of ghost who steals."

"We didn't have a choice," I protested.

"Maybe not, but it's still against the law. I'm sure it bothers him."

"I feel guilty for asking him to do it," I admitted.

My phone rang and I answered it. "Daniel?"

"It's me."

"Did you get it or were we too late?"

"I got it."

He sounded distant—not quite like himself. "Are you okay?"

"I feel like a criminal."

"You used to be a spy. Just think of this as another mission."

"Yeah, but I never stole anything."

"You stole information."

"Not funny."

I stepped into the hallway so I could continue our conversation without all the ears in my apartment. "Don't beat yourself up over this. You knew Paul well. What would he have done in this situation?" I asked. "I've never met him, but I bet he would steal a watch to keep it from a traitor."

"I know you're right, but I still feel bad. I'm headed home right now. We can take Paul's watch apart and see if it has a code. If it does, we can start trying to crack the two pieces."

"I'll be here. See you in a bit." I couldn't wait for him to get back. I don't know if it was the soul saver connection or my real feelings for him, but I hated every minute he wasn't with me.

"Actually, you probably won't be here when he gets back."

I started to open my apartment door, but let go of the handle and whirled around at the sound of the unfamiliar voice behind me. "Who are you?"

"I'm the guy you've been trying to avoid."

"Benjamin Church," I whispered.

The man—ghost—in front of me smiled and nodded once. He had a round face with a longish nose. He didn't look anything like the

227

paintings I'd seen of him online. Of course, the paintings depicted him in colonial clothing and powdered wigs. I'd pictured him older, too. I knew I couldn't run from him—I mean, the guy could walk through walls—but I still wanted to get somewhere where I wasn't alone with him.

I whirled around to grab the handle to my door, but another ghost appeared behind me, blocking my way. My heart threatened to burst from my chest from its incessant pounding. I took a deep breath and forced myself to look menacing. I'm sure it wasn't very effective. I dropped my hands to my sides and clenched them into fists, hoping their trembling wouldn't be as noticeable. "What do you want from me?" I hissed.

"Do you have the watch?"

The amused look on Church's face annoyed me. "No."

"I didn't think you would. Daniel's smarter than that." He took a step toward me. I wanted to take a step back, but that would have put me closer to the creep blocking my rear side. "Unfortunately, he wasn't smarter than me. My sources told me he found a soul saver. A girl he spends all his time with these days. Too bad he chose *this* morning to leave you alone. I can't very well take a ghost, but I can take a girl."

My heart pounded so hard my chest ached, and I reached for the wall to keep myself from falling over when my knees started to shake. I opened my mouth to scream, but the man behind me covered my mouth with his hand before any sound came out.

And then everything went black.

Chapter 25

I woke up in an unknown dark space. My head hurt and my stomach churned. *Did they drug me?* As my mind slowly started to clear, I tried to take in as much of my surroundings as I could.

My hands were tied together behind my back and wherever I was, I didn't have enough room to stretch my legs out from their curled position. Church and his thug had stuck something over my mouth—probably duct tape. My stomach flip flopped at the realization that I couldn't speak or move. I forced myself to calm down. Puking with my mouth covered would kill me.

When the waves of nausea finally cleared, I went back to my surroundings inventory. Judging by the vibrations below me and the sounds around me, I was in a moving vehicle of some sort, probably a trunk. I sniffed the air. It smelled of rubber and oil. Yep. Definitely a trunk.

I don't know how long we drove, or how long we'd driven before I woke up, but every second felt like an eternity. The vehicle mercifully came to a stop and I heard car doors slam. I kicked at the sides of my prison, hoping that if we'd stopped in a public place, someone would hear me and come to my rescue. The top of the

229

trunk popped open. I squinted against the light coming from a single bulb dangling from the ceiling of a large room.

"Look who woke up," Church said, leaning over me. "Haul her out of there, boys."

Two men, the one from back at my apartment and another I didn't recognize, grabbed me by the armpits and pulled me out of the trunk. I turned my head in all directions, trying to get an immediate feel of my new surroundings. We were in a warehouse of some sort. A table littered with rusty tools was shoved up against one wall while an old leather couch sat directly across from it. Another door on the opposite end of the room, slightly ajar, led to some unknown place. I hoped for a bathroom. The men propelled me forward and shoved me onto the couch. Church pushed a button on the wall and the floor-to-ceiling garage door descended, locking us in. My only hope at escape would be the man door next to the garage door . . . if it happened to be unlocked.

"You can take the tape off her now. No one will hear her all the way out here," Church ordered.

I pretended the news didn't bother me, but in reality, it scared me to death. If no one could hear me, was I so far out of the city that I'd be lost even if I did manage to escape?

Thug Number One stepped forward and gripped the duct tape covering my mouth. He yanked it off in one swipe, jerking my head back as he did so. It hurt—a lot. I bit my lip and kept my emotions pushed down inside my chest.

"I think I'll text your boyfriend to let him know where you are and what we want. Then, all we have to do is wait," Church said. "As soon as your boyfriend delivers his watch, I'll let you go. Or maybe not. Maybe you'll have value for a while longer. Or better yet, I'll save myself the trouble of returning you and just drop you in the ocean."

"If that's your plan, you might as well kill me now and save yourself some time," I said. "Daniel's not going to give up his watch."

Church crossed the room toward the couch, keeping his eyes on me the entire time. I tried to concentrate on the sound of his shoes scraping against the cement floor rather than his piercing stare. When he arrived at the couch, he leaned in, his face just inches from mine. "*You* might think the watch is the most important thing to him, but *I* think you underestimate the power of your femininity."

"Excuse me?" I fought the urge to kick him in the groin as he leaned over me. There was no way I could take on three ghosts by myself.

"If my sources are correct, Daniel's got a thing for you. Besides that, he's faithful. He always does the right thing."

"Your sources?"

Church stepped back and my chance at kicking him floated away. "I believe you know one of them. Does the name Myles Westing ring a bell?"

I clenched my jaw. "The man's a weasel. I wouldn't trust him if I were you."

Church threw his head back and laughed. "It's me he shouldn't trust. He thinks I'm going to share my bounty with him."

"Why do you want the watch so much anyway? Is it really worth that much? I hate to tell you this, but it doesn't even work anymore." I hoped to keep him talking while I came up with an escape plan. Up to that point, I had zero ideas.

"I'm not stupid and despite your obvious youth, I don't think you are either."

"What's that supposed to mean?"

"You know why I want the watch."

"I *really* don't know why." I had an *idea* . . . but I didn't know all the details.

Church leaned back and rested against the side of the car still parked in the middle of the warehouse. He crossed his arms over his

231

chest and looked at me. "I need Avery's piece of the code."

I raised my eyebrows and feigned surprise. "Code? I don't know anything about a code. That doesn't even make any sense." I think it worked.

Church raised his eyebrows. "You mean to tell me Avery didn't tell his precious soul saver about the code in his watch?"

"Oh, I get it. You mean the engraving. I've seen that. It says Daniel Avery—1775."

Church exchanged looks with his men. "If Daniel doesn't know about the code, what makes you so sure he wouldn't give up the watch in exchange for you?"

Good point. "Because it was a gift from General Washington, one of the greatest men to ever live. Why would he give it up to someone who betrayed their fellow countrymen?"

Church glared at me. "Washington was a joke. Think of how many men died in that war because everyone was too selfish to pay their dues to the crown."

My mouth dropped open. "You've been around for hundreds of years and you're telling me you don't think the United States of America is better off than it was under British rule?" *Am I seriously debating history with a ghost?*

Church's expression didn't change. "Name one thing wrong with the current Great Britain."

I didn't expect that question. My mouth opened automatically to respond but I didn't have an answer so I closed it again. Even Daniel admitted he liked visiting England. My mind whirled, trying to come up with another response, but we were interrupted by a ringing phone somewhere in the warehouse. One of the thugs pulled a cell phone from his pocket and looked at the ID. "It's him, Ben."

Him? Do they mean Daniel? I desperately wanted to see him, but I didn't want him giving up the one thing we had going for us in our quest for his extrication.

Church grabbed the phone from the man and answered it. "Did you get it?" Church listened to the voice on the other end of the line. His face turned an angry shade of gray and he slammed his fist into the side of the car, cursing into the phone. I cringed at the string of expletives coming from his mouth.

He put the phone back to his ear. In a quiet voice that somehow seemed scarier than his real voice, he uttered, "Find it, or so help me, you'll lose everything." He tossed the phone to the man who'd originally handed it to him and began pacing the room. I avoided making eye contact with him and instead focused on an oil stain on the cement floor. The longer Church paced, the more nervous I became. When he came to an abrupt stop and turned in my direction, I kept my eyes down. I could see his feet moving toward me and hear the scrape of his shoes on the ground. "Look at me," he hissed.

I didn't obey.

"I said look at me!" He grabbed me by the chin, his sharp fingers digging into the sides of my face and forced my head up. My heart pounded a rhythm I didn't recognize. "I'm going to give you one chance to be honest with me. Where's the watch?"

Didn't we just go over this? "I told you, Daniel isn't going to—"

His fingers tightened on my chin, making it hard to breathe as he cut my words off. "I'm not talking about Avery's watch. I'm talking about Revere's. The one you wrote about in that notebook."

"I don't have that watch. I've never even touched it." *And that really is the truth.*

Church let go of my face, shoving my head into the back of the couch in the process. I wanted to rub some of the soreness out of my jaw, but I couldn't with my hands still tied behind my back. He walked to the car, opened the passenger side door, and began rummaging around. His body blocked my view of his actions, but when he turned around he held my notebook in his hands—the

233

notebook Myles stole for him. He flipped through the pages and then stopped. "Is this not your notebook and your handwriting?"

I shrugged.

"Let me read what you've written on this page." Church tapped the notebook with his long index finger. He cleared his throat and began to read. "Known spies are Daniel Avery, Benjamin Church, Matthew Heinrichsen, and Paul Revere. Fifth man is still unknown." He paused and looked up at me. "Do we agree that you wrote that?"

I still didn't say anything.

Church continued. "Next to each name you were kind enough to write the location of each watch. Daniel Avery: In owner's possession. Benjamin Church: Presumed in owner's possession. Matthew Heinrichsen: Heinrichsen family collection, current owner unknown. Paul Revere: Paul Revere House, upstairs bedroom." He closed the notebook and tossed it onto the hood of the car. "Now, what was that you said about not knowing where Revere's watch is?"

I swallowed hard, my mind racing. "I know where the watch is, but I don't have it. We saw it in an upstairs room at the Paul Revere House. You didn't expect us to *steal* it did you?" He'd already mentioned that Daniel was faithful and honest. Encouraging that line of thinking might be the best thing to do.

"Funny . . . because one of my guys just left the museum and guess what? The watch isn't there anymore. I wonder where it went." Church returned to the couch, his imposing body invaded my personal space. Even though my heart beat faster, the adrenaline building up inside begged me to lash out.

I closed my eyes and took a deep breath before answering. "Have you tried checking with your source? You know, Myles Westing? The guy that knew about the watches? I'm telling you, he can't be trusted. How long before he's blackmailing you for Revere's watch?" I didn't mind throwing Myles under the bus. In fact, I almost grinned when the idea came to me to put the blame on him.

Church stood up straight and motioned toward Thug Number Two, the one who hadn't been with the other two when they kidnapped me. He must have been guarding the warehouse or driving the getaway car. "Heston, come with me. We're going to get Revere's watch. Dunn, you guard the princess."

Without another glance in my direction, Heston and Church jumped into the car and peeled out of the warehouse. The large mechanical door came down from the ceiling again and closed me in with the man called Dunn. I didn't appreciate the way he looked at me, his eyes lingering longer than necessary. I leaned back against the cushions of the couch and turned away from him.

"How'd you find out about ghosts?" Dunn asked. He had a gruff voice that rattled when he spoke.

"I'm a soul saver. I thought your boss already established that," I answered.

"You're kind of young for that, aren't you?"

"Age has nothing to do with it."

He stopped talking for a moment, drumming his fingers on his thigh, but then he cleared his throat and asked, "How does one go about getting extricated?"

With that question, I finally looked up, meeting his eyes. If the man was interested in being extricated, it might be motivation to let me go. "It's not that hard really, if you know the right people to help you," I lied. Extrication was *not* easy—as I'd learned more than once.

"Can all ghosts be extricated?"

"Of course!" Another lie. For all I knew, the keys to some ghosts' extrications were long gone and they were stuck on earth forever.

"Huh."

I could see from his expression that Dunn was giving some serious thought to the subject. "Why are you helping Church?" I asked.

"Everyone I cared about in life is gone. It doesn't matter what I do now. Besides, I need the money." Dunn's openness surprised me.

"You're a ghost. Can't you just take what you need?"

Dunn shuffled his feet on the dirty floor and played with a wrench he picked up off the table. "Not all ghosts are thieves."

"Meaning . . . you're not a thief."

He gave a small nod.

"Let me get this straight. You're not a thief, but you willingly kidnap innocent teenage girls?"

Dunn glared at me. "Church did that. Not me."

"But you're the one still holding me here." *I might be getting through to him!*

Dunn continued to stare at me.

"Just let me go. You can tell him I tricked you, or I managed to get my hands apart, or whatever. I'm sure you're smart enough to think of something convincing."

Dunn stared at me for an eternity before responding. "Sorry. I can't. He'll make my already pathetic life even more miserable."

"Can you at least untie me? I need to use the bathroom. I promise I won't run." *For at least a few seconds.*

Dunn pushed himself up from his chair and walked toward me. *Did I really just talk him into letting me go?*

He grabbed me by the shoulders and hauled me off the couch. Turning me around, he began loosening the rope around my wrists.

"Thanks for doing this," I said.

"Don't get too excited. I'm not a fool. You have one minute." He shoved me into the small bathroom and pulled the door shut. Seeing the nasty toilet, I knew I'd be okay for a while longer. I turned in a circle, trying to find something useful. The only thing in the room besides the toilet was a dirty pedestal sink with an incessant drip. There wasn't even a mirror. *So much for breaking off a piece of the glass like they do in the movies.* Bathroom escape? Fail.

When I emerged, Dunn tossed the rope previously attached to

my wrists to the side and dragged me to the table cluttered with tools. I struggled to stay on my feet. He rummaged around the table before producing a pair of handcuffs. The key to unlock them rested inside the lock. He placed one cuff around my wrist and then dragged me back to the couch, clamping the other cuff around one of the pipes behind the couch. I saw him toss the key onto the table across the room.

Smart, Jamie. You might have been able to get out of the ropes on your own, but there's no way you're picking the lock off the handcuffs. At least I could move around a little more since only one arm was cuffed. I rubbed my wrists as best I could, trying to relieve some of the soreness the rope had caused.

Time dragged while Church and Heston were gone. I considered letting myself fall asleep, but I wanted to be awake in case an opportunity to escape appeared. When the heavy garage door rose again, I sat up straight on the couch. Would Daniel be with them?

"Any luck, Ben?" Dunn asked when Church emerged from the driver's side door.

Church slammed the door and shook his head. "Westing denies having Revere's watch."

"Was he telling the truth?"

"He kept slipping into ghost form, but we roughed him up enough when he was visible that I think he would have caved if he really did have it."

"And we scared him enough that he won't be coming around asking for his share of the pot, either," Heston sneered.

"Are the watches really worth that much?" I said.

The men turned quickly, remembering I was there.

"The watches are irrelevant. It's the codes I told you about that are important. That's where the real money will be."

Church's phone rang and he looked down at the screen. "Your boyfriend's calling."

Daniel! My heart leaped and I sat as far forward on the couch as I could, hoping to catch more of the conversation.

"Are you ready to make a trade? Your watch for the girl?" Church said into the phone. I couldn't hear Daniel's response through the phone and had to guess what was being said by watching Church's facial expressions. He listened intently for a minute, mumbling into the mouthpiece now and then, before turning and looking right at me. With a roll of his eyes, he pressed the speaker phone and motioned to me. "Say something, girl. He wants proof you're alive."

"Jamie? Are you there? Are you okay?"

I almost cried when I heard Daniel's voice and I didn't feel quite so alone. Scooting to the edge of the couch, as far as the handcuffs would let me go, I yelled into the phone. "Daniel! Don't give them your watch! It's not worth it! You've got to find Revere's watch, too. Someone stole it from the museum and you've got to find it before Church does!" I yelled the words as fast as I could, trying to get as much information as possible passed to Daniel before Church decided I'd said enough. When I came up for a breath, Church yanked the phone away and shoved me against the back of the couch. My head hit the pipe my hand was cuffed to. Instead of cringing or rubbing my head, I smiled at him.

Church turned the speaker off and put the phone back to his ear. He turned away from me and muttered into the phone. I strained to hear him, but couldn't quite make out the words. Before he ended the conversation, he turned back and looked at me one more time, making sure he had my full attention before saying, "You have one hour to be here with your watch or the girl is history. Understand?"

Chapter 26

When I'm in the process of saving a soul, it's almost as if my mind and my body aren't my own anymore. Something about the power of my connection to the ghosts makes me feel as if I would do anything to help them, including sacrifice my own life for their freedom. I'd heard of parents throwing themselves in front of buses or jumping into flood waters to try to save their children, knowing that they'd most likely not survive the event. My dad had told me many times that he'd do anything for me. I never doubted his sincerity. As I sat in the warehouse, handcuffed to a pole, my thoughts were only of Daniel's safety. My own mortality never crossed my mind.

Even though I'd insisted to Church that Daniel wouldn't give up the watch for me, I knew it wasn't true. He *would* come and he would do whatever he thought necessary to get me out of the situation. Daniel was good.

Church, Dunn, and Heston leaned against the car, playing a game of cards on the hood while they waited for Daniel's arrival. My eyes took in every inch of the warehouse, hoping to find something useful. Other than the couch, the table littered with tools, and the insignificant bathroom, the only thing that broke up the monotony of the room was a small window on the far side of the room above the table. The glass didn't look as if it had ever been cleaned. Though flimsy, and probably easy to break, the hole wouldn't be big enough for me to fit through . . . *if* I managed to get out of the handcuffs and across the room without anyone noticing. If I made it that far, I might as well just run out the door. As far as I knew, it wasn't locked.

The window opened from the bottom up. Dunn had raised it earlier, just enough to get a small breeze coming through the room. My limited glimpse of the outside world showed that the sun was beginning to set. I'd been in Church's grasp for an entire day. The diminishing light cast shadows around the room, making everything more deceiving than it had been earlier.

Time crawled and I found myself thinking of Juliet waiting for her Romeo. Lines from the play we'd read in freshman English coursed through my brain. *"So tedious is this day as is the night before some festival to an impatient child who hath new robes and may not wear them."* Shakespeare knew what he was writing about. I decided to give in and take a nap when an out-of-place movement across the room caught my eye. I gasped when I thought I saw a face peering through the window.

"What's wrong with you now?" Heston barked at me.

"I . . . I . . . saw a spider crawling across the floor. It was big and hairy and—"

"Where'd it go?" Heston snickered. "You can have it for your dinner. If your boyfriend doesn't show up soon, it'll be your last meal." He grinned and looked to his companions, probably hoping they'd laugh at his sense of humor. They didn't take the bait.

My stomach growled at the mention of food, but I pushed my hunger from my mind. I glanced at the window again. With the low light I couldn't be positive, but I was pretty sure a face was still there. Whoever the face belonged to put a finger to their lips. They didn't need to worry, though. I had no intention of giving them away. *Who is it? It can't be Daniel. He wouldn't risk the other ghosts seeing his aura.*

Did the person belonging to the shadowy face come to rescue me, or was it just a coincidence? I'd been shown many times that summer that coincidences are rare. Fate does things on purpose. I might as well give the nameless face a little help. "Hey! Speaking of dinner, when do I get to eat? I'm starving. You guys have kept me locked up here all day and you haven't given me anything to eat. Even prisoners of the state get more food than that." All three men turned and stared at me, scowling. I pretended to meet their eyes, but really my attention was directed at the face in the window, just past them. I took a deep breath. *Please let this work.* "I saw Dunn put the handcuff keys on the table over there. Can't you at least unlock me so I can put my arm down? I'm not going anywhere. I promise."

"Nice try, girl," Church said. "The sooner your boyfriend gets here, the sooner you can go . . . or not."

My idea worked. Before Church even finished speaking, a hand slithered through the window, feeling around on the table for the keys. My mind raced, trying to think of another way to help whoever the hand belonged to.

"I think I *left*," I enunciated the word, "my wallet at home. I hope Daniel has money for bus fare." I tried not to smile as the hand moved to the left on the table.

Church looked at me with a confused stare. "That's what you're worried about right now? If I were you, I'd be more concerned about what's going to happen if your boyfriend doesn't show up soon."

I shrugged. "It might be a little *forward*, but I like to be prepared." The hand moved forward, managing to grab the keys. "Yes!" I squealed.

Church gave me another confused look, but turned his attention back to the card game on the hood without saying anything else.

The hand slowly lifted the small ring of keys from the table, but they clanked together as they rose. My mouth dropped open as all three heads started to turn toward the window as if operated by one unseen being. There was only one thing I could think to do.

I screamed.

It worked. All eyes turned to me instead of the window. "What is *wrong* with you?" Heston demanded. He stomped toward the couch and glared at me.

"I saw the spider again. It ran in front of me."

Heston stuck his face next to mine. "Yeah? Well, maybe we should blindfold you. Then you won't be seeing anything. There could be spiders crawling all over you and you'd never even know it."

"Stop messing with the girl and get over here," Church yelled. "You're not scaring anyone and it's your turn."

Heston growled at me one more time and then returned to the card game. He didn't make it all the way through his next turn before a sharp knock sounded on the warehouse door.

Daniel! I desperately wanted to see him and my heart pounded as I waited for Dunn to open the door. The burning in my chest only increased when I saw Daniel's face, and a small whimper escaped my throat. His eyes fell on me immediately and he crossed the room in three giant strides.

He grabbed my free hand as he fell to his knees in front of me. "J, I'm so sorry. I had no idea they'd do something like this. I've been so worried about you all day. Did they hurt you? Are you okay?"

I took my time responding. Tears had sprung to my eyes and I didn't want Daniel to hear my voice crack. "It's okay. They didn't hurt me." *At least not very much.*

"Did you bring the watch? She doesn't leave with you unless I've got it in my hand." Church's voice broke up our joyous reunion.

Daniel rose and turned to face the man who was the ultimate cause of his death. He clenched and unclenched his fists at his side.

242

"It's been well over two hundred years since I've seen you. And you know what?" Daniel took a step toward the traitor. Church didn't respond, but then, I don't think Daniel expected a response. "I still can't figure out why you would betray your friends, your neighbors, your land. Were you bribed? Was it blackmail? Please make me understand." Daniel sat down on the couch next to me and pulled me close. I leaned into his side, relishing the comfort of his nearness.

Church crossed his arms over his chest and leaned back against the car. "You make it sound like it was a simple decision. Believe me, it wasn't something I did without giving it a lot of thought. I knew I'd be going against my friends and neighbors, but they—*you*—had it all wrong. We should have never broken off to form our own country. I did what I believed was best, and you did what you believed was best. You can't judge a man for following his convictions."

Daniel shrugged. "I can judge whoever I want."

"Not everything is as one-sided as you think, Avery."

Daniel changed the subject. "Did you really die in a shipwreck? And where have you been all these years?"

Church walked over to the table and grabbed one of the rusty folding chairs leaning against it. The chair creaked when he sat down and I found myself wishing it would cave in on him. "Nope. That's the beauty of it all. There were a lot more people on my side—our side— than anyone ever knew about. My banishment from the colonies was actually my ticket to freedom. Mine and the others banished with me, that is. Our boat never arrived at its destination, but that doesn't mean we were all destroyed in some tragic shipwreck. Some of us lived for another decade before we passed. England welcomed us with open arms. After all, we'd dedicated our lives in service to her."

"So why, after all these years, do you want my watch? What significance could *my* pocket watch possibly have for you?"

"I'm surprised you haven't figured it out yet. I thought you were smarter than that, Avery. As I told your soul saver earlier, it's not the

243

watch I care about, but the code it contains."

"Code?"

"Give me the watch and I'll show you."

Daniel looked at me and then reached for his pocket.

"No!" I grabbed Daniel's arm. "You can't give it to him. It'll ruin your chances of extrication. I can *feel* it."

Daniel placed one palm on my cheek and I leaned into his touch. "Shh. It'll be okay. I'd rather stay here forever than have something bad happen to you," he whispered.

He stood from the couch and lifted my free hand with both of his, brushing it softly with his lips. "We've got this under control," he whispered. Before letting go of my hand, he pressed something into my palm. I waited until he joined Church and his men by the car to look at what I held.

The keys to the handcuffs.

That was his hand that came through the window? How did the other ghosts in the room not see his aura?

"You want it? Here you go," Daniel hissed. I looked up just in time to see him toss his watch to Church. I cringed when the doctor grabbed it from the air, a glint of pure evil in his eyes. "It's all yours. Let Jamie go and you won't have to worry about us anymore. We'll leave peacefully."

"Not so fast," Church said. "Don't you want to know why I've been hunting these things down?"

Daniel hesitated, looking briefly at me. "The thought *has* crossed my mind."

Church held Daniel's watch up to the overhead lights. "It's a thing of beauty, really."

Daniel's watch had been completely put back together. That must have been why it took him so long to come to my rescue. He must have spent the entire day trying to fix the thing in order to maintain our innocence. If Church didn't know that we knew about the code, our chances of getting away unharmed were much higher.

"I didn't know about the secret behind the watches at first," Church continued. "In fact, it was only by accident that I found out it was more than just a sentimental gift."

"Oh?" Daniel continued his fake naivety.

"Yes. You see, after I died, I lost track of my watch. Later, when I'd been dead long enough to figure out how to make myself visible to mortals, I tracked some of my stuff down and reclaimed it. The watch was among some of my personal effects that had been doled out to a friend." Church dangled Daniel's watch from his fingers by the chain. It swung back and forth, mesmerizing me like a pendulum. "Fifty years after I got it back, I dropped it. Like this." Church took Daniel's watch and hurled it at the cement floor.

"No!" I heard myself yell. *All that hard work for nothing.*

Daniel didn't show any emotion. "You wanted my watch just so you could destroy it? How extremely honorable of you."

Church bent down and retrieved the casing from the pile of broken pieces littering the floor. "It's the engravings I want. See? Daniel Avery—1775. But on the other side? History speaks to us." Church leaned closer to Daniel and showed him the casing.

Daniel raised his eyebrows and opened his mouth, pretending to see the code for the first time. His acting skills were much better than mine. "What does it mean?" he asked.

"It means our dear friend General Washington left us all a message."

"Do you know how to read it?" Daniel asked excitedly, adding to his pretend innocence.

I realized then that I still held the keys to the handcuffs. All eyes in the room were on Church and the watch. I quickly inserted the key into the cuff attached to the pipe and slid my hand out. I left my hand draped over the couch so my freedom wouldn't be as noticeable if someone glanced at me. I didn't want to risk running

245

until Daniel managed to get his watch back.

"The code can't be completely solved unless we have all the watches together," Church explained. "Part of the key to solving it is on each watch."

"Do you have any idea what solving it means?" Daniel asked.

Church leaned back in the chair and it creaked again. "Washington, the old fool, trusted me completely. He confided in me that he would be hiding a stash of munitions and valuables so they wouldn't fall into British hands. He gave me my watch and thanked me for being a loyal friend. Three days later, you blew my cover."

"And I've never regretted it for a day."

"You know what I think?"

Daniel shrugged.

"I think the codes on these watches lead to the hiding place of Washington's treasure."

Daniel laughed out loud. "Don't tell me you honestly believe the valuables are still hidden. If the code on the watches really led to the cache, I guarantee Washington moved them the moment he found out about your deception."

"Not if he didn't know where the cache was to begin with."

Daniel raised his eyebrows. "You're telling me you think Washington couldn't remember where he hid his stuff?"

"No. I'm telling you he never knew in the first place."

Chapter 27

Explain yourself," Daniel demanded after hearing Church's theory that Washington didn't know where the valuables were hidden.

"When Washington told me he'd be hiding everything, he also said he planned to do it in a way that would prevent it from being stolen by someone who knew its location. He didn't let me in on all the details, but he said he came up with a plan to have someone else unknowingly bury it and note the location's coordinates. The coordinates were given to him in a sealed envelope. Washington passed the envelope to a separate and impartial person and had them divide the coordinates into six pieces. That person wrote a code around those six pieces. At the time Washington was telling me this, I didn't understand that he'd just passed me a piece of those coordinates. Believe me, if I'd known I would have immediately set out to solve it. As it so happened, you turned me in and I completely forgot about the coded treasure until I broke my watch decades later."

Daniel no longer needed to fake his surprise and shock. "You *really* think Washington's treasures are still hidden?"

"Of course. If they'd ever been found, don't you think it would have made the news. I did my research. No mysterious caches of munitions or valuables dating to the time of the war have ever been uncovered. At least, nothing worth mentioning."

"How do you know the person who wrote the code, or the person who buried the valuables, weren't traitors like you?" Daniel demanded.

"Call it intuition. Washington wasn't a fool in everything. I'm sure he knew to cover his tracks with those men."

Valuables hidden by Washington himself? I couldn't wrap my brain around it. Finding something like that would be priceless. But something Church said earlier kept nagging at me. "Wait a second," I said, carefully keeping my freed arm on the couch next to the handcuffs. "You said Washington divided the coordinates into six pieces. I thought there were only five spies in your little group?"

"You've done your homework," Church said. "There *were* only five spies. Washington couldn't completely relinquish control over the cache. He kept one of the code pieces for himself. If he wanted to dig up the valuables, he just had to gather his spies and he'd have all the information he needed. Unfortunately for him, he didn't know how fast his spy ring would fall to pieces. Lucky for him, he learned to hone his methods and it helped him win his war."

"You've got your watch and now Daniel's watch. Do you have others?" I asked, hoping we were ahead of him.

A slow smile spread across Church's face. "I've been at this for a while." He opened the trunk of the car and returned to Daniel's side with a small lock box.

I was in the trunk with the watches the whole time? I was so close!

Church pulled a chain out from beneath the collar of his shirt. A single silver key dangled from the end of it and he used it to open the case. "Here's my watch, casing only of course." He pulled it from the box and held it up for Daniel to see, but not close enough for him to grab it. "And here's Matthew Heinrichsen's watch. You didn't know about him before the other day, did you?"

Daniel shook his head.

"Heinrichsen. Matthew Heinrichsen," Church answered. "When I figured out that he was one of the five, I easily got if from his family's collection. They didn't even have it protected."

"So there's you, me, Washington, this Heinrichsen guy...and...?" Daniel said.

"And your dearest pal of all, Mr. Paul Revere himself.'"

Daniel shook his head back and forth. "Jamie wrote his name in the notebook just as an idea of someone to look into."

"Nice try. Jamie also wrote in the notebook that you'd already found his watch in his museum."

"I worked for him during my time as a spy and he never gave anything away about being one himself," Daniel said. "Wouldn't I notice if he was spying at the same time that I was?"

"Not if he was a good spy. I think he was one of Washington's better men."

"That makes five known watch recipients. If neither of us knows who the sixth watch was given to, how do you expect to crack the code?"

Church laughed and stuck his hand into the case again. He pulled out another watch and stuck it in Daniel's face. "Who said I didn't know who had the other watch?"

My heart fell. Church had five of the six watches. I only hoped Daniel hid Paul Revere's watch somewhere it couldn't be found.

"I think this person was the most surprising spy. To me, at least," Church said. "This watch belonged to Lydia Canterman."

"A *woman*?" I gasped.

Church nodded. "No one expected a woman. It was the perfect cover. Lydia was—"

"—one of the serving girls at the Green Dragon Tavern," Daniel said, finishing Church's sentence. "We used to have meetings there. I had no idea she was involved."

"It surprised me too, Avery." Church dropped the watch into the box and locked it with his key. "I think it's time for you to go now."

"Not so fast. I want to make a deal first."

I jerked my head up at Daniel's words. *What does he think he's doing?*

Church nodded. "I see. You find out that your watch has more than sentimental value and all of a sudden you're interested. Well, guess what?" Church sneered. "I don't make deals."

"How do you plan to solve the code once you have all the watches?"

"It might take a while, but . . . I'm not going anywhere anytime soon. I've been studying the art of codes and methods used back then. I just need that last watch of Revere's."

"Let me help you solve the code and I won't take anything from the cache. You can have everything."

Heston snickered on the other side of the car. Church glared at him and he quieted immediately. "You expect me to believe that you don't want anything out of this?" Church asked.

"I do want something," Daniel said quietly. "I want to be extricated. I honestly believe I just have to be part of solving the code and then I'll extricate. I won't even be around to claim any of the so-called treasure."

Church tilted his head and stared intently at him. Daniel held his ground, meeting Church's gaze and returning it. The only sound that could be heard was the dripping faucet in the bathroom on the far side of the room. My heart beat in rhythm with the sound.

Please say yes. We can't lose access to those watches.

"I already told you," Church said. "I don't make deals. Not—"

"Aaaggghhh!" An ear-splitting scream filled the warehouse,

echoing off each wall.

I jumped off the couch, forgetting to pretend I still wore handcuffs. It didn't matter, though. The attention wasn't on me. My eyes darted to the window again and that time I knew for sure that my mind hadn't invented a face. Church stomped across the room and threw open the door to the warehouse. An arm came through, swinging a tire iron. Surprised, Church jumped back, but not in time to dodge the weapon. The metal connected with his head and he fell backward onto the concrete, bleeding from a gash in his forehead.

My mouth dropped. "Steven?"

"Jamie! Look out!" Daniel yelled.

My head came up just in time to see Heston lunging for me. I jumped to the side and he crashed headfirst into the edge of the couch instead. My size had its advantages. From my vantage point, I couldn't see Church. I had no idea which form he was in.

"Jamie, where are you?" Steven called from the other side of the car. "I knocked him out, but as soon as he comes to, he'll switch into ghost mode and heal. We've got to hurry."

I tried to run in the direction of Steven's voice, but Dunn blocked my way. Daniel jumped between us and swung his fist. Dunn changed into ghost form long before the punch reached him and Daniel followed suit. I lost track of both of them.

"I really need to find something that allows me to see ghosts," I muttered, crouching by the side of the couch.

"Jamie?" a high-pitched voice called.

"Mom!" I'd never been more excited to see her. "How did you know where I was?"

"Daniel brought us with him. We've got to get out of here." She grabbed my arm and pulled me toward the door just as Heston got to his feet.

A vein in his forehead pulsed as he dove for me again, grabbing onto my arm. With Mom pulling on me from one side and Heston on the other, I felt like the rope in a tug-of-war. Both arms were occupied so I used the next best thing I had. I brought my knee up and shoved it into Heston's gut as hard as I could. He lost his grip on my arm as he stopped to clutch at his middle. The split second it took him to go invisible and then return to human form was all Mom and I needed to make our getaway.

As we rounded the car, I saw Church's legs poking out from behind it. He moaned and moved around. We only had seconds before he'd heal himself.

"This way!" Steven called.

Mom jumped over Church's body and ran for the door Steven held open. I jumped, but not in time. Church grabbed my leg as I rose over his body and pulled down. I crashed to the ground, hitting my head on the cement. The room moved in circles and I fought to keep from throwing up. Church shot to his feet and stood over me, a long knife in his hand. I closed my eyes, hoping whatever he had planned for me would end quickly.

"Drop. It."

I recognized that voice. Daniel reappeared between me and Church just as I opened my eyes.

"And give up my chance to punish your girlfriend? Not a chance," Church hissed.

Daniel pulled his arm back and brought it forward, his fist connecting with Church's face. I heard a crunch, but both men disappeared before I could assess the damage. In another split second, they were back again, circling each other as if they were boxers in the ring. I pushed with my legs until I'd scooted far enough back to give them some breathing room.

"Leave, Jamie," Daniel said without ever taking his eyes off Church.

"Not without—" I started to say, but he cut me off.

"Leave! He can't hurt me. I'll find you later."

Even though I knew his words were true, I still hesitated. A movement by the door caught my eye. Portia stood at the edge motioning frantically for me to come. My ankle and head throbbed, but I managed to roll onto all fours and crawl toward the door. Behind me, another punch connected with someone's body, producing a sickening thud. I flinched. Both ghosts disappeared again before I had a chance to see which was the victim.

I used the doorframe to pull myself into a standing position. Steven arrived and lifted me under the arms as I hobbled toward the idling minivan. Mom sat behind the wheel and relief washed over her face when the back door slid open and I climbed in with Steven. Portia followed us and slammed the door shut. Mom hit the gas and the van lurched forward down a gravel road.

"Stop! We've got to help Daniel," I insisted. "He's alone with *three* of them."

Portia grabbed my hand and held it. "Daniel will be fine. He's a ghost. They can't hurt him. Just like he can't hurt them. He'll distract them long enough for us to get out of here and then he'll meet up with us somewhere."

"What happened back there?" Mom's voice betrayed her terror. "You were right behind me. I ran and then I turned around and you were gone."

"Church happened, that's what." I groaned. "He's still got Daniel's watch. I can't believe it. If I hadn't been kidnapped, we'd still have it. It's all my fault."

"It's not your fault," Mom said. "Church would have found a way to get to you no matter how careful you were."

"And don't worry about the watch," Portia said. "Or should I say watches."

"Huh?" I looked up at her through my tears. In her lap she held the box of watches Church had shown Daniel.

I grabbed the box from her. "How'd you get this?"

253

"Easy. Everyone else was preoccupied. No one saw the tiny brunette slither under the car, grab the box, and slip the key out of the unconscious Church's pocket. Sometimes my size has its advantages."

Chapter 28

I could kiss you!" I squealed as I clutched at the box of watches.

Portia grinned. "I'd settle for a hug."

I threw my arms around her. "Thank you, thank you, thank you!"

"Where are we going?" Steven asked. He'd climbed over the middle console to sit in the front passenger seat.

"Nowhere in particular. Right now, I'm just getting us away from that warehouse," Mom answered.

"We can't go back to our apartment. Or Daniel's either, for that matter," I said. "It has to be somewhere they'd never expect."

"I haven't been to Hawaii in a while," Mom laughed.

I rolled my eyes. "Somehow I don't think we'll be much help to Daniel from Hawaii."

"It needs to be somewhere public," Steven said. "If Church and his men find us, it'll be harder for them to get what they want if we're out in the open."

"At the same time," Portia began, "if we're out in the open, we'll be easier to spot."

I frowned. "I don't know how Daniel's going to find us if we're not at one of our apartments. I lost my phone when they kidnapped me. It's probably in the trunk of Church's car. Daniel won't be able to call."

"You mean this phone?" Mom's purse rested on the console between the seats. She reached into it and pulled out my phone.

I grabbed it from her hand. "Where did you get this?"

"It was on the floor outside our apartment. You went outside to talk to Daniel on the phone and never came back. We started to worry. Portia went into the hall to look for you and found the phone. When Daniel showed up a little while later and you weren't with him, we knew it hadn't been dropped accidentally."

"I don't think I've ever seen someone come unglued like Daniel did when he found out you were missing," Portia said. "I thought he might die of despair . . . if he weren't already dead, of course."

"None of us were surprised when Daniel got a text from Dr. Church a little while later," Steven said.

"Did they hurt you, Jamesie? Are you sure you're okay?" Mom asked again.

"I'm fine. Maybe a little bruised, but it's not a big deal." Honestly, without as much adrenaline pumping through me as before, my body had started to register the pain of all my bumps and bruises. I touched a hand to my forehead. A huge knot had formed where my head collided with the cement floor moments before. I didn't mention it to Mom. Worrying her unnecessarily wouldn't make it any better.

Steven turned around in his seat. "Are your experiences with ghosts always this crazy?"

I shook my head. "No. Sometimes they're worse. Too bad I can't still use witchcraft. I would have saved myself long before any of you showed up to rescue me."

"We can't keep aimlessly driving around," Mom complained.

"Someone's got to come up with a plan."

"What about a library? We can sit and study the watches together and it will be easy for Daniel to access," Portia suggested.

I looked at my phone. "It's almost eleven. I doubt any of the libraries in the area are open this late."

"Anyone else hungry?" Steven asked. "We could find a diner. They usually have late hours."

"I'm starving, but that only buys us a little time. No diner is going to want us to stick around until we solve the code."

"You think of everything, don't you?" Steven grinned.

"Like I always tell Peter, I'm a realist."

Mom laughed. "Good thing one of us in this vehicle is."

My mind drifted to thoughts of Peter. I missed having him around. I could count on him for anything during an extrication and no matter how odd I acted, he always forgave me. As much as I liked spending time with Daniel alone, I knew things needed to change. Our relationship wouldn't last forever. I had to stop trying to solve his problems by myself and accept help from those who offered. And that included Peter.

We drove around for ten more minutes trying to come up with a reasonable plan. We'd finally decided to get a hotel room when I remembered something my dad told me earlier in the week. "I know where we can go!" I yelled.

Portia jumped.

"Dad's attending a seminar in Providence this weekend. The city isn't that far from home, but since I'm gone, he said he'd just get a hotel room there instead of going back to Marion each night. Staying at home will be a lot more comfortable than a cramped hotel room."

"You're sure he's gone?" Mom asked. "If he's there, showing up on his doorstep could get a little . . . awkward."

"Once Dad has a plan, he stays with it."

"True." Mom nodded. "Marion it is."

"What about Dan—?" I started to say. As if on cue, my phone rang. "Daniel?" I answered. "Are you okay?"

"I'm fine. I think I finally lost them."

"Where are you? We'll come get you. We thought it would be best if we went to—"

"Wait," Daniel cut me off. *"Don't say it unless you're positive none of the ghosts followed you. I lost track of one of them before I even got out of the warehouse."*

I swallowed hard and looked at the dark faces in the van. *Is a ghost in here with us? Did someone else just hear our entire plan?* "I won't say anything else. Where are you?" I asked again.

"Just stop driving and I'll find you."

"How do you plan to do that?"

The other end of the line was silent for an extra beat. *"Don't be mad, but I . . . uhh . . . installed a tracker app on your phone."*

"You did *what?*"

"I'm sorry. I freaked out when they grabbed you this morning. I put it there so when I got you back, you wouldn't disappear on me again."

I probably should've been mad, but it made sense—not to mention the fact that he cared enough not to lose me again.

Mom pulled over and parked in the parking lot of a strip mall. Most stores were closed, but a pizza joint still flashed its neon sign, letting all who might have the late night munchies know they were still open for thirty more minutes. My stomach growled just thinking about it. Steven must have felt the same way because after five minutes of waiting for Daniel to show up, he jumped out and disappeared into the building with a promise to return with food.

Twenty minutes after we parked, I noticed a figure walking across the parking lot toward the van. It only took a second to recognize the profile. Even though we'd only known each other for a short time, I'd come to appreciate the way he walked with his head held high. I threw the van door open and jumped out. As soon as he saw me, he picked up his pace. In that moment, my life resembled a scene from one of those annoying chick flick movies, but I didn't care.

"J," he whispered into my hair after he'd reached my side and pulled me into a tight hug. "This day has been the longest day of my life. All I could think about was what Church might be doing to you. If they weren't already dead, so help me I would have killed them all again."

I swallowed back tears, but kept my arms around him. The need to be in his presence deepened the longer I knew him. "It all turned out fine. You saved me."

"Barely. Turns out I'm an awful protector."

I lifted my head from his shoulder and looked straight into his eyes. "This is all part of my job description. I agreed to help you knowing full well that it could get dangerous. I mean, no offense, but Church doesn't hold a candle to the demonic beings I've fought in the past."

Daniel's lips turned up slightly. "Unfortunately, I don't think we're through with him yet. Until we get all of the watches back we can't—"

I pressed my fingers to his lips. "Don't say anything else until you see what Portia did."

By the time we arrived in Marion, it was one in the morning. My head throbbed, partially from the bump on the cement and partially from twenty-four hours without any sleep. When Mom parked in the driveway of the only place I truly knew as home, I almost cried. The thought that I could sleep in my own bed—or sleep, period—never sounded so good. I dragged myself from the van and up the front porch. "Do you think you can do a walkthrough of the house? You

259

know, make sure there aren't any other dead residents?" I asked Daniel.

"Sure. Be right back."

"Don't forget the attic," I called as Daniel disappeared from view.

Daniel searching my house for ghosts brought back memories of Nick, Sophia, and Haven doing the same thing for me. Thinking back to my time with the others almost seemed like dreams.

Daniel didn't return for at least ten minutes. I was starting to worry that something happened to him when the front door opened. "It's clear," he said, taking my hand and pulling me inside. The others followed close behind. None of us dared return to our apartments to pack clothes or toiletries so I raided my bathroom and closet for things that might fit Mom and Portia. I offered to dig through Dad's closet for Steven, but he declined.

"Mom and Portia, you can sleep in the guest room," I instructed after giving everyone a grand tour of the house. "Steven, is the couch okay?"

"The couch will be fine. Thanks," he answered.

"Daniel, we can sit in the kitchen and look at the codes," I said.

He shook his head. "Absolutely not. You're completely exhausted. The watches can wait until morning."

I tried to protest, but Daniel put a finger over my lips.

"Fine." I sighed. "I'll go to bed. But just for a little while."

Daniel squeezed my hand. "Goodnight. Just call down the stairs if you need me."

I returned the hand squeeze and dragged myself up the stairs to my room. I kicked my shoes off and tugged open the dresser drawer holding extra pairs of pajamas. The contents of the drawer looked as if they'd been dumped out and stuffed back in. I never put my clothes away without folding them. Dad raised me better than that. *Did Camille do this when she came over to get Daniel's watch?*

I tugged open the drawer holding jeans. Since it was summer, I'd only packed one pair for the trip to Boston. Each pair was stuffed into the drawers in the same way as the pajama drawer. Seeing that, I quickly opened and closed each drawer in my dresser. All were in a similar state of disarray. I slammed the last drawer shut and ran to my desk. The drawers had mini organizer bins so I always knew where to find a pencil, paperclip, or tape. The entire contents looked as if it had been poured out and stirred up.

Someone's been in my room.

A soft tapping sounded on my door and I jumped. "Who's there?"

"It's me."

I ran to open the door for Daniel. He took one look at my worried face and asked, "What's wrong?"

"Someone searched my room."

"How do you know?"

"All my drawers are messed up."

"Could it have been your dad looking for something?" Daniel asked.

I shook my head. "No way. I know you haven't met him, but he's clean and organized beyond normal. I've never seen him look through my stuff, but if he did, he'd *never* leave it this way."

"Is anything missing?"

I shrugged. "Not that I noticed. I don't have anything valuable. Everything important came to Boston with me."

My eyes fell on the trunk resting by the foot of my bed. I *really* didn't want to open it. The trunk belonged to one of my murdering ancestors. I tried not to think about him. It was the same trunk where I found Daniel's watch. With a determined sigh, I crossed the room and opened the lid of the trunk. The contents looked a little scattered, but I honestly couldn't remember what condition the trunk had been in the last time I closed it. If something was taken, I wouldn't know.

Kneeling by the trunk, I dropped my head into my hands resting on the lid. My eye caught the corner of something sticking out from under the bed. I reached for the crumpled paper.

"What's that?" Daniel asked.

"I don't know." I turned the paper over in my hand. "It's a business card. That answers the question of who's been in my room." I passed the card to Daniel.

"Myles."

I nodded.

"Maybe his threats weren't so idle after all. He must have come here after Church roughed him up." Daniel reached out and placed a hand on my shoulder. "Don't worry about him. I've checked the house and he's gone. If someone comes back, I'll still be here. I'm not leaving you alone again."

"Just don't let those watches out of your sight."

He patted the box tucked under his arm. "Are you kidding me? I'm not even letting go of them."

I sat down on the edge of my bed, trying to stifle a yawn.

"I better let you get some sleep. I actually came up here to get your internet password. I thought I could do some code research while you're sleeping."

I gave him the password and he turned to leave.

"Daniel," I said quietly.

He stopped, his hand on the doorknob. "Yeah?"

"Are you scared?"

He tilted his head and looked at me. "Scared of what?"

"Death. I mean, the permanent kind."

He dropped his hand from the doorknob and sat next to me on the bed. "I'm not sure how to answer that question."

"This summer, I . . ." I paused. "I've been forced to look at death differently. Before I became a soul saver, I'd never lost anyone I cared deeply about before. When someone's a ghost, it's like their life has changed, but they're still themselves and they're still around.

262

When a person is extricated, there's no coming back. It's so . . . permanent."

Daniel set the box of watches on the bed and took my hand in his. "It only feels permanent while you're still living. When you die, you'll see everyone again."

"So you believe in heaven then?" I asked.

"Of course. Don't you?"

I thought for a second. "I think I do."

Daniel rubbed his thumb along the palm of my hand and I closed my eyes, savoring the comforting feeling. "You asked if I was scared."

I opened my eyes again.

"I am. I'm terrified."

I smiled. "Even though you believe in heaven?"

He nodded. "I haven't seen my family for hundreds of years. It would be nice to see them again, but . . . their memories have faded in my mind. The thought of leaving those I care about *now* is harder to fathom than the idea of seeing my own family again."

I had to ask. "Who is it you care about now?"

He slowly trailed his fingers up my arm, stopping when they brushed my cheek. My entire body trembled. Taking my hands, he pulled me close and gently pressed his lips to mine. The kiss was so soft and subtle that I would have thought I imagined the whole thing if it weren't for the fact that my lips still tingled long after he pulled away.

Daniel clasped both of my hands and touched his forehead to mine. "I don't know if I can leave you. And I'm not sure I still want to be extricated," he whispered.

Chapter 29

I pulled my head back from Daniel's, hoping a few inches distance between us would help me think more clearly. It didn't work. My mind was still a jumbled mess. "You don't want to be extricated?"

"I don't know. I've been around for hundreds of years already, what's a few more years going to do?" he said. "You and I can be together, J."

"But you don't age. I do. Wouldn't that be kind of, you know, creepy?"

He laughed. "Not at first. Maybe when you die—hopefully in a long time from now—you and I can be together as ghosts."

"That's assuming I become a ghost."

"If you're my soul saver, and you die before I finish my business, you'll have to come back. And if that doesn't work, I've got all the watches. I can just keep them somewhere safe until I decide it's time to solve their codes."

I smiled and shook my head.

He laughed out loud. "I know, I know. It sounds ridiculous. It *is* ridiculous." He stopped smiling and became serious again. "J, I've never felt this way about anyone before. Part of me wonders if we're

264

both wrong about my extrication. What if fate put us together because we really are meant to be soul mates—on earth?"

I swallowed hard. "I feel the same way about you, but . . ."

"But?"

"I'm not convinced that your attraction to me, or mine to you," my cheeks burned, "isn't strictly based on our connection as soul saver and ghost." I took a deep breath and plunged forward again. "We've only known each other for a few days. It doesn't make sense that we would feel this way about each other. I felt this way with all my ghosts."

Daniel grinned sheepishly. "Is this your way of breaking up with me?"

My mouth dropped open. "*What*?"

"Relax. I'm kidding. I know you're right and I know I have to be extricated. It's just hard to think straight when I'm with you." Daniel stood and stepped toward the door again. "You better get some sleep or you won't be any help to us in the morning."

"Stay with me," I said. "You can use my computer. I'm so tired I won't even notice if the lights are on. I'll feel safer that way."

Daniel changed course and sat down at my desk. "I'll be right here when you wake up."

I woke to the sound of birds tweeting outside my bedroom window. In the Boston apartment, I woke to the sounds of the city. I didn't realize until that point that I missed my Marion room so much. My eyes fluttered open and I looked at the clock on my bedside table. Half past nine. Besides the birds, I couldn't hear any other sounds and I wondered if everyone else in the house still slept.

Remembering Daniel's promise not to leave me, I suddenly sat up in my bed. "Daniel?"

He was next to my side in a flash. "I'm right here. What's wrong?"

I shook my head. "Nothing. I just . . . I didn't see you at first."

"I've been here all night. Just like I promised."

I laid down again and stretched my arms over my head. In the morning light, things didn't seem so bleak. "Were you bored all night? I shouldn't have made you stay up here."

"It was fine. The time flew by. Look." He walked to the desk and came back with one of the watches. "I took Paul's watch apart last night to get to the casing. I've copied the codes from all the watches down and emailed them to myself and to you. And I printed off copies. Even if Church and his men find us and demand the watches back, we'll still have all the codes. We just have to solve it before them."

I ran my fingers over Paul Revere's watch. "I can't believe you fixed your watch yesterday and then Church threw it on the ground again at the warehouse."

Daniel laughed. "It wasn't really my watch. At least, not all of it. After I found out Church had taken you, I got to work engraving a new casing. Your mom and her partners helped. I didn't know how things were going to go down at the warehouse, but I didn't want Church to get my code. I engraved a fake code on the fake watch. The real one never left my possession nor did Paul's. Getting the rest of the watches from Church was just a bonus."

I grinned. "I had no idea."

"Good thing some of the silversmithing skills I learned from Paul all those years ago stuck. The hardest part was making it look old enough. If Church hadn't been blinded by his greed, he would have seen right through my bluff."

"I guess it doesn't matter now." I swung my legs over the side of the bed and realized I still wore the clothes I'd been wearing for two days straight. "You didn't happen to solve the code, too, did you?"

"Nope."

"Good. That'll give us something to do today. But first, I'm going to go take a shower. I'll meet you downstairs in a bit."

"Yes, Ma'am," he joked. He gave me a quick kiss on the cheek and darted out of the room. After that goodbye, I was fully awake.

By the time I showered and dressed, I was the last to make it downstairs. Daniel had all six watches spread out amongst remnants of half-eaten breakfasts on the dining table.

I grabbed an apple from the bowl on the counter and washed it at the sink, munching on it while I loaded everyone's dishes into the dishwasher.

"What do you think, Jamie?" Mom asked.

I hadn't been listening to their conversation. "About what?" I asked.

"About the books. We got lucky."

"Umm . . . sure." I still didn't know what she referred to. I looked at Daniel, but he just shrugged.

"I had the books I got from the library in the van instead of the apartment," Steven said. The books were spread out on the table in front of him. Portia sat next to him, staring at her laptop with creased brows.

"Did you find something interesting in the books?" I asked Steven.

He smiled. "It's all interesting. I don't know yet if it's important, but . . ."

Daniel pulled a chair out for me and I sat down next to him. "We're looking into ciphers from the Revolutionary War that have already been solved."

I sat on the chair and tucked my legs under myself. "When I was a kid, I used to have a bottle of invisible ink. Camille and I would write messages back and forth to each other. That's about as much knowledge as I have of secret codes."

"They used invisible ink back then, too," Portia said without

267

looking up from her laptop.

"Ha ha. Very funny," I said.

Portia eyed me over the top of her screen. "I'm serious, Jamie. See." She turned her computer so I could see it and pointed to the screen. "They'd write secret messages on unimportant letters, papers, and books. Sometimes they'd write the messages in the margins and sometimes they'd write them between the lines of a letter. The recipient could hold the paper over a candle and the secret message would appear."

"No way."

Daniel laughed. "It really happened. Sadly, there's no way invisible ink can be the answer to our problem. It wouldn't have worked on the metal of the watches. And even if it had, it would have rubbed off years ago."

I reached into the center of the table and picked up one of the watches. On the back, Daniel had stuck a piece of masking tape with the initials MH—Matthew Heinrichsen. Each piece of the code contained numbers and letters in what, at first glance, seemed to be an unorganized manner. "Do you think the fact that the letters and numbers aren't in lines and they aren't all the same size means something?" I asked.

"Probably. Which makes it even more complicated."

"With our luck, it's not even going to be a code. Maybe the person who made the watches was just messing around."

"If the story were made up, Church wouldn't be trying so hard to get his hands on them," Mom said.

"Is every watch exactly the same?" I asked.

"Pretty much," Daniel answered. "The backs have slight variances in their designs. The cutouts and holes are different, but I think it's because they were handmade. The artist changed it a little with each one."

I sighed and went to work like everyone else, staring mindlessly at the papers and watches in front of me. Four hours later, we hadn't made any progress. Portia had given up and returned to the guest room to take a nap. Steven sat on the couch with a book in his hands, but his eyes were closed and his head lolled to the side. I didn't have a clue where Mom had disappeared to.

I pushed away from the table and turned to Daniel. "Do you think we're making this harder than it has to be?" I tucked my bare legs up under my chin and wrapped my arms around them. "We've compared these numbers and letters to all the codes we can find and they don't even come close to meaning anything."

"I don't think the codes on the watches are going to be the same as ones used later in the war. It was just so early. I mean, Washington had only been general for a few months before I died. I'm sure his schemes weren't as elaborate in the beginning as they were later on. So yes, we're probably making it harder than it has to be."

"Let's think this through rationally then. What is it we think the code is going to reveal?" I asked.

"The location of a supposed cache of valuables."

"Right. How would that location be described?"

Daniel narrowed his eyebrows.

"I mean, would it tell us to take a left at widow Smith's house and then walk ten paces until we see a giant oak and begin digging?"

Daniel laughed. "Not a chance."

"Okay. Then how would it have been written back then? In modern times, we can type a latitude and longitude into any GPS and find the spot we need within a couple of feet of accuracy. Without electronics, would they have known how to pinpoint locations like that back then?"

Daniel jumped up and began pacing back and forth in front of the table. "J, You might be on to something. Did you know General Washington was a surveyor?"

269

I shook my head.

"He was. Before the war. And I think after the war, too. Maybe Church is wrong and Washington did have knowledge of where the cache was. Maybe he surveyed the spot himself."

"So . . . we're looking for coordinates then?"

Daniel abruptly sat back down and grabbed the pages of codes. One by one he lined them up across the table. "Possibly. There *are* more numbers than letters."

"Except there are way more numbers than necessary on each watch. How do we determine which ones are the coordinates?" I picked up one of the actual watches and stared at it. My heart beat faster and the palms of my hands began to sweat. I felt like we were on the verge of a breakthrough. "Daniel," I whispered. "This is it. I feel it."

He looked up at me. "Really?"

I nodded.

"How do we narrow it down?"

"Let's think in simple terms. We're pretty sure Washington didn't hide the valuables until after he arrived in Cambridge, right?"

"Correct."

"Then that means we don't have much leeway on latitude and longitude. If we look up the basic coordinates of Boston, we can see if there are any similar numbers on the watch casings and go from there."

"You're a genius." Daniel squeezed my shoulder and reached for Portia's laptop. I watched over his shoulder as he searched for the coordinates. "Got it! The basic longitude of the Boston area is 71 degrees west and the basic latitude is 42 degrees north."

I leaned over the table and searched the pages of numbers and letters. "Are those numbers on any of the watches?"

Daniel grabbed one of the papers. "Right here. There's a 71!"

I snatched the paper next to it. "This one has a 42." My heart pounded. "We're really going to get it."

"What next?" Daniel asked.

"I have no idea. Knowing the most generalized latitude and longitude doesn't get us very far. Boston is what? Ninety square miles? And I don't think that includes the Cambridge area."

"The rest of the numbers on the watches probably pinpoint the location. We just need to figure out which ones to use."

I sighed. "Back to the drawing board."

Mom came into the kitchen. "Anyone want lunch? What's your dad got stashed away?" She opened the pantry door and stuck her head in.

"I think we found something, Lillian," Daniel called.

Mom's head shot back out. "Seriously?"

Daniel grinned. "Want to hear our theory?"

Steven must have been listening from the couch because he jumped up and made it to the table before Mom. "Tell us."

We explained our theory to Mom and Steven and then again to Portia when she came downstairs. Everyone agreed that it made sense. We nibbled on sandwiches and drank lemonade while thinking through the new theory. When nothing but crumbs remained on my plate, I stood to take it to the sink. My hip bumped the table, knocking one of Steven's books to the ground. "Sorry," I mumbled as I bent to pick it up, my eyes falling to the open page. With trembling hands, I dropped the dishes to the floor and picked up the book. "Guys. I know how to solve the codes."

Chapter 30

I shoved everything aside and set the open book on the table where everyone could see it. "Steven, remember how you discovered that Matthew Heinrichsen was one of the spies?" I asked.

"I dropped the book in the library and it fell open to the page with a picture of his watch," Steven answered.

I pointed at the book on the table. "I think history just repeated itself."

Daniel leaned over the book and read to himself. "This has to be it. And I was starting to think we'd never solve it."

"Let's just hope Church didn't solve part of the code with the watches he already had."

"I doubt Church had fate helping him." Daniel pushed the book across the table to my mom.

Steven read over her shoulder. "Masked letters were sometimes used to send coded messages during the Revolutionary War. This type of letter was most often used by the British, but it is believed the Americans used the method on occasion. To send a masked

272

letter, a person would make a template in a unique shape and place it over a sheet of paper. The secret message was then written within the shape. When the paper was removed, the sender could then fill in the paper with sentences and words to make it seem as if it were ordinary correspondence. The mask, or template, was usually sent ahead of the letter rather than with the coded letter so it would not be able to be deciphered if intercepted." Steven stopped reading and looked at Daniel. "If Jamie's right, that means we have to find the templates somewhere. Did General Washington ever give you anything else? Something that might not have seemed important at the time?"

Daniel frowned and shook his head. "Not that I can think of."

I put my hand up. "Remember, this was just the beginning of the use of secret codes in the war. They were simpler. If I'm right, the templates came with the watches. We already have all of them."

Portia gasped. "The engravings on the back of the watches!"

I grinned. "Bingo."

"So the difference in the casings had nothing to do with the artists desire to be different?" Mom said.

"I think the differences were intentional," I answered.

Daniel grabbed the closest watch and peeled the masking tape labeled with a P and an R off the back. "We'll try Revere's watch first." He traced the watch onto a piece of paper, carefully marking the holes in the design before looking up? "Got any scissors?"

I jumped up and got a pair from one of the kitchen drawers. Daniel carefully cut around the circle and inside each hole. The process was tedious. I would have butchered the paper if I'd tried it myself.

"Ready?" Daniel said, holding the miniature template.

I held up both hands with my fingers crossed. "Ready."

He placed the paper over the inside casing. I knew immediately that the method worked. Daniel grinned from ear to ear as if it were

273

Christmas morning. "One down, five more to go."

Portia looked at the numbers showing through the cut template. "We know which numbers and letters to use, but we still don't know what order to put them in, do we?"

"Clockwise. You read them clockwise since it's a watch." I spoke with a surety. I don't know how I knew, but I knew.

"Then the letters and numbers from this watch are 42, 35, N."

"Sounds like the latitude to me," Mom said. "Didn't you say that's roughly where Boston falls on the grid?"

"Uh huh." I nodded.

Portia grabbed another watch and peeled the tape off. "Let's see what Washington's watch has to say."

Ten minutes later, we had another template ready.

"The code from his watch is only made up of letters. R, I, P, M."

Portia frowned. "That means absolutely nothing."

"Keep going, maybe it will mean something after we have all the watches finished," I insisted.

Cutting out each tiny template was painstaking work and it took a full hour before we had the rest of the six codes completed. We lined the codes up along the table.

"Here's what we have when they're together," I said. "M, H, S; J, 42, 35, N; R, I, P, M; 71, 5, W, 1; 7, 7, 5, Y; S, G, G, W."

"Does that jumble mean anything to anyone?" Daniel asked.

Steven shook his head. "Not yet."

"We have to figure out what order to put them in," Portia said. "Alphabetical, the date the watches were received, the order in which each person agreed to be a spy, by birthday . . . it could be so many things."

"Which one is yours again?" I asked Daniel.

He pointed to the code at the end of the line.

"They need to be placed in order of the age of the recipient," I insisted. Again, the words came out of my mouth without any prior thought. The whole soul saver thing was starting to trip me out.

"Which person was the oldest?" Mom asked.

I glanced at Daniel but he only shrugged. "I don't remember discussing age with them. I'm sure I was the youngest. And Lydia Canterman was probably the next youngest. She was around twenty at that time."

Mom pulled Lydia's code from the line and placed it just before Daniel's.

"What about the other four?" Steven asked.

"I honestly don't know. Portia?" Daniel looked at her as she rapidly typed on her keyboard.

"Already on it." Her eyes scanned the computer screen. "Okay, Church was born in 1734, Revere was born in 1735, and Washington was born in 1732."

Mom shuffled the papers into the correct order.

"What about Matthew Heinrichsen?" I asked.

"I'm sure his birth date is in the book." Steven grabbed the library book from the table and flipped through the pages. "Here it is. June 7, 1746. His code goes in the middle."

Mom adjusted the papers again, adding Heinrichsen's code to the line.

"So now we have, R, I, P, M; J, 42, 35, N; 71, 5, W, 1; 7, 7, 5, Y; M, H, S; S, G, G, W," I said.

Daniel pointed at the last page, the one belonging to him. "GGW must stand for General George Washington."

"That makes sense. What about the first code? It's only letters, too."

"RIP usually means Rest In Peace," Steven commented.

My heart sped up. "Rest in Peace M. J. That's got to be it!"

"Then who is M. J.?" Portia asked.

"No idea," Daniel said. "But maybe we're not supposed to know. Maybe that's part of the mystery of the code."

275

"What's next, Jamie?" Mom asked.

"The latitude and longitude. So far we have Rest In Peace M. J., followed by a latitude and longitude and then 1, 7, 7, 5. That part is obvious. It's the year. Right?"

All heads nodded so I continued, "We know it ends with General George Washington, but I can't figure out what Y, M, H, S means. It sounds like a high school, but I highly doubt that has anything to do with it."

"Your most humble servant," Daniel whispered. "It has to be. It was a common way to end correspondence back in my day. "Your most humble servant, General George Washington."

"We did it," I breathed. "We solved the code."

"Do you feel any different?" I asked Daniel. After deciphering the code, we retreated to the swing on my back patio. All of us agreed to take a break while Portia made some much needed dinner. Mom and Steven helped her in the kitchen.

"What do you mean?"

"Well, we thought your extrication might happen just by solving the code. With other ghosts I've helped, their extrications came almost immediately after completing their unfinished business. They felt a kind of pulling sensation that they couldn't fight. Within moments, they were gone."

"I don't feel anything like that, but . . ."

"But?"

"I do feel like my time is almost up. I feel like nothing is important anymore, like I don't need to worry about the daily grind. Does that make any sense?" Daniel explained.

"I think so."

"If solving the code didn't extricate you, there's only one logical next step. You know that, right?"

Daniel pushed with his legs, causing the swing to move back and forth. I leaned back against the cushioned seat and closed my eyes, enjoying the breeze of the early evening on my face.

"I do know. We have to dig up the cache."

I nodded, still keeping my eyes closed. "Yep. Somehow my experiences with ghosts always lead me to dark secluded places where I have to dig around for things. I should have known from the very beginning that this would happen."

Daniel laughed and pushed the swing harder. "I'm looking forward to it. Do you know how long it's been since I've done something exciting?"

"Umm . . . a day? Wasn't it just yesterday that you saved me from my kidnappers?"

"Touché." He grabbed my hand and laced his fingers through mine. "I meant it's been a long time since I've gone on a secret mission for Washington."

"If we follow the coordinates tonight, and get lucky, you might be just a few hours away from your extrication."

I felt Daniel's fingers tremble in my hand ever so slightly. "I'm very much aware of that." He squeezed my hand and I leaned my head onto his shoulder. It felt comfortable and natural, as if we were lifelong friends rather than barely more than strangers. I even drifted off to sleep, peacefully swinging with my soul mate.

"Dinner's ready!" Mom called from just inside the patio doors.

I stood and reached for Daniel's hand.

"I think I'll just stay out here a little longer . . . if that's okay. I'm enjoying the evening's weather. And you might find this surprising, but I'm not very hungry."

"Horribly surprising," I said sarcastically. "I'll let you know when we've finished."

I sat at the table with mom and her partners. We mostly ate in silence, each of us contemplating the events of the last few days and the events about to happen.

"Are we going tonight for sure?" Mom asked.

I glanced at Portia and Steven who in turn gazed at me. "I think we should. The longer we wait to find the cache, the sooner we risk Church finding us. Besides, Dad will be back in the morning and I'd rather leave a note that we stopped by rather than have him come home to find us still here. It will save a lot of explanation."

"Not to mention, I *really* need a change of clothes," Portia added.

"What's our plan of attack then?" Mom said.

"I did an internet search for the coordinates while you were outside, Jamie," Steven said. The coordinates fall just outside of Boston. It appears to be a fairly undeveloped area, although I'm sure it's private property."

"It won't be the first time I've trespassed," I muttered.

"Excuse me?" Mom said with raised eyebrows.

"Ghost business. I'm sure you've done the same."

Steven laughed out loud. "We've done some crazy stuff, but nothing compares to working with you."

I shrugged. "What can I say? I tend to attract ghosts with a lot of baggage."

"What was that about my baggage?" a voice behind me said.

"Daniel! I didn't hear you come in."

"It's because I'm a ghost," he grinned. "I'm stealthy like that." He sat down next to me and put his arm on the back of my chair.

"It'll be dark soon. For obvious reasons, we can't be digging around in the daylight. If we're going to go tonight, we need to leave soon."

Portia cleared her throat. "Daniel, how sure are you that Church or his men haven't been hanging around here?"

"Pretty sure. I've done quite a few checks. But . . . I can only see their aura if nothing else is blocking them, like doors and walls."

I involuntarily glanced at the closed pantry door.

"I think we should split up tonight just in case they're following us," Steven said. "If we leave in a couple of groups, they'll be confused and they might follow the wrong group."

"We should have at least two people per group, though. It's safer that way," Mom added.

"Which means we can only have two groups," Portia concluded.

"I might be able to convince Peter and Camille to help tonight," I said.

"That's a good idea, J. They already know about ghosts and they've helped you in the past, right?" Daniel said.

I nodded. "Maybe if they dress like you and me, and leave together, it will confuse anybody watching our apartment."

"Except that Peter won't have an aura," Portia said.

"No, but maybe someone watching won't think of that. If they see two teens leaving with my mom, they might not even think about auras. We could even have them carry the box the watches came in—emptied of course."

"If your friends go with Lillian, then Portia and I can leave together," Steven said. "That leaves the two of you as a group to actually go where the coordinates lead. Daniel will be able to tell if you're being followed by any ghosts."

"I'll call Peter and Cam right now." I ran upstairs to my bedroom, hoping for a little privacy. "Peter?" I said when his familiar voice answered.

"Hey. How are things going with Daniel? I've been wondering."

"I would have called sooner, but things got crazy." I thought about my kidnapping the day before. Eventually I'd tell him about it, but I didn't want to get into it right then. "I need a favor. How do you feel about helping with another extrication?"

"You know I'm always game."

I spent the next few minutes explaining the basics of what we

279

found out since we last spoke and what kind of favor I needed from him. He agreed to come with us.

I called Camille next. Convincing her was easier than I expected. She must have been really bored without me around, because once I assured her she'd be getting the easy job, she agreed without any hesitation.

"Mom said I have to be home by two tomorrow. Is that going to be a problem?" Camille asked when I answered the door a half hour later. She stepped through the door and dropped her duffel bag on the entryway floor.

"I'm sure that will be fine," I answered. Camille's eyes weren't on mine, though.

Her mouth fell open slightly and she fought to hold back a grin as she looked over my shoulder. "You must be Daniel. I'm Camille."

Daniel reached out and shook the hand she offered. Camille, ever the flirt, let her hand linger in his longer than necessary.

"Jamie!" Camille hissed after Daniel disappeared into the kitchen again. "I changed my mind. I'm not going to help you extricate him. Have you looked him? That would be a crime to society if he dies."

"A crime to society? He's already dead, Cam."

"Give me one hour with him and I'll convince him to stay."

My jaw dropped. "Are you kidding me?"

Camille tilted her head to the side and grinned. "Oh . . . that's right. You already claimed him."

"That's not how this works, okay? It's his time to go."

Camille shrugged. "Whatever you say."

Peter arrived next. "I brought two hoodies so Camille could wear one, too," he said, tossing one of the jackets at Camille on the couch. "Where exactly are we going?"

"We're all going to Boston and then you and Camille are going to leave with my mom," I said. "It doesn't really matter where you go, we just need to throw the other ghosts off our trail."

"Can we go to a mall? I could really use a manicure." Camille frowned as she stared at her hands."

"I love that idea," Mom squealed. "I was thinking the same thing."

"Take me with you," Peter mouthed to me. "Please!"

I smiled apologetically at him. "Steven and Portia will leave next. Any ideas where you'll be going?"

Portia looked at Steven. "We could go to a movie? Or check out a different restaurant."

"Sure. I'm up for anything," Steven answered.

"That leaves Daniel and me. We'll follow the coordinates." I couldn't help but look at Peter. He was the most understanding and accepting guy I'd ever known, but his eyes still held a look of hurt or betrayal . . . or maybe both.

Chapter 31

We arrived in Boston two hours later. Everyone but Daniel and I went up to the apartment. Daniel and I waited in a tiny coffee shop across the street from the complex. Night had fallen and the thought of what we were about to do made me sick to my stomach. I ordered a milkshake, but just played with the straw instead of drinking it. I wanted closure for Daniel, but I didn't want him to leave, and running into ghosts of the unsavory kind wasn't something I was thrilled about.

I jumped when my cell phone rang on the table next to me. "Mom?" I answered.

"*Good thing we didn't come back here last night. The apartment is trashed.*"

"I'm so sorry."

"*It's not your fault . . . and it's not Daniel's fault either. This is all part of the business.*"

"Did they take anything?"

"*Not that we can tell at first glance. I think they just emptied drawers out and searched cupboards. Your suitcases have been dumped. Camille's trying to pick them up for you.*"

282

"Tell her thanks."

"*I will. Portia and Steven are getting ready to leave. They're going to head south on foot. Peter, Cam, and I will give them a ten or fifteen minute head start and then we'll leave in the van.*"

From our little table in the coffee shop, I could see the parking spot where Mom left the minivan. We'd know exactly when they left.

"You ready for this?" Daniel asked.

"I don't know if it's the kind of thing you can get ready for."

"Kind of like extrication. It's weird to think I might not be here in a few hours."

"Don't remind me. If you're gone, that means I'll go into mourning and that's hard to get out of."

Daniel's eyebrows shot up. "Don't mourn me. I died a long time ago."

"Sorry. It's part of the job description."

"Do you want to find another ghost soon?"

I folded my arms over my chest and looked down at them. "It's hard to say. I like the adventure and the friendships and all of that, but . . . it's been a long summer so far. I could use a break."

Daniel laughed. "Well, if my extrication doesn't—"

"There they are!" I hissed, cutting off Daniel's words. I pointed out the window at three figures heading toward the minivan. I recognized Mom's purple jacket. Camille and Peter were behind her. Their hoods were up, blocking their faces, and they were holding hands. *Wait . . . what?*

Daniel must have seen the shock on my face because he whispered, "Don't worry. They're just trying to play the part. It was Camille's idea."

I didn't bother mentioning to him that Camille was the biggest flirt at Old Rochester High School. "Are they being followed?" I asked.

Daniel leaned closer to the window. "I'm not sure yet." His eyes scanned the parking lot and the road in front of the complex. "There! Do you see that? By the tree?"

My eyes followed to the spot he pointed. "I see a tree."

"You don't see a glow by it?"

I shook my head.

"That's what I thought. I was pretty sure it was a ghost's aura, but it could have been a reflection from the streetlight."

"Is the ghost following them?"

"It's moving toward the van." Daniel stood from his chair and pressed his nose against the glass. "It's in the van with them."

My heart beat harder. "I'm texting Peter." I pulled out my phone and began to type. *"Careful of your words. You've got a tail."* I shoved my phone back in my pocket and took a deep breath. "I think that's our cue."

Before leaving Marion, Daniel and I had borrowed a car from my ghost friends, Jack and Rita. They were some of my favorite people— dead or alive. They offered to accompany us to the cemetery, but I declined their help. Donating a car was favor enough.

"I used to own a car," Daniel said as we drove.

"What happened to it?"

"Upkeep and maintenance were frustrating. And with how much traveling I was doing at the time, I didn't get much use out of it anyway. That was back in the 1970s."

"You're telling me you haven't driven since the 70s?" I double-checked the tightness of my seatbelt.

Daniel laughed. "I never said that. I've rented cars almost everywhere I've gone. I just haven't owned one in a long time." He stopped talking and looked at me. "You're shivering."

"Sorry."

"Don't apologize, just turn the heat up."

"I'm not cold."

"J, you're shaking."

"I'm . . . nervous."

"Want to call the whole thing off?"

"No! I mean, no." I took a deep breath. "I don't know why, but something about this whole situation feels different this time. I think it's because we don't know what we're going to find. Whatever it is, it will be historically significant. I've never been a part of something so important."

Daniel reached across the seat and grasped my hand. We drove in silence for the rest of the ride. He navigated each turn as the GPS instructed. We left the city and found ourselves in a sparsely populated area. The night couldn't have been darker and I started to wonder if something happened to the moon. I thought I had my trembling under control until the GPS spoke again. *"Arriving at destination."*

Daniel parked under a large tree on the side of the road and turned off the car. "Can you see anything out there?"

"Not really. I see an old gate, but that's about it."

"There's a sign falling off its post over there." Daniel pointed. "I'm going to check it out." He jumped out of the car and trudged through the weeds. I couldn't tell from his reaction what he read. He returned to the car and opened my door. "Not to freak you out, but ... it's an old cemetery."

Of course it is. What else would it be? I lifted one leg out of the car and took a deep breath. I had to give myself a pep talk before I could pull the other leg out of the car. "Come on, Jamie. You've spent the night in a creepy cemetery before. You've got this."

"Do I even want to know?" Daniel smiled.

"Probably not."

Daniel walked to the back of the car and grabbed the two shovels we'd brought out of the trunk. I pulled a flashlight out of the bag I carried and then slung the bag over my shoulders. Daniel grabbed my free hand and we began taking one cautious step after another toward the cemetery. The entrance was marked by a tall wrought-iron gate. The clasp meant to lock it had long since been broken off and weeds had built up around the edges of the gate. Daniel gave it a good shove to get it moving. Its hinges creaked as it slowly swung open. That one solitary noise almost made me turn around and run back to the car. If it weren't for Daniel's firm grasp on my hand, I would have been gone for sure.

Beyond the gate, moss-covered headstones dotted the tall grass. The light from my flashlight bouncing off them created shadows. Sometimes it seemed as if the shadows moved.

"Do you see any . . . ghosts?" I asked.

"Not yet." Daniel squeezed my hand. "In a place as old as this, I wouldn't be surprised if there weren't any resident ghosts left."

"How do we know where M. J. is?"

"We don't know. We'll just have to read all the headstones."

"Of course," I mumbled. I aimed the flashlight at the nearest stone, a granite obelisk. "Henry Isling, 1734. Do you think that's the year he was born or the year he died?"

"I have no idea. Same thing on this one." Daniel read the headstone next to Henry's. "Samuel T. Wick, 1758."

Daniel leaned the shovels against a headstone and pulled another flashlight from my bag. "Here's one for someone named Elizabeth, but the last name is worn off. It does have RIP, though."

We wandered through the headstones, carefully examining each one. The burials didn't seem to be organized in any way. Headstones were turned in all directions—some close together and others with large spaces in between. In the dark, my senses were heightened and I turned at every sound, the flapping of a bird's wings, the rustle of the leaves overhead, the shuffling of Daniel's feet on the ground. We covered the entire space of the cemetery twice without finding any clues to the message on the watch.

"I'm starting to think Church was wrong," Daniel called from across the cemetery.

"What do you mean?" I called back.

"Church is convinced that General Washington didn't know where the cache was hidden, right? Maybe he did know. If so, I guarantee he pulled the cache as soon as he found out Church was a traitor. Everything's probably been gone for two hundred years."

"I still have the feeling we're in the right place," I whispered, not necessarily intending for Daniel to hear me. "What about this name? I don't think I saw this one before," I called as I read from another headstone. "Betsy Howe, Loving Daughter, Died 1741."

"I remember it. I read it when I searched that end of the cemetery the first time," Daniel answered.

I sighed and took another step forward, but my foot caught on a rock and I crashed to the ground. Daniel was by my side in a flash.

"You okay?"

"I'm fine." I could feel a trickle of blood running down my leg, but I ignored it. *Can I just have one soul saving experience where I don't end up damaged? Is that really too much to ask for?*

I accepted Daniel's hand to stand up, but then pulled it away and knelt back down. "I didn't trip over a rock. It's another headstone. The headstone had toppled from its base and the weeds and grasses had grown up around it. I used my bare hands to brush some of the dirt and debris away while Daniel aimed his flashlight at the stone. When the name revealed itself, a shock went through my entire body. My heart stopped, but when it started again, its rhythm was so prominent I felt every thump inside my head. "M. Jennings, 1775," I read.

Daniel dropped to his knees next to me. "This is the only M. J. in the entire cemetery."

"So . . . what do we do now? Do we . . . dig?" I swallowed hard, trying to keep my stomach down where it belonged.

"I guess so."

"What happens when all we unearth is a dead body?"

"On the bright side, it will have been buried long enough that all we'll find is bones. Not . . . other stuff."

"Is that supposed to make me feel better?"

"If you want, I can dig while you wait in the car?"

I aimed my light in the direction of the cemetery entrance. From where we were, I couldn't even see the car. "No way. I'm staying with you."

"Then let's do this." Daniel walked back to the headstone where he'd left the shovels earlier and brought them to me. "I have a feeling this isn't going to be easy."

"At least it rained a couple of days ago. Maybe the ground won't be too hard." My words were just wishful thinking. It seemed as if each time I stuck my shovel in the ground, I hit rocks. I'd never seen soil with so much gravel in it. Daniel and I talked at first, but after a while, we halted all conversation. My back ached and my hands had blisters after only thirty minutes of work.

"Why don't you take a break, J," Daniel finally said.

"I'm fine. I don't need a break."

"You don't heal like I do. When I get tired, I just flash in and out and I'm good to go again." Daniel reached over and took the shovel from my hands. "Just sit for a minute."

I gave in and sat down with my back leaning against Betsy Howe's headstone. I hoped she didn't mind. I didn't mean to do it, but my eyes closed as I listened to the song of Daniel's shovel in the dirt nearby. *Crunch, scoop, scrape. Crunch, scoop, scrape.* Crickets chirped and somewhere not far away, an owl hooted, reminding me that we weren't completely alone. I'd almost drifted off to sleep, when a twig snapped somewhere behind me. The noise couldn't have come from Daniel. Without thinking I jumped from my position and dove toward his comforting arms. "Did you hear that?"

He didn't answer. I watched his face as he focused on the trees just beyond our location. "There's no use hiding. I can see you," he called to someone I couldn't see.

A low chuckle echoed toward us. "I figured if I stayed hidden long enough, the two of you would do all the work."

I'd never forget the voice of my one time captor—Dr. Benjamin Church.

"You're alone tonight," Daniel said. I think it was for my benefit since I couldn't see ghost auras. For all I knew there could have been thirty more guys hiding in the trees.

Dr. Church stepped out of the shadows in his human form. "If I do this alone, I get all the glory—and wealth."

Daniel tossed his shovel to the ground. "We haven't found anything yet, if that's what you're wondering."

"I assumed that's why you were still digging."

"You can have everything that's buried here if you just leave Jamie and her family alone."

"Oh, I'm definitely getting everything," Church sneered. "There was never a question about that." He took another step toward us and Daniel moved in front of me. "I plan to convince the world that I'm actually a descendant of the *traitorous* Dr. Benjamin Church. My name will be remembered for finding Washington's treasure rather than my deeds of centuries ago. Deeds that I'm not ashamed of, mind you."

"No one will believe you. You're a ghost," I hissed.

"And what ghost will rat me out?" Church chuckled. "None, I say. Because no one will believe them."

Church folded his arms in front of his chest. "I never said you could stop digging."

I picked up my abandoned shovel and hurled it at him. "Dig it yourself."

The light from the two small flashlights didn't cover a lot of area, but I could see the anger on Church's face. "She's a little feisty, isn't she Avery? Back in our day, a woman behaving in that way wouldn't be tolerated. Maybe I should teach her a lesson on how a real lady should act."

He picked up the shovel at his feet and took a step toward me, but Daniel met him halfway, swinging the shovel as a growl escaped his throat.

Church backed away and held up his hands as if surrendering. "I see how this is going to go. I'll help you for now, but when whatever is buried here is unearthed, all alliances are off."

Daniel didn't say anything, but he resumed his rhythmic shoveling. Church picked up the shovel I'd thrown at him and fell into sync next to Daniel. The pile of discarded dirt grew higher and higher and as the hole deepened, so did my anxiety. Finally, Daniel plunged his shovel into the dirt, but instead of the familiar grind of gravel on metal, we heard the sound of hollow wood.

"Jackpot," Church said.

I grabbed one of the flashlights off the ground and aimed it into the hole. Aged gray wood barely showed among the loose dirt. "We're not going to get it out unless we completely uncover it," Daniel said. He and Church worked feverishly, their pace increasing with the prospect of what lay ahead. When the edges appeared, Daniel jumped into the hole and used his hands to finish wiping the remaining dirt and debris from the wooden lid.

"Is it a treasure chest or something?" I asked.

Daniel remained quiet.

"Daniel?"

He silently climbed back out of the hole, his eyes never leaving the wooden box.

"It's not a treasure chest. It's a coffin."

Chapter 32

I gasped and jumped back, stumbling over Betsy Howe's headstone again. "A *coffin*? We just unburied a *coffin*?"

"We're in a cemetery. What did you think we were going to find?" Church said.

"What better place to hide valuables," Daniel mumbled. "Or a body."

Church shuffled from one foot to the other. "Are you going to open it or not, Avery?"

"Be my guest," Daniel answered, motioning toward the coffin.

Church jumped into the hole and used the shovel to pound on the lock holding the casket closed. The weathered lock broke off with only three hits of the shovel. "Just so we're clear, if you take even one thing out of here, I'll kill the girl."

Daniel repeatedly opened and closed his fist. I slipped my hand in his and squeezed, trying to keep him calm. He said the valuables didn't matter to him, but deep down I knew that letting Church—the traitor—have them, would be the worst possible punishment for Daniel.

Church reached for the coffin's lid and I grabbed Daniel's arm

291

with my free hand, my fingers digging into his flesh. I could feel a scream working its way up my throat from the pit of my stomach. If the coffin held human remains, the scream would find its way out.

Church reached for the lid. "Almost two and a half centuries later, I finally get to see what Washington hid."

I buried my face in Daniel's sleeve. "Tell me when the horror is over," I whispered.

He reached up and pulled my hands from my eyes. "I think you'll want to see this, J."

I opened one eye first and then the other. Both flashlights were aimed inside the opened coffin. Instead of a dead body, the box had been filled to the brim with gold, silver, jewels, and rolled up parchments.

"Wooh!" Church yelled. "I knew it! I knew Washington never got around to unburying all of this. I just became one of this country's wealthiest men."

Daniel slipped his arm around my waist and pulled me close to his side.

I leaned my head against his chest. "I'm sorry we didn't save it from him," I whispered.

Daniel ran his fingers through my hair. "If I know you, you'll find a way to stop him and let the real truth come out. You know, when I'm gone."

"I'm glad you have so much confidence in me, but without your help, I don't think I can win a fight with him."

Daniel rested his chin on top of my head. "Church looks at this stuff and sees wealth. I look at it and see a priceless gift for our nation."

"What are you two doing up there?" Church still stood in the hole next to the coffin, both fists full of his greatest dream come true. "Stop shaking things around."

"We're not doing anything," I said, baffled by Church's odd

behavior.

"I have the weirdest sensation. It feels like something is pulling on me," Church said. His eyes darted to the coffin. "The treasure has a curse on it. Avery, get me out of here!"

Church threw the jewels back into the coffin and clawed at the dirt, trying to haul himself out of the hole. "How do I break the curse?" he hissed.

Watching the evil villain of Daniel's story have a panic attack was one of the greatest moments of my life and I couldn't help but smile. I knew exactly what was going on. "I hate to tell you this," I said. "No, actually, I'm elated to tell you this. There's no curse. At least, not in the sense that you're thinking. You're about to be extricated."

"No!" Church yelled. "Not after all this!"

"Goodbye doctor," Daniel said.

Church flickered in and out one last time and then he was gone, nothing left of him but a pile of clothes lying in the dirt.

Daniel and I exchanged looks. "That's . . . it?" Daniel said.

I nodded. "He's gone. And he's never coming back."

Daniel bent and picked up some of the coins that had fallen into the dirt when Church extricated. "It happened so fast." He looked up at me and I thought I detected sadness in his eyes. "I feel it, J. I'm leaving, too," he whispered.

"We were right. This was your unfinished business."

Daniel straightened and took both of my hands in his. "I'm going to miss you so much," he whispered.

"Not for long. You'll be able to see your siblings, your parents, your friends—" My voice cracked so I stopped talking.

Daniel wrapped his arms around me and pulled me close. I took a deep breath, trying to memorize his scent so I could think of him after he'd gone.

"I know you'll do the right thing with this stuff," Daniel said slowly. Speaking was getting harder for him as he fought the pull I knew he felt.

I nodded and mumbled into his chest. "We'll take care of it."

Daniel lifted his head and tilted my chin up. "I love you, Jamie Peters, as a true friend."

I forced a smile as the tears began to fall in little rivulets down my cheeks. "I love you too, Daniel."

And then he was gone.

I fell to me knees, the sobs coming out in bursts. I could barely breathe. The familiar pain of losing a ghost was something I would never get used to. I cried for a long time, the tears seeming to have no end. Time passed, but still I couldn't move. When I felt someone's arm slide around my shoulders, I gasped and pulled away. But the arm held me close.

Peter.

Mom and Camille hovered a few feet away.

"You'll get through this," Peter whispered into my hair. "You're Jamie Peters. You're strong and smart and I'm pretty sure you're the world's greatest soul saver."

"It hurts so much," I said.

"I know. If I could take your pain away, I would do it in a heartbeat."

I knew he meant every word of it.

"How did you know to come here?" I asked.

Mom knelt next to us. "The ghost that followed us got angry when he found out Peter and Camille weren't you and Daniel. It was the same guy, you know, the big one, from the warehouse the other day. He made himself visible and threatened us if we didn't give him Daniel's location or else the watches."

"Your mom was awesome, Jamie," Camille said. "She didn't take his crap and totally stood up to him."

"Sounds just like her daughter," Peter said.

"Anyway, just when I thought I better give something up to him to protect all of us, he disappeared," Mom said.

"Only he didn't just disappear," Camille said excitedly. "He extricated! One second he was there and then . . . poof! He was gone."

"The same thing happened with the ghost following us." We all turned at the sound of Steven's voice. He and Portia were picking their way through the headstones. He let out a low whistle when he saw the inside of the hole we dug.

"Yeah," Portia said, peering down at the treasure-filled coffin. "We figured that could only mean one thing. Jamie and Daniel found the cache and it caused everyone to extricate."

I forced a half smile. "That's pretty much what happened."

Portia squeezed my free hand—the one not wrapped around Peter. "I'm sorry, sweetie," she said quietly. "I know it doesn't mean much, but we all know what you're feeling. Saying goodbye to ghosts is never easy and I'm sorry you have to go through this."

"Thanks, Portia." I took a deep breath and forced my wobbly legs to stand. I stepped toward the gaping hole and aimed a flashlight into it. "So . . . what do we do with General Washington's treasure?"

Chapter 33

Mom!" I called. "Have you seen my blue sneakers with the pink stripes? I need to pack them." Déjàvu. I distinctly remembered yelling the same thing to my dad six weeks earlier when packing to go to Boston with mom. *Has it really only been six weeks?*

"Have you looked behind the couch? Maybe we missed them when we were cleaning up the destruction from Church and his men," Mom called from the kitchen.

I looked behind the couch. "They're not there!"

Tossing a blanket aside, I found my shoes, still covered in dirt from the night spent in the cemetery. I sunk to the ground and pulled the shoes into my lap, forcing myself to take deep breaths. Sometimes the littlest things triggered my emotions, but it was time to let Daniel go and move on.

After we left the cemetery that night, we found a public phone and called the police, reporting vandalism at the colonial cemetery. We didn't leave our names and we made sure to get rid of all evidence linking back to us. As an afterthought, we took all six of the watches—in varying condition—and dumped them into the coffin with the rest of the valuables. I wanted the name of Daniel Avery to

296

go down in history in one way or another. Mom suggested we leave Church's watch out, but I couldn't do it. As horrid as the man had been, I couldn't change the real story.

News of the mysterious grave made it into the papers and the TV stations the next day. In the few weeks since, treasure seekers and history buffs had poured into Boston from all over the world, each giving a theory as to the why and how of the cache.

But only a few of us knew—or would ever know—the real truth.

I thought about writing an anonymous letter to the Boston Globe, detailing Daniel's life, but I knew it would just be considered another quack job.

"You ready to go?" Mom asked, coming into the living room.

"I think so." I looked around the little apartment one last time. "It will be weird to be back in Marion again."

"It won't seem so weird once school starts up next week."

"Maybe." I opened the front door and stepped out, calling goodbye to Steven and Portia. I still had a key to Daniel's apartment—technically Uncle Charlie's—and I inserted it into the keyhole. "I just want to take one more look around."

"I'll give you a minute," Mom said.

I stepped into the apartment and shut the door behind myself. I ran my fingers over the books on his bookshelf and inhaled deeply. I could almost smell him, proof that he hadn't been a figment of my imagination. I no longer had his watch, but I wanted something to remind me of him. I gazed at the titles of the books, but then took a closer look at my hand. The ring Daniel bought me on our first date glinted in the light. That was all I needed.

I stepped back into the hall and slid the key under the door. Daniel was gone and he wasn't coming back.

"So . . . how long before you're helping another ghost?" Mom teased as we threw my bags into the back of the van.

"For now, I'm okay if I never see another ghost in my life—with

297

the exception of Jack and Rita."

Mom grinned. "Famous last words, Jamie. Famous last words."

Author's Note

As with all the books in the Soul Saver series, *On Liberty's Watch* is based on real events from our nation's past. My main ghost, Daniel Avery, is completely fictional, but many of the characters he interacted with in his life were real.

I learned so much more than I ever knew before about Paul Revere and tried to portray him as accurately as possible. His family members were real, his shop was real, and we all know that his famous midnight ride was real. Paul was also a member of the Mechanics—an organization within the Sons of Liberty—who were known to meet at the Green Dragon Tavern in Boston.

Dr. Joseph Warren was an influential man during the early days of the revolution, but sadly, just like in the story, he was killed at the Battle of Bunker Hill. It was Warren who sent William Dawes and Paul Revere on their famous ride. In *On Liberty's Watch,* Paul Revere identified Warren's body shortly after the battle. In reality, the body wasn't identified by Revere until many months later. How? By dental forensics. Revere had fashioned a false tooth for Warren and recognized it on the body.

Robert Newman, the sexton from the story who helped Daniel light the lanterns in the Old North Church, was the real man who

299

carried them to the top of the steeple in 1775. I learned while researching him that he had a connection to my second Soul Saver book, *Haven Waiting*. Robert Newman's great-grandfather, William Burroughs, was hung for witchcraft in Salem in 1692.

Much has been written about General George Washington over the years and using him as a character was a daunting task. Washington is known for his use of spies during the Revolutionary War and I knew it would be the perfect job for Daniel. In the story, the letter Washington dictated to a scribe while Daniel listened is word for word one of the letters he sent to General Gage during the early months of the Revolutionary War.

General Gage and Major General Howe, officers for the British army, both served in Massachusetts during the siege of Boston. Were they bad guys? I guess that depends on whose side you were on. War can confuse any situation.

Dr. Benjamin Church, my villain in *On Liberty's Watch*, really did betray his friends and fellow Sons of Liberty when he sent correspondence to the wrong side. Although he might not be as infamous as someone like Benedict Arnold, I found his story to be just as fascinating. In 1778, Dr. Church was named in the Massachusetts Banishment Act and boarded a ship destined for the French island, Martinico, but he never arrived. To this day, the location of that ship is not known. Did all aboard lose their lives in a stormy ocean, or did the ship secretly dock somewhere else like in my story? Perhaps Dr. Church *didn't* really die aboard its decks.

That's one mystery we'll never be able to solve, but as long as there are unsolved mysteries from history, I'll keep finding ghosts to give us the "answers."

ABOUT THE AUTHOR

 Tifani Clark grew up on a farm in southeastern Idaho (yes, that's where they grow all the potatoes) as the middle of five children. She had a lot of space to imagine and daydream and often pictured herself as a character in one of the many books she read. She was habitually found pretending to be Scarlet O'Hara. Tifani loves mysteries and hates it when one goes unsolved. She is married to the love of her life and is the mother to four fabulous children. When not writing, she enjoys playing the violin and piano and traveling to new places. She especially enjoys visits to national parks and places of historical significance.

www.ingramcontent.com/pod-product-compliance
Lightning Source LLC
Chambersburg PA
CBHW051409170626
46809CB00006B/2080